Every Breath

ALSO BY NICHOLAS SPARKS

NICHOLAS SPARKS

Every Breath

sphere

For Victoria Vodar

SPHERE

First published in the United States in 2018 by Grand Central,
an imprint of Hachette US
First published in Great Britain in 2018 by Sphere

1 3 5 7 9 10 8 6 4 2

A CIP catalogue record for this book
is available from the British Library.

Hardback ISBN 978-0-7515-6775-5
Trade Paperback ISBN 978-0-7515-6776-2

Printed and bound in Great Britain by
Clays Ltd, Elcograf S.p.A.

Papers used by Sphere are from well-managed forests
and other responsible sources.

MIX
Paper from
responsible sources
FSC® C104740
FSC
www.fsc.org

Sphere
An imprint of
Little, Brown Book Group
Carmelite House
50 Victoria Embankment
London EC4Y 0DZ

An Hachette UK Company
www.hachette.co.uk

www.littlebrown.co.uk

ACKNOWLEDGEMENTS

For me, the creation of any novel is a bit like I imagine childbirth to be: a process of anticipation, terror, grinding exhaustion, and eventually, exhilaration...an experience that I'm glad I don't have to endure by myself. By my side every step of the way, from gestation to squalling birth, is my longtime literary agent, Theresa Park, who is not only incredibly talented and intelligent, but has been my closest friend over the last quarter century. The team at Park Literary & Media is hands down the most impressive, knowledgeable, and visionary in the business: Abigail Koons and Blair Wilson are the architects of my international career; Andrea Mai finds innovative ways for me to partner with retailers like Target, Walmart, Amazon, and Barnes & Noble; Emily Sweet manages my myriad social media, licensing, and brand partnership endeavors; Alexandra Greene provides essential legal and strategic support; and Pete Knapp and Emily Clagett ensure that my work remains relevant to a constantly evolving readership.

At the publisher that has debuted every one of my books

since *The Notebook*, there have been many changes over the decades, but during the past several years I've been grateful to have my work championed by Hachette Book Group CEO Michael Pietsch. Grand Central Publishing Publisher Ben Sevier and Editor-in-Chief Karen Kosztolnyik have been recent but very welcome additions to the team, bringing with them fresh ideas and new energy. I'll miss GCP's VP of Retail Sales, Dave Epstein, who—together with his boss Chris Murphy and PLM's Andrea Mai—helped shape the retail strategy for my last few books. Dave, I wish you many peaceful days of fishing during your retirement. Flag and Anne Twomey, you bring magic and class to each of my book jackets, year after year. To Brian McLendon and my extremely patient publicist, Caitlyn Mulrooney-Lyski, thank you for shepherding the marketing and publicity campaigns for my books with such care; and to Amanda Pritzker, your attentiveness and effective collaboration with the team at Park Literary are much appreciated.

My longtime publicist at PMK-BNC, Catherine Olim, is my fearless protector and straight-shooting advisor, and I treasure her counsel. The social media whizzes Laquishe "Q" Wright and Mollie Smith help me stay in touch daily with my fans and have encouraged me to find my own voice in this ever-shifting world of virtual communication; I'm grateful for your loyalty and guidance over the years.

In my film and TV endeavors, I've had the same remarkable team of representatives for 20+ years: Howie Sanders (now at Anonymous Content), Keya Khayatian at UTA, and my dedicated entertainment attorney Scott Schwimer. (Scottie, I hope you enjoy your namesake in this book!) Any author would be lucky to have his or her Hollywood projects shepherded by this Dream Team.

   And finally, to my home team: Jeannie Armentrout; my assistant, Tia Scott; Michael Smith; my brother, Micah Sparks; Christie Bonacci; Eric Collins; Todd Lanman; Jonathan and Stephanie Arnold; Austin and Holly Butler; Micah Simon; Gray Zurbruegg; David Stroud; Dwight Carl-blom; David Wang; my accountants, Pam Pope and Oscara Stevick; Andy Sommers; Hannah Mensch; David Geffen; Jeff Van Wie; Jim Tyler; David Shara; Pat and Billy Mills; Mike and Kristie McAden; longtime friends, including Chris Matteo, Paul DuVair, Bob Jacob, Rick Muench, Pete DeCler, and Joe Westermeyer; my extended family, including Monty, Gail, Dianne, Chuck, Dan, Sandy, Jack, Mike, Parnell, and all my cousins, nephews, and nieces; and finally my children, Miles, Ryan, Landon, Lexie, and Savannah...
I say a prayer of thanks for your presence in my life, every day, and with every breath.

KINDRED SPIRIT

*T*here are stories that rise from mysterious, unknown places, and others that are discovered, a gift from someone else. This story is one of the latter. On a cool and blustery day in the late spring of 2016, I drove to Sunset Beach, North Carolina, one of many small islands between Wilmington and the South Carolina border. I parked my truck near the pier and hiked down the beach, heading for Bird Island, an uninhabited coastal preserve. Locals had told me there was something I should see; perhaps, they'd even suggested, the site would end up in one of my novels. They told me to keep my eye out for an American flag; when I spotted it in the distance, I'd know I was getting close.

Not long after the flag came into view, I kept my eyes peeled. I was to look for a mailbox called Kindred Spirit. The mailbox—planted on a pole of aging driftwood near a saw grass–speckled dune—has been around since 1983 and belongs to no one and everyone. Anyone can leave a letter or postcard; any passerby can read whatever has been placed inside. Thousands of people do so every year. Over time, Kindred Spirit has been a repository of hopes and dreams in written form . . . and always, there are love stories to be found.

The beach was deserted. As I approached the isolated mailbox on its lonely stretch of shoreline, I could just make out a wooden bench beside it. It was the perfect resting place, an outpost of reflection.

Reaching inside the mailbox, I found two postcards, several previously opened letters, a recipe for Brunswick stew, a journal that appeared to have been written in German, and a thick manila envelope. There were pens, a pad of unused paper, and envelopes—presumably for anyone who was inspired to add their own story to the contents. Taking a seat on the bench, I perused the postcards and the recipe before turning to the letters. Almost immediately, I noticed that no one used last names. Some of the letters had first names, others had only initials, and still others were completely anonymous, which only added to the sense of mystery.

But anonymity seemed to allow for candid reflection. I read about a woman who, in the aftermath of a struggle with cancer, had met the man of her dreams at a Christian bookstore, but worried that she wasn't good enough for him. I read about a child who hoped to one day become an astronaut. There was a letter from a young man who planned to propose to his sweetheart in a hot air balloon, and still another from a man who wanted to ask his neighbor on a date but feared rejection. There was a letter from someone recently released from prison who wanted nothing more than to start his life over. The final missive was from a man whose dog, Teddy, had recently been put to sleep. The man was still grieving, and after finishing the letter, I studied the photograph that had been tucked inside the envelope, showing a black Labrador retriever with friendly eyes and a graying muzzle. The man had signed his initials A.K., and I found myself hoping he would find a way to fill the void that Teddy's absence had left behind.

By then, the breeze was steady and the clouds had begun to darken. A storm was rolling in. I returned the recipe, postcards, and letters to the mailbox and debated opening the manila envelope. The thickness indicated a substantial number of pages, and the last thing I wanted was to get caught in the rain as I trekked back to my truck. Flipping over the envelope as I debated, I saw that someone had printed on the back The Most Amazing Story Ever!

A plea for recognition? A challenge? Written by the author, or by someone who'd examined the contents? I wasn't sure, but how could I resist?

I opened the clasp. Inside the envelope were a dozen or so pages, photocopies of three letters, and some photocopied drawings of a man and woman who clearly looked to be in love with each other. I set those aside and reached for the story. The first line made me pause:

The destiny that matters most in anyone's life is the one concerning love.

The tone was unlike the previous letters, promising something grand, it seemed. I settled in to read. After a page or so, my curiosity became interest; after a few more pages, I couldn't put the story aside. Over the next half hour, I laughed and felt my throat tighten; I ignored the uptick in the breeze and clouds that were turning the color of charcoal. Thunder and flickers of lightning were reaching the distant edge of the island when I read the final words with a sense of wonder.

I should have left then. I could see sheets of rain marching across the waves toward me, but instead, I read the story a second time. On that reading, I was able to hear the voices of the characters with utter clarity. By the time I read the letters and examined the drawings, I could feel the idea taking shape that I might somehow find the writer and broach the possibility of turning his story into a book.

But finding that person wouldn't be easy. Most of the events had taken place long in the past—more than a quarter century earlier—and instead of names, there were only single initials. Even in the letters, the original names had been whited out before the pages were copied. There was nothing to indicate who the writer or artist might have been.

A few clues remained, however. In the part of the story dating back to 1990, there was mention of a restaurant with a deck out back and an indoor fireplace, where a cannonball allegedly salvaged from one of Blackbeard's ships sat atop the mantel. There was also reference to a cottage on an island off the North Carolina coast, within walking distance of the restaurant. And in what seemed to be the most recently written pages, the writer spoke of a construction project currently under way at a beach house, on a different island altogether. I had no idea whether the project was now finished, but I had to start somewhere. Though years had passed, I hoped the drawings would eventually help me identify the subjects. And, of course, there was also the Kindred Spirit mailbox on the beach where I sat, which played a pivotal role in the story.

By then, the sky was positively threatening and I knew I was out of time. Sliding the pages back into the manila envelope, I returned it to the mailbox and hurried to my truck. I barely beat the downpour. Had I waited another few minutes, I would have been drenched, and despite having my windshield wipers on high, I could barely see through the glass. I drove home, made myself a late lunch, and stared out the window, continuing to think about the couple that I'd read about on the pages. By evening, I knew that I wanted to go back to Kindred Spirit and examine the story again, but weather and some business travel prevented me from returning for nearly a week.

When I finally made it back, the other letters, the recipe, and the journal were there, but the manila envelope was gone. I wondered what had become of it. I was curious as to whether a stranger had been as moved by the pages as I'd been and had taken them, or if perhaps there was some sort of caretaker who occasionally purged the mailbox. Mainly, I wondered whether the author had had second thoughts about revealing the story and come to retrieve it himself.

It made me want to talk to the writer even more, but family and work kept me busy for another month, and it wasn't until June that I found time to begin my quest. I won't bore you with all the details regarding my search—it took the better part of a week, countless phone calls, visits to various chambers of commerce and county offices where building permits were recorded, and hundreds of miles on the truck. Since the first part of the story took place decades ago, some of the reference points had long since disappeared. I managed to track down the location of the restaurant—it was now a chic seafood bistro with white tablecloths—and used that as a starting point for my exploratory excursions, in order to get a sense of the area. After that, following the trail of building permits, I visited one island after the next, and on one of my many walks up and down the beach, I eventually came across the sound of hammering and a power drill—not uncommon for salted and weather-beaten homes along the coast. When I saw an older man working on a ramp that led from the top of the dune to the beach, though, I felt a sudden jolt. I remembered the drawings, and even from a distance suspected that I had found one of the characters I had read about.

Walking over, I introduced myself. Up close, I became even more certain it was him. I noted the quiet intensity I'd read about and the same observant blue eyes referenced in one of the letters. Doing the math, I figured him to be in his late sixties, which was the right age. After a bit of small talk, I asked him point-blank whether he'd written the story that had ended up in Kindred Spirit. In response, he deliberately turned his gaze toward the ocean, saying nothing for perhaps a minute. When he turned to face me again, he said that he would answer my questions the following afternoon, but only if I was willing to lend him a hand on his construction project.

I showed up with a tool belt early the following morning, but the tools proved unnecessary. Instead, he had me haul plywood, two-by-fours, and pressure-treated lumber from the front of the house to the back, up over the sandy dune, and onto the beach. The pile of lumber was enormous, and the sand made every load seem twice as heavy. It took me most of the day, and aside from telling me where to place the lumber, he didn't speak to me at all. He spent the day drilling and nailing and working beneath a searing early-summer sun, more interested in the quality of his work than my presence.

Shortly after I'd finished hauling the last load, he motioned for me to take a seat on the dune and opened a cooler. Filling a pair of plastic cups from a thermos inside, he handed me a cup of iced tea.

"Yeah," he finally offered. "I wrote it."

"Is it true?"

He squinted, as if evaluating me.

"Some of it," he admitted, in the accent I'd heard described in the pages. "Some might dispute the facts, but memories aren't always about facts."

I told him that I thought it might make for a fascinating

book and launched into a series of passionate arguments. He listened in silence, his expression unreadable. For some reason, I felt anxious, almost desperate to persuade him. After an uncomfortable silence during which he seemed to be weighing my proposition, he finally spoke: He was willing to discuss the idea further, and perhaps even agree to my request, but only on the condition that he be the first to read the story. And if he didn't like it, he wanted me to bury the pages. I hedged. Writing a book takes months, even years, of effort—but he held firm. In the end, I agreed. Truth be told, I understood his reasoning. If our positions had been reversed, I would have asked the same of him.

We went to the cottage then. I asked questions and received answers. I was provided again with a copy of the story, and I was shown the original drawings and letters that enlivened the past even more.

The conversation rolled on. He told the story well and saved the best for last. As evening fell, he showed me a remarkable item—a labor of love—that enabled me to visualize the events with detail and clarity, as if I'd been a witness to all that had happened. I also began to see how the words would appear on the page, as if the story were writing itself and my role was simply to transcribe it.

Before I left, he requested that real names not be used. He had no desire for fame—he considered himself a private person—but more than that, he knew that the story had the potential to open old, and new, wounds. The events, after all, hadn't taken place in isolation. There were living people involved, some of whom might be upset by the revelations. I have honored his request because I believe that the story has larger value and meaning: the power to remind us that there are times when destiny and love collide.

I began working on the novel soon after that first evening we spent together. In the year that followed, whenever I had questions, I called or visited. I toured the locations, or at least those that hadn't been lost to history. I went through newspaper archives and examined photographs taken more than twenty-five years earlier. To flesh out even more details, I spent a week at a bed and breakfast in a small coastal town in eastern North Carolina and traveled as far as Africa. I was fortunate in that time seems to move more slowly in both of those regions; there were moments when I felt as if I had actually journeyed deep into the past.

My trip to Zimbabwe was especially helpful. I'd never been to that particular country and was overwhelmed by the spectacular wildlife. The country had once been called the breadbasket of Africa, but by the time of my visit, much of the agricultural infrastructure had decayed and the economy had collapsed for largely political reasons. I walked among crumbling farmhouses and fallow fields, dependent on my imagination as to how verdant the land had been when the story first began. I also spent three weeks on various safaris, absorbing everything around me. I spoke to guides and scouts and spotters, discussing their training and their daily lives; I speculated on how challenging it must be for them to maintain families, since they spend most of their time in the bush. I confess, I found Africa utterly seductive. Since those trips, I've often felt the urge to return, and I know I will before long.

In spite of all the research, there's much that remains unknown. Twenty-seven years is a long period of time, and to re-create verbatim an ancient conversation between two people is impossible. Nor is it possible to recall with accuracy each and every step a person takes, or the position of the clouds in the sky, or the rhythm of the waves as they roll up on the shore. What

I can say is that what follows next is the best I can possibly do under such constraints. Since I made further alterations for the purposes of privacy, I'm comfortable describing this book as a novel and not a work of nonfiction.

The genesis, research, and creation of this book has been one of the more memorable experiences of my life. In some ways, it's transformed the way I think about love. I suspect that most people harbor a lingering sense of What if I'd followed my heart?, and there's no way to ever really know the answer. A life, after all, is simply a series of little lives, each of them lived one day at a time, and every single one of those days has choices and consequences. Piece by piece, those decisions help to form the people we become. I've captured some fragments to the best of my ability, but who is to say that the picture I've assembled is a true portrait of who the couple really was?

There will always be doubters when it comes to love. Falling in love is the easy part; making that love last amid life's varied challenges is an elusive dream for many. But if you read this story with the same sense of wonder that I felt when writing it, then perhaps your faith in the uncanny force that love can exert on people's lives will be renewed. You might even find your way to Kindred Spirit one day, with a story of your own to tell . . . one that has the power to change someone else's life in ways you never imagined possible.

Nicholas Sparks
September 2, 2017

PART I

TRU

On the morning of September 9, 1990, Tru Walls stepped outside and surveyed a morning sky that was the color of fire near the horizon. The earth was cracked beneath his feet and the air was dry; it hadn't rained in more than two months. Dust clung to his boots as he made his way to the pickup he'd owned for more than twenty years. Like his footwear, the truck was covered in dust, both inside and out. Beyond a fence topped with electric wire, an elephant pulled branches from a tree that had toppled earlier that morning. Tru paid it no attention. It was part of the landscape of his birth—his ancestors had emigrated from England more than a century earlier—and he was no more startled than a fisherman spotting a shark as the daily catch was pulled in. He was lean, with dark hair and squint lines at the corners of his eyes earned by a life spent in the sun; at forty-two, he sometimes wondered whether he'd chosen to live in the bush or the bush had chosen him.

The camp was quiet; the other guides—including Romy, his best friend—had left earlier that morning for the main lodge, where they would ferry guests from around the world into the bush. Tru had worked at the lodge in Hwange National Park for the past ten years; prior to that, his existence had been more nomadic, with changes in lodges every couple of years as he'd gained more experience. As a rule, he'd avoided only those lodges that allowed hunting, something his grandfather wouldn't understand. His grandfather—who was referred to by everyone as the Colonel, though he never served in the military—claimed to have killed more than three hundred lions and cheetahs in his lifetime while protecting livestock on the massive family farm near Harare where Tru had been raised; his stepfather and half brothers were steadily making progress toward that same number. In addition to cattle, Tru's family cultivated various crops, harvesting more tobacco and tomatoes than any other farm in the country. Coffee, too. His great-grandfather had worked with the legendary Cecil Rhodes—mining magnate, politician, and emblem of British imperialism—accumulating land, money, and power in the late nineteenth century, before Tru's grandfather took over.

His grandfather, the Colonel, inherited a thriving enterprise from his father, but after World War II, the business expanded exponentially, making the Walls family one of the wealthiest in the country. The Colonel had never understood Tru's desire to escape what was by then a bona fide business empire and life of considerable luxury. Before he'd died—Tru had been twenty-six at the time—he'd once visited a reserve where Tru had been working. Though he had slept at the main lodge rather than the guide camp, seeing Tru's living quarters had been a shock to the old man. He'd surveyed a dwelling that he probably regarded as little better than a shack, without insulation or telephones. A kerosene lantern provided lighting, and a small communal generator powered a miniature refrigerator. It was a far cry from the home where Tru had been raised, but the austere surroundings were all Tru needed, especially as evening descended and an ocean of stars appeared overhead. In fact, they were a step up from a few of the previous camps where he'd worked; in two of those, he'd slept in a tent. Here, at least, there was running water and a shower, which he considered something of a luxury, even if they were in a communal bathroom.

On this morning, Tru carried his guitar in its battered case; a lunch box and thermos; a handful of drawings he'd made for his son, Andrew; and a knapsack containing a few days' worth of clothing, toiletries, drawing pads, colored and charcoal pencils, and his passport. Though he'd be gone for about a week, he figured it was all he would need.

His truck was parked beneath a baobab tree. A few of his fellow guides were fond of the dry, pulpy fruit. They'd mix it into their porridge in the morning, but Tru had never developed a taste for it. Tossing his knapsack onto the front seat, he checked the bed of the truck, making sure there was nothing in the back that could be stolen. Though he'd leave the truck at the family farm, there were more than three hundred field workers there, all of whom made very little money. Good tools were prone to vanishing into the ether, even under the watchful eyes of his family.

He slid behind the wheel and slipped on his sunglasses. Before turning the key, he made sure he hadn't forgotten anything. There wasn't much; in addition to the knapsack and guitar, he carried with him the letter and photograph he'd received from America, along with his plane tickets and his wallet. In the rack behind him was a loaded rifle in case his truck broke down and he found himself wandering in the bush, which remained one of the most dangerous places in the world, especially at night, even for someone as experienced as he. In the glove compartment were a compass and a flashlight. He made sure his tent was beneath the seat, again in case of emergency. It was compact enough to fit in the bed of his truck, and though it wouldn't do much to keep predators at bay, it was better than sleeping on the ground. *All right, then,* he thought. He was as ready as he'd ever be.

The day was already growing warm and the interior of the truck was even hotter. He'd avail himself of the "two-twenty" air-conditioning: two windows down at a speed of twenty miles an hour. It wouldn't help much, but he'd long since grown used to the heat. He rolled up the sleeves of his tan button-up shirt. He wore his usual trekking pants, which had grown soft and comfortable over the years. The guests hanging around the swimming pool back at the main lodge would likely be in bathing suits and flip-flops, but he'd never been comfortable in that attire. The boots and canvas pants had once saved his life when he'd crossed paths with an angry black mamba; if he hadn't had the proper clothing, the venom would have killed him in less than thirty minutes.

He glanced at his watch. It was a little after seven, and he had a long couple of days ahead. Cranking the engine, he backed out before heading toward the gate. He hopped out, pulled the gate open, rolled the truck through, and then closed the gate again. The last thing the other guides needed was to return to camp and find that a pride of lions had settled in. It had happened before—not at this particular camp but at another where he'd worked, in the southeastern part of the country. That had been a chaotic day. No one had been quite sure what to do other than bide their time until the lions figured out how long they intended to stay. Fortunately, the lions had vacated the camp to go on the hunt later in the afternoon, but ever since then, Tru made a point to check the gates, even when he wasn't driving. Some of the guides were new, and he didn't want to take any chances.

Shifting the truck into gear, he settled in, trying to make the ride as smooth as possible. The first hundred miles were on rutted gravel roads pocked with potholes, first on the reserve, then winding past a number of small villages. That part would take until the early afternoon, but he was used to the drive, and he allowed his mind to wander as he took in the world he called home.

The sun glinted through wispy clouds that trailed over the tree line, illuminating a lilac-breasted roller as it broke free from the tree branches on his left. Two warthogs crossed the road ahead of him, trotting past a family of baboons. He'd seen those animals thousands of times, but he still marveled at how they could survive when surrounded by so many predators. Nature had its own insurance policy, he knew. Animals that were low on the food chain had more young; female zebras, for instance, were pregnant for all but nine or ten days a year. It was estimated that female lions, on the other hand, had to mate more than a thousand times for every cub that reached its first birthday. It was evolutionary balance at its finest, and though he witnessed it daily, it still struck him as extraordinary.

Often, guests would ask him about the most exciting things he'd seen while guiding. He'd recount what it was like to be charged by a black rhino, or how he'd once witnessed a giraffe bucking wildly until finally giving birth in an explosive discharge that had surprised him in its violence. He'd seen a jaguar cub dragging a warthog nearly twice its size high into a tree, only inches ahead of a pack of snarling hyenas who'd caught the scent of the kill. One time, he'd followed a wild dog that, abandoned by its own kind, had bonded with a pack of jackals—the same pack it used to hunt. The stories were endless.

Was it possible, he wondered, to experience the same game drive twice? The answer was both yes and no. A person could go to the same lodge, work with the same guide, leave at the same time, and drive the same roads in exactly the same weather in the same season, but always, the animals were in different places, doing different things. They moved to and from watering holes, watching and listening, eating and sleeping and mating, all of them simply trying to survive another day.

Off to the side, he saw a herd of impalas. Guides would joke that those antelopes were the McDonald's of the bush, fast food in abundance. They were part of every predator's diet, and guests usually grew tired of photographing them after a single game drive. Tru, however, slowed the truck, watching as one after another made an impossibly high and graceful leap over a fallen tree, as if choreographed. In their own way, he thought, they were as special as the big five— lion, leopard, rhino, elephant, and water buffalo—or even the big seven, which included cheetahs and hyenas. Those were the animals that guests most wanted to see, the game that inspired the most excitement. The thing was, spotting lions wasn't particularly difficult, at least when the sun was shining. Lions slept eighteen to twenty hours a day, and they could usually be found resting in the shade. Spotting a *moving* lion, on the other hand, was rare, except at night. In the past, he'd worked at lodges that offered evening game drives. A few had been hair-raising, and many had been blinding, the dust from a hundred buffalo or wildebeest or zebra swirling as they'd stampeded from lions. It had been impossible to see more than inches in any direction, forcing Tru to stop the jeep. Twice, he'd realized that his vehicle was suddenly sandwiched between the pride of lions and whatever they'd been hunting, sending his adrenaline skyrocketing.

The road grew steadily rougher, and Tru slowed even more, weaving from one side to the other. He was headed for Bulawayo, the second-largest city in the country and home to his ex-wife, Kim, and their son, Andrew. He had a house there as well, which he'd bought after his divorce. In retrospect, it was obvious that he and Kim hadn't been well suited for each other. They'd met ten years ago at a bar in Harare, when Tru had been between jobs. Later Kim would tell him that he'd struck her as exotic, which along with his last name was enough to pique her interest. As for her, she was eight years younger and beautiful, with an easygoing yet confident charm. One thing led to the next, and they'd ended up spending much of the next six weeks together. By then, the bush was calling to Tru again and he'd wanted to end the relationship; instead, she'd told him she was pregnant. They got married, Tru took a job at Hwange because of its relative proximity to Bulawayo, and Andrew came along not long after that.

Though she'd known what Tru did for a living, Kim had assumed that when they had a child, Tru would find a job that didn't keep him away for weeks on end. Instead, he continued to guide, Kim eventually met someone else, and their marriage came to an end less than five years after it had started. There were no hard feelings on either side; if anything, their relationship had improved since their divorce. Whenever he picked up Andrew, he and Kim would visit for a while, catching up like the old friends they were. She'd remarried and had a daughter with her second husband, Ken; on their last visit, she'd told Tru she was pregnant again. Ken worked in the finance office of Air Zimbabwe. He wore a suit to work and was home every night for dinner. That's what Kim wanted, and Tru was happy for her.

As for Andrew...

His son was ten now, and the one great thing to come out of the marriage. As fate would have it, Tru contracted the measles when Andrew was a few months old, leaving him sterile, but he had never felt the need for another child. For him, Andrew had always been more than enough, and he was the reason Tru was detouring to Bulawayo instead of heading straight to the farm. With blond hair and brown eyes, Andrew resembled his mother, and Tru had dozens of drawings of him tacked to the walls of his shack. Over the years, he'd added photographs—on almost every visit, Kim would hand Tru an envelope filled with them—different versions of his son blending together, evolving into someone entirely new. At least once a week, Tru would sketch something he'd seen in the bush—usually an animal—but other times, he would draw the two of them, trying to capture a memory from their previous visit.

Balancing family and work had been a challenge, especially after the divorce. For six weeks, while he worked at the camp, Kim had custody and Tru would be entirely absent from his son's life: no calls, no visits, no impromptu soccer matches or ice cream runs. Then, for two weeks, Tru would assume custody and play the role of full-time father. Andrew would stay with him in his house in Bulawayo, Tru ferrying him to and from school, packing lunches and making dinner, and helping with homework. On the weekends, they did whatever Andrew chose, and in each and every one of those moments, Tru would wonder how it was possible to love his son as deeply as he did, even if he wasn't always around to show it.

Off to the right, he spotted a pair of circling buzzards. Searching for something left over from the hyenas last night, perhaps, or maybe looking for an animal that had died earlier in the morning. Lately, many of the animals had been struggling. The country was in the midst of yet another drought, and the watering holes in this area of the reserve had gone dry. It wasn't surprising; not far to the west, in Botswana, lay the vast Kalahari Desert, home of the legendary San people. Their language was thought to be one of the oldest in existence, heavy on knocks and clicks, and sounded almost alien to outsiders. Despite having virtually nothing in the way of material things, they joked and laughed more than any other group of people he'd ever met, but he wondered how long they would be able to maintain their way of life. Modernity was encroaching and there were rumors that the government of Botswana was going to require that all children in the country be educated in schools, including the San. He guessed that would eventually spell the end of a culture that had existed for thousands of years.

But Africa was always changing. He'd been born in Rhodesia, a colony of the British Empire; he'd watched the country descend into civil unrest, and he had still been a teenager when the country finally split, eventually becoming the nations of Zimbabwe and Zambia. Like in South Africa—which was regarded as a pariah because of apartheid in much of the civilized world—in Zimbabwe, much of the wealth was concentrated among a tiny percentage of the population, almost all of them white. Tru doubted that would last forever, but politics and social inequality were subjects he no longer discussed with his family. They were, after all, part of that privileged group, and like all privileged groups, they believed they deserved their riches and advantages, no matter how brutally the original wealth and power might have been accrued.

Tru eventually reached the limits of the reserve and passed the first of the small villages, home to about a hundred people. Like the guide camp, the village was fenced for the safety of both the people and the animals. He reached for his thermos and took a drink, resting his elbow on the windowsill. He passed a woman on a bicycle loaded down with boxes of vegetables, then a man who was walking, most likely headed for the next village, about six miles away. Tru slowed and pulled over; the man ambled to the truck and got in. Tru spoke enough of the man's language to keep a conversation going; in all, he was relatively fluent in six languages, two of them tribal. The other four were English, French, German, and Spanish. It was one of the qualities that made him an employee sought after by lodges.

He eventually dropped the man off and continued his drive, finally reaching a road paved in asphalt. He stopped for lunch soon after, simply pulling off the road to eat in the bed of his truck in the shade of an acacia tree. The sun was high by then and the world around him was quiet, no animals in sight.

Back on the road after lunch, he made better time. The villages eventually gave way to smaller towns, then larger ones, and late in the afternoon, he reached the outskirts of Bulawayo. He'd written Kim a letter, telling her when he'd be arriving, but mail in Zimbabwe wasn't always predictable. Letters usually reached their destination, but timeliness wasn't something that could be counted on.

Pulling onto her street, he parked behind Kim's car in the driveway. He approached the door and knocked; moments later, she answered, clearly expecting him. As they hugged, Tru heard his son's voice. Andrew tumbled down the stairs, leaping into Tru's arms. Tru knew that the time would come when Andrew considered himself too old for such displays of affection, so he squeezed tighter, wondering whether any joy could ever surpass this.

"Mummy told me that you're going to America," Andrew said to him later that night. They were sitting out front, on a low wall that served as a fence between Kim's house and the neighbor's.

"I am. But I'm not staying long. I'll be back next week."

"I wish you didn't have to go."

Tru slipped his arm around his son. "I know. I'll miss you, too."

"Then why are you going?"

That was the question, wasn't it? Why, after all this time, had the letter arrived? Along with a plane ticket?

"I'm going to see my father," Tru finally answered.

Andrew squinted, his blond hair bright in the moonlight. "You mean Papa Rodney?"

"No," Tru said. "I'm going to see my biological father. I've never met him."

"Do you want to meet him?"

Yes, Tru thought, then, *No, not really.* "I don't know," he finally admitted.

"Then why are you going?"

"Because," Tru said, "in his letter, he told me that he was dying."

After saying goodbye to Andrew, Tru drove to his house. Once inside, he opened the windows to air the place out, unpacked his guitar, and played and sang for an hour before finally turning in for the night.

He was out the door early the following morning. Unlike those in the park, the roads to the capital city were relatively well maintained, but it still took most of the day to get there. Tru arrived after dark to see lights shining in the stately home that his stepfather, Rodney, had rebuilt after the fire. Nearby were three other houses—one for each of his half brothers and the even larger main house where the Colonel had once lived. Technically, Tru owned the main house, but he made his way toward a smaller shack structure near the fence line. In the distant past, the bungalow had once housed the chef and his wife; Tru had fixed up the place in his early teen years. While he'd still been alive, the Colonel had seen that the bungalow was cleaned somewhat regularly, but that no longer happened. There was dust everywhere, and Tru had to shake the spiders and beetles from the sheets before crawling into bed. It mattered little to him; he'd slept in worse conditions countless times.

In the morning, he avoided his family. Instead, he had Tengwe, the crew foreman, drive him to the airport. Tengwe was gray haired and wiry and knew how to coax life out of the ground in the harshest conditions imaginable. His six children worked at the farm, and his wife, Anoona, prepared meals for Rodney. After his mother's death, Tru had been closer to Tengwe and Anoona than even the Colonel, and they were the only ones at the farm he ever missed.

The roads in Harare were clogged with cars and trucks, carts and bikes and pedestrians; the airport was even more chaotic. After checking in, Tru boarded a flight that would take him first to Amsterdam, then to New York and Charlotte, and finally to Wilmington, North Carolina.

With layovers, he was in transit for nearly twenty-one hours before he stepped onto U.S. soil for the first time in his life. When he reached the baggage claim area in Wilmington, he spotted a man holding a sign with his name on it, above the name of a limousine service. The driver was surprised by the lack of checked luggage and offered to carry both the guitar case and the knapsack. Tru shook his head. Stepping outside, he could feel his shirt beginning to tack to his back in the thick, humid air as they trudged to the car.

The drive was uneventful, but the world beyond the car windows was foreign to him. The landscape, flat and lush and verdant, seemed to stretch in every direction; he saw palms intermingled with oaks and pine trees, and grass the color of emeralds. Wilmington was a small, low-lying city featuring a mix of chain stores and local businesses that eventually gave way to a historic area with homes that looked at least a couple of hundred years old. His driver pointed out the Cape Fear River, its brackish waters dotted with fishing boats. On the roads, he saw cars and SUVs and minivans, none of them straddling the lanes as they did in Bulawayo, avoiding carts and animals. No one was riding a bicycle or walking, and nearly every person he saw on the city sidewalks was white. The world he'd left behind felt as distant as a dream.

An hour later, Tru crossed a floating pontoon bridge and was dropped off at a three-story home nestled against a low-rising dune in a place called Sunset Beach, an island just off the coast near the South Carolina border. It took him a moment to understand that the entire bottom floor was comprised of garages; the whole structure seemed almost grotesque compared to the much smaller house next door, which displayed a FOR SALE sign out front. He wondered whether the driver had made a mistake, but the driver checked the address again and assured him that he was in the right place. As the car pulled away, he heard the deep, rhythmic pulsation of ocean waves rolling ashore. He tried to remember the last time he'd heard that sound. A decade at least, Tru guessed as he climbed the steps to the second floor.

The driver had given him an envelope containing the key to the front door, and he stepped past the foyer into an expansive great room with pine flooring and a wood-beamed ceiling. The beach house decor looked like something staged for a magazine, every throw pillow and blanket placed with tasteful precision. Large windows offered a view of the back deck and an expanse of sea grass and dunes beyond, stretching to the ocean. A spacious dining area extended off the great room, and the designer kitchen included custom cabinetry, marble countertops, and premium appliances.

A note on the counter informed him that the refrigerator and pantry had been stocked with food and drinks, and that if he needed to go anywhere, he could call the limousine company. Should he be interested in ocean activities, a surfboard and fishing gear could be found in the garage. According to the note, Tru's father hoped to arrive on Saturday afternoon. He apologized that he wasn't able to get there sooner, although no explanation was offered for the delay. As he set the note aside, Tru was struck by the idea that perhaps his father was as ambivalent about their meeting as Tru was... which raised the question as to why he'd provided the airline ticket in the first place. Well, Tru would soon find out.

It was Tuesday evening, so Tru would have a few days to himself. He hadn't anticipated that, but there wasn't much he could do at this point. He spent the next few minutes exploring the house, learning the layout. The master bedroom was down the hall from the kitchen, and it was there that he left his belongings. Upstairs, there were additional bedrooms and bathrooms, all of which appeared pristine and unused. In the master bathroom he found fresh towels along with soap, shampoo, and conditioner, and he treated himself to an extra-long shower, lingering beneath the spray.

His hair was still damp as he stepped onto the back deck. The air remained warm, but the sun was sinking lower and the sky had fanned into a thousand shades of yellow and orange. Squinting into the distance, he could just make out what looked to be a pod of porpoises playing in the waves beyond the breakers. A latched gate gave way to steps that descended to a planked walkway over the grasses; following the steps, he trekked out to the final dune, discovering more steps leading to the beach.

There were few people about. In the distance, he saw a
woman trailing behind a small dog; in the opposite direction, a few surfers floated on their boards near a pier that
stretched into the ocean like a pointed finger. He started toward the pier, walking on the compact sand near the water's
edge, musing that until recently, he'd never heard of Sunset
Beach. He wasn't sure he'd ever thought about North Carolina at all. He tried to recall whether any of his guests over
the years had come from here, without luck. He supposed it
didn't make any difference.

At the pier, he took the stairs up and strolled to the end.
Resting his arms on the railings, he gazed over water that
stretched to the horizon. The sight of it, the immensity of it,
was almost beyond comprehension. It reminded him that
there was an entire world out there to explore, and he wondered if he would ever get around to doing it. Maybe when Andrew was older, they'd spend some time traveling together...

As the breeze picked up, the moon began its slow ascent
into an indigo sky. He took it as a cue to head back. He
assumed his father owned the place. It might have been
a rental, but the furnishings were too pricey to trust to
strangers, and besides, if that was the case, why not simply
put Tru up at a hotel? He wondered again about the delay
until Saturday. Why had he flown Tru out so far in advance?
If the man was indeed dying, Tru speculated that it could
be something medical, which meant there was no guarantee
about Saturday, either.

But what would happen when his father did show up?
The man was a stranger; a single meeting wasn't going to
change that. Nonetheless, Tru hoped he'd be able to answer
some questions, which was the only reason Tru had decided
to come in the first place.

Entering the house, he fished out a steak from the re-frigerator. He had to open a few of the cabinets before he found a cast-iron fry pan, but the stove, as fancy as it was, functioned similarly to the ones back home. There were also various food items from a place called Murray's Deli, and he added what appeared to be some kind of cabbage salad as well as potato salad to his plate. After he ate, he washed the plate, glass, and utensils by hand and grabbed his guitar before returning to the back deck. He played and sang softly to himself for an hour while the occasional shooting star passed overhead. He thought about Andrew and Kim, his mother and grandfather, before finally becom-ing sleepy enough to go to bed.

In the morning, he did a hundred push-ups and a hun-dred sit-ups before trying and failing to make some coffee. He couldn't figure out how the machine worked. Too many buttons, too many options, and he had no idea where to add the water. He decided to visit the beach instead, hoping to stumble upon a place to buy a cup.

Like the evening before, he had the beach mostly to him-self. He thought about how pleasant it was to spontaneously take a walk. He couldn't do that at Hwange, not without a rifle, anyway. He breathed deeply when he reached the sand, tasting salt in the air, feeling like the foreigner he was.

He slipped his hands into his pockets, taking in the morning. He had been walking for fifteen minutes when he spotted a cat crouched on top of a dune, next to a deck that was under repair, the steps to the beach still unfin-ished. At the farm, there had been barn cats, but this one looked as though it spent most of its time indoors. Just then, a small white dog raced past him, barreling toward a flock of seagulls that burst into the air like a small explosion. The dog eventually veered toward the dune, spotted the cat, and took off like a rocket. The cat jumped up to the deck as the dog scrambled up the dune in pursuit, both of them vanishing from sight. A minute later, he thought he heard the distant screech of car tires, followed by the sound of a dog yelping and crying.

He glanced behind him; halfway down the beach, he saw a woman standing near the water, no doubt the dog's owner, her gaze fixed on the ocean. He guessed she was the same woman he'd spotted the night before, but she was too far away to have seen or heard what had happened.

Hesitating briefly, Tru started after the dog, his feet slipping in the sand as he scaled the dune. Stepping onto the deck, he followed the walkway, eventually reaching a new set of steps leading on one side up to the house's deck and on the other, down to the ground. He went down, winding between two houses that were similar in style to the one where he was staying. Climbing over a low retaining wall, he continued to the road. No car in sight. No hysterical people or dog lying in the road, either. That was good news, as an initial matter. He knew from experience that wounded animals often sought shelter if they were still able to move, nature's way of allowing them to heal while hiding from predators.

He walked along one side of the road, searching the bushes and around trees. He didn't see anything. Crossing the street, he repeated the process and eventually came across the dog standing near a hedge, its rear leg bobbing up and down. The dog was panting and shaking, whether from pain or shock, Tru couldn't tell. He debated whether to go back to the beach and try to find the woman, but he was afraid the dog might hobble away to parts unknown.

Removing his sunglasses, he squatted down and held his hand out.

"Hey there," he said, keeping his voice calm and steady, "You all right?"

The dog tilted its head and Tru slowly began to inch toward it, speaking in low, steady tones. When Tru was close, the dog stretched out, trying to sniff his hand, before taking a couple of hesitant steps forward. When the dog finally seemed convinced of his good intentions, it relaxed. Tru stroked its head and checked for blood. Nothing. On its collar tag, Tru saw the name *Scottie*.

"Hi, Scottie," he said. "Let's get you back to the beach, shall we? Come on."

It took some coaxing, but Scottie finally began to follow Tru back toward the dune. He was limping, but not to the point where Tru thought anything might be broken. When Scottie stopped at the retaining wall, Tru hesitated before finally reaching down and scooping him into his arms. He carried him between the houses and up the steps to the walkway, then eventually over the dune. Scanning the beach, he spotted the woman, much nearer now.

Tru eased down the dune and started toward her. The morning remained bright, but the woman seemed even brighter, amplified by the sunny yellow fabric of her sleeveless top fluttering in the wind. He watched as the gap between them continued to close, studying her as she drew near. Despite the confusion on her face, she was beautiful, with untamed auburn hair and eyes the color of turquoise. And almost at once, something inside him began to stir, something that made him feel a bit nervous, the way he always felt in the presence of an attractive woman.

HOPE

Hope stepped from the back deck to the walkway that led over the dune, trying to keep her coffee from spilling. Scottie—her aptly named Scottish terrier—strained at the leash, eager to reach the beach.

"Stop pulling," she said.

The dog ignored her. Scottie had been a gift from Josh, her boyfriend of the past six years, and he barely listened on his best days. But since arriving at the cottage the day before, he'd been positively wild. His paws scuffled madly against the sandy steps as they descended to the beach, and she reminded herself that she needed to bring him to another one of those weekend obedience training programs, though she doubted it would do any good. He'd flunked out of the first two already. Scottie—the sweetest and cutest dog in the world—seemed to be a bit of a dim bulb, bless his heart. Then again, maybe he was just stubborn.

Because Labor Day had come and gone, the beach was quiet, most of the elegant homes dark. She saw someone jogging near the pier; in the opposite direction, a couple strolled near the water. She leaned over, setting the foam cup in the sand while she released Scottie from the leash, watching as her dog sprinted away. She doubted anyone would care. Last night, she'd seen two other dogs off leash, and in any case there weren't too many people around to complain.

Hope started walking and took a sip of her coffee. She hadn't slept well. Usually, the endless roar of the waves lulled her immediately to sleep, but not last night. She'd tossed and turned, woken multiple times, and had finally given up for good when sunlight began streaming into her room.

At least the weather was perfect, with blue skies and a temperature more typical of early autumn than late summer. On the news last night, they had predicted storms over the weekend, and her friend Ellen was crazy with worry. Ellen was getting married on Saturday, and both the wedding and the reception were supposed to be outdoors at the Wilmington Country Club, somewhere near the eighteenth green. Hope figured there was probably a backup plan—no doubt, they'd be able to use the clubhouse—but when Ellen had called last night, she'd nearly been in tears.

Hope had been sympathetic on the phone, but it hadn't been easy. Ellen was so caught up in her own worries that she hadn't so much as asked how Hope was doing. In a way, that was probably a good thing; the last thing Hope wanted to talk about right now was Josh. How was she supposed to explain that Josh was going to be a no-show for the wedding? Or that—as disappointing as a rained-out wedding could be—there were definitely worse things?

Right now, Hope was feeling a bit overwhelmed by life in general, and spending the week alone at the cottage wasn't helping. Not only because Josh wasn't around, but because it was probably the last week she'd ever spend here. Her parents had listed the cottage with a Realtor earlier in the summer, and they'd accepted an offer ten days ago. She understood why they were selling, but she was going to miss this place. Growing up, most of her summers and holidays had been spent here, and every nook and cranny held memories. She could recall washing the sand from her feet with the garden hose, watching storms from the window seat in the kitchen, and the scent of fish or steaks being grilled on the barbecue on the back deck. She remembered swapping late-night secrets with her sisters in their shared room, and it was here that she'd kissed a boy for the very first time. She had been twelve years old and his name was Tony; for years, his family had owned the cottage three doors down. She'd had a crush on him most of the summer, and after they'd split a peanut butter and jelly sandwich, he'd kissed her in the kitchen while her mom had been watering plants on the deck.

The memory still made her smile, and she wondered what the new owners intended to do with the place. She wanted to imagine that they wouldn't change a thing, but she wasn't naive. During her childhood, the cottage had been one of many similarly sized homes along this stretch of shoreline; now there were only a few cottages remaining. In recent years, Sunset Beach had been discovered by the wealthy, and more than likely, the cottage would be razed and a new, much larger home constructed, like the three-story monstrosity right next door. It was the way of the world, she supposed, but it nonetheless felt like part of her was being razed as well. She knew it was crazy thinking— a little too *woe is me*—and she chided herself for it. Playing the martyr wasn't like her; until recently, she'd always thought of herself as a glass-half-full, *because today is a new day* kind of girl. And why not? In most ways her life *had* been blessed. She had loving parents and two wonderful older sisters; she was an aunt to three boys and two girls, who were a source of constant joy and surprise to her. She'd done well in school, and she enjoyed her work as a trauma nurse in the ER at Wake County Medical Center. Despite the few pounds she wanted to lose, she was healthy. She and Josh—an orthopedic surgeon—had been dating since she was thirty, and she loved him. She had good friends and owned her own condominium in Raleigh, not far from her parents. From the outside, everything looked just peachy.

So why was she feeling so wonky right now?

Because it was one more trying thing in an already trying year, beginning first and foremost with her dad's diagnosis, that particular soul-crushing bombshell arriving in April. Her dad was the only one who hadn't been surprised at the news from the doctor. He'd known something was amiss when he no longer had the energy to jog in the woods behind his house.

Her dad had exercised in those woods for as long as she could remember; despite the construction engulfing Raleigh, the area had been designated a greenbelt, which was one of the reasons her parents had bought their home in the first place. Over the years, various developers had tried to overturn the city's decision, promising jobs and tax revenue; they did so without success, partly because her father had opposed them at every meeting of the city council.

Her dad adored the woods. Not only did he run there in the mornings, but after he finished at the school, he would walk the paths he'd followed earlier in the morning. When she was a little girl, she would tag along with him after work, chasing butterflies or tossing sticks, hunting for crawdads in the small creek that wove toward the path in places. Her dad was a high school science teacher who knew the names of every bush and tree they passed. He would point out the differences between a southern red oak and a black oak and in that instant, the distinctions were as obvious as the color of the sky. Later, though, if she attempted it on her own, the information jumbled together. The same thing would happen when they stared at constellations in the sky; he'd point out Hercules, Lyra, or Aquila and she'd nod in wonder, only to squint in confusion at the same sky a week later, trying to remember which one was which.

For a long time, she'd believed her dad to be the smartest man in the world. When she would tell him that, he'd always laugh and say that if that were true, then he would have figured out a way to earn a million dollars. Her mom was a teacher, too—second grade—and it wasn't until Hope graduated from college and began paying her own bills that she realized how much of a financial challenge it must have been for them to raise a family, even on their combined income.

Her dad had been a coach to the high school's cross country and track teams as well. He never raised his voice, but nonetheless led his teams to numerous conference championships. Along with her sisters, Hope had participated in both sports all four years of high school, and though none of them were stars, Hope still jogged a few times a week. Her older sisters ran three or four days a week, and for the past ten years, Hope had joined her dad and her sisters at the annual Turkey Trot on Thanksgiving morning, all of them working up an appetite before sitting down at the table. Two years earlier, her dad had won his age-group bracket.

But now, her dad would never run again.

It had started with occasional twitches and a slight, if no-
ticeable, fatigue. For how long, she wasn't exactly sure, but
she guessed that it had been a couple of years. In the twelve
months after that, the runs in the woods became jogs, and
then finally walks.

Old age, his internist suggested, and it made sense. By
then, her dad was in his late sixties—he'd retired four years
earlier—and he had arthritis in his hips and feet. Despite
a life of exercise, he took medication for slightly elevated
blood pressure. Then, last January, he'd caught a cold. It was
a normal, run-of-the-mill cold, but after a few weeks, her
dad had still found it harder to breathe than usual.

Hope had gone with him to another appointment with
his internist. More tests were done. Blood work was sent to
the labs. He was referred to another doctor, then another. A
muscle biopsy was taken, and when the results came back,
there was the suggestion of a potential neurological problem. It was at that point that Hope began to worry.

More tests followed, and later, Hope sat with the rest of
her family as the diagnosis of amyotrophic lateral sclerosis
was pronounced. Lou Gehrig's disease, the same disease that
put Stephen Hawking in a wheelchair, caused the death
of neurons that control voluntary muscles, the doctor explained. Muscles gradually weakened, resulting in loss of
mobility, swallowing, and speaking. And, then, finally,
breathing. There was no known cure.

Nor was there any way to predict how quickly the disease
would progress. In the months since the diagnosis, her father had seemed little changed, physically. He still went for
his walks in the woods, still had the same gentle spirit and
unwavering faith in God, still held hands with her mom as
the two of them sat on the couch and watched television

in the evenings. That gave her hope that he had a slow-progressing version of the disease, but she worried all the time. How long would her dad remain mobile? How long would her mom be able to handle his care without help? Should they start building ramps and add a railing for the shower? Knowing there were wait lists for the best places, should they start researching assisted-living facilities? And how would they ever pay for it? Her parents were anything but wealthy. They had their pensions and small savings, and they owned their home and the beach cottage, but that was it. Would that be enough, not only for her father's medical care but for her mom's remaining years as well? And if not, what would they do?

Too many questions, with little in the way of answers. Her mom and dad seemed to accept the uncertainty, as did her sisters, but Hope had always been more of a planner. She was the kind of person who would lie awake at night anticipating various possibilities and making hypothetical decisions about pretty much everything. It made her feel like she was somehow better prepared for whatever might come, but on the downside, it led to a life that sometimes cascaded from one worry to the next. Which was exactly what happened whenever she thought about her dad.

But he was doing okay, she reminded herself. And he might be okay three or five or even ten years from now; there was no way to tell. Two days ago, before she'd left for the beach, they'd even gone on a walk, just like they used to. Granted, it was slower and shorter than their walks had been in the past, but her dad could still name all the trees and bushes, and he shared his knowledge one more time. As they were walking, he'd stopped and leaned over, lifting a fallen leaf that presaged the arrival of autumn.

"One of the great things about a leaf," he said to her, "is that it reminds you to live as well as you can for as long as you can, until it's finally time to let go and allow yourself to drift away with grace."

She liked what her dad had told her. Well...*kind of*. No doubt he'd viewed the fallen leaf as a teachable moment, and she knew there was both truth and value in what he said, but was it really possible to face death without any fear at all? To gracefully drift away?

If anyone could do it, her dad probably could. He was just about the most even-keeled, balanced, and peaceful person she'd ever met, which was probably one of the reasons he'd been married to her mom for fifty years and still liked to hold her hand and smooch when he thought the girls weren't paying attention. She often wondered how the two of them could make being in love seem both intentional and effortless at the same time.

That had left her in a funk, too. Well, not so much because of her mom and dad, but because of Josh. As much as she loved him, she'd never gotten used to the on-again, off-again nature of their relationship. Right now they were in the off-again position, which was the reason that Hope was spending the week at the cottage alone except for Scottie, with only a pedicure and time with the hairstylist on the agenda until the rehearsal dinner on Friday night.

Josh was supposed to have come with her this week, and as the date of the trip had approached, Hope had become ever more certain they needed some time alone together. For the last nine months, the practice where he worked had been trying to hire two more orthopedic surgeons to handle the surging patient load, without luck. Which meant Josh had been working seventy- to eighty-hour weeks, and had been on call constantly. Even worse, his days off weren't always in sync with hers, and lately, he seemed to feel a greater-than-usual need to blow off steam in his own way. On his few free weekends, he tended to prefer hanging out with his buddies, boating or water-skiing or overnighting in Charlotte after hitting the bars, instead of spending time with her.

It wasn't the first time that Josh had drifted into a phase like this one, where Hope sometimes felt like an afterthought. He'd never been the type who sent flowers, and the tender gestures her parents shared every day probably seemed utterly foreign to him. There was also, especially at times like these, a bit of Peter Pan about him, a quality that made her wonder whether he would ever really grow up. His apartment, filled with IKEA furniture, baseball pennants, and movie posters, seemed more suitable for a graduate student, which made sense, since he hadn't moved since he'd started medical school. His friends—most of whom he'd met at the gym—were in their late twenties or early thirties, single, and as handsome as Josh was. Josh didn't look his age—he'd be forty in a few months—but for the life of her, she couldn't understand how hanging out at bars with his buddies, who were most likely there to meet women, was something he would still find appealing. But what was she supposed to say to him? "Don't hang out with your friends"? She and Josh weren't married, they weren't even engaged, and he'd told her all along that what he wanted in a partner was someone who wouldn't try to change him. He wanted to be accepted for who he was.

She understood that. She wanted to be accepted for who she was, too. So why did it matter if he liked to hang out with his buddies at bars?

Because, she heard a voice inside her answer, *right now we're not technically together and anything is possible. He hasn't always been faithful during previous breakups, has he?*

Oh yeah. *That.* It had happened when they'd broken up the second and third times. Josh had come clean both times and told her what had occurred—women who'd meant nothing to him, terrible mistakes—and he'd sworn it would never happen again. They'd been able to move past it, she'd thought, but...now they were broken up again, and she could feel those old fears cropping up. Even worse, Josh and his friends were in Las Vegas, no doubt living it up and doing whatever it was that guys did while they were there. She wasn't sure exactly what a guys' weekend in Las Vegas might entail, but strip clubs came immediately to mind. She strongly doubted that any of them were lining up to see Siegfried and Roy. Las Vegas was nicknamed Sin City for a reason.

The whole situation still irritated her. Not only because he'd abandoned her this week, but because breaking up, even temporarily, had been so unnecessary in the first place. Couples argued. *That's what they did.* And then afterward, they discussed the situation, learned from their mistakes, tried to forgive, and moved on from there. But Josh didn't seem to understand that notion, and it left her questioning whether the two of them still had a future.

Sometimes she asked herself why she still wanted him in her life, but deep down, she knew the answer. As furious as she was with him and as frustrating as she found some of his ingrained traits, he was whip-smart and handsome enough to make her heart lurch. Even after all these years, Hope could still get lost in his dark violet eyes. Despite his weekends with the guys, she knew he loved her; a few years earlier, when Hope had been in a car accident, Josh had raced immediately from work and refused to leave her hospital bedside for two straight days. When her dad needed referrals to a neurologist, Josh had taken control of that situation, earning the gratitude of her entire family. He looked after her in little ways, taking her car in for oil changes or to rotate her tires, and every once in a while he would surprise her with a home-cooked dinner. At family gatherings and with her friends, Josh remembered details of everyone's lives and had a gracious knack for making them feel at ease.

They also shared the same interests. They both enjoyed hiking and concerts and had the same taste in music; in the past six years, they'd traveled to New York City, Chicago, Cancun, and the Bahamas, and every one of those getaways had validated her reasons for being with him. When life with Josh was good, it felt like everything she wanted, forever. But when it wasn't good, she admitted, it was terrible. She suspected there might be something addictive about those dramatic ups and downs, but she had no way to know for sure. All she knew was that as unbearable as life with him sometimes felt, she couldn't quite imagine life without him, either.

Up ahead, Scottie was trotting and sniffing, weaving toward terns and sending them into deeper water. Changing directions, he raced for the dune for no reason that Hope could deduce. When they got back to the cottage, he'd probably spend the rest of the morning comatose with exhaustion. Thank God for small favors.

She took another sip of coffee, wishing things were

different. Her parents made marriage seem effortless; her sisters were cut from the same cloth. Even her friends seemed to float along in their relationships while she and Josh were either soaring or sinking. And why had her most recent argument with Josh been their worst ever?

Thinking back, she suspected that she had been as much to blame as he was. He was stressed about work, and she was admittedly stressed about...well, their future, actually. But instead of finding solace in each other's company, they had let the stress slowly amplify over a period of months until it finally blew. She couldn't even remember how the argument had started other than that she'd mentioned Ellen's upcoming wedding, and Josh had grown quiet. It was clear he was upset about something, but when she asked what was wrong, Josh told her it was nothing.

Nothing.

She hated that word. It was a way to end conversations, not begin them, and maybe she shouldn't have pressed him about it. But she had, and for whatever reason, what had originally begun as the mere mention of a friend's wedding turned into shouts and screams, and the next thing she knew, Josh was storming out the door to spend the night at his brother's house. The following day, he'd told Hope that he thought they needed to take a break to evaluate things, and a few days after that, he'd texted to say that he and his buddies were heading to Las Vegas the week of the wedding.

That had been almost a month ago. They'd talked on the phone a few times since then, but those calls had done little to soothe her, and he hadn't called at all in nearly a week. She wished she could roll back the clock and start over, but what she really wanted was for Josh to feel the same way. And for him to apologize. His reaction to the argument had been so over-the-top; it felt as though it hadn't been enough to sink the knife in her heart; he'd needed to twist it as well. Things like that didn't bode well in the long run, but would he ever change? And if not, where did that leave her? She was thirty-six years old, unmarried, and the last thing she wanted was to start over in the dating scene. She couldn't even imagine it. What was she supposed to do—hang out at bars while guys like Josh's friends hit on her? No, thank you. Besides, she'd devoted six years to Josh; she didn't want to believe that it had been a waste of time. As crazy as he could sometimes make her feel, he had so many good qualities…

She finished her coffee. Up ahead, she saw a man walking near the water's edge. Scottie raced past him, closing fast on another flock of seagulls. She tried to immerse herself in the ocean view, watching the ripples shift from yellow to gold in the morning light. The waves were mild and the sea was calm; her dad would tell her that it likely meant a storm was coming, but Hope decided not to mention that to Ellen if her friend called again. Ellen wouldn't want to hear it.

Hope ran a hand through her hair, tucking loose strands behind her ear. There were wispy clouds on the horizon, the kind that would likely burn off as the morning progressed. It would be a perfect afternoon for a glass of wine, maybe some cheese and crackers, or even oysters on the half shell. Add some candles and some sultry R&B, and…

Why was she thinking such things?

With a sigh, she focused on the waves, recalling that as a little girl, she used to play in them for hours. Sometimes she rode a boogie board, other times it was fun diving under them as they broke overhead. More often than not, her dad would join her in the water for a while, and the memories brought with them a tinge of sadness.

Soon, she thought, her dad would never enter the ocean again.

Staring out over the water, Hope reminded herself that she was fretting over first-world problems. It wasn't as though she were worrying about whether she'd eat today, or have a safe place to sleep. The water she drank didn't heighten her risk of contracting cholera or dysentery; she had clothing, and an education, and the list went on and on and on.

Her dad—what with his leaf story and all—wouldn't want her to worry about him. And as for Josh, more than likely, he'd come around. Of their four previous breakups, none had lasted longer than six weeks, and in each case, it had been Josh who'd suggested that they start over. As for Hope, she was a big believer in the philosophy *If you love something, set it free, and if it comes back it loves you.* Common sense told her that begging someone to stay was often the same as begging someone to love you, and she was wise enough to know that never worked.

Turning from the water, she began to meander down the beach again. Shading her eyes, she searched for Scottie up ahead but couldn't find him. She scanned the area behind her, wondering how he could have slipped past her, but he wasn't there, either. Other than her, the beach was empty, and she felt the first twinge of worry. On previous walks, it had sometimes taken her a few seconds to locate him, but he wasn't the kind of dog that would simply run off. It occurred to her that he might have chased some birds into the water and gotten caught in an undertow, but Scottie never swam in the ocean. And yet, he was...gone.

It was then that she spotted someone walking over the dune a short distance up the beach. Her dad still would have made a big deal about that. Dunes were fragile and people were supposed to use the public access paths if there were no steps to the beach, but . . . whatever. She had more immediate concerns . . .

She peered ahead and behind, her gaze returning to the man. He'd reached the beach, and she thought she'd ask him whether he'd seen Scottie. It was doubtful, but she didn't know what else to do. Veering in his direction, she absently noticed that he seemed to be carrying something. Whatever it was blended in with the white shirt he was wearing, and it took her a moment to realize that he had Scottie in his arms. She picked up her pace.

The man walked toward her, moving with an almost animal-like grace. He was dressed in faded jeans and a white button-up shirt, the sleeves rolled to the elbows. As he approached, she noticed his shirt was unbuttoned at the top, revealing chest muscles that indicated both exercise and an active life. He had dark blue eyes, like the sky in late afternoon, and coal-black hair that was turning gray near his ears. When he offered a sheepish smile, she noted the dimple on his chin and an unexpected familiarity in his expression, one that strangely made her feel as if they'd known each other all their lives.

SUNSET BEACH

T ru had no inkling of what Hope was thinking as she approached, but it was impossible for him to turn away. She was dressed in faded jeans, sandals, and a yellow sleeveless blouse that dipped to a low V in front. With smooth, lightly tanned skin and auburn hair framing high cheekbones, she drew his gaze with irresistible force. Her eyes widened with some effusive emotion—Relief? Gratitude? Surprise?—when she finally came to a breathless stop in front of him. Equally at a loss for words, they faced each other without speaking before Tru finally cleared his throat.

"I'm assuming this is your dog?" he inquired, holding Scottie toward her.

Hope heard an accent, something that sounded British or Australian but wasn't quite either. It was enough to break the spell, and she reached for Scottie.

"Why are you holding my dog?"

He explained what had happened as he handed her the dog, and watched as Scottie licked her fingers, whining with excitement.

When he finished, he detected a note of panic in her tone. "Are you saying that he was hit by a car?"

"All I know is what I heard. And he was favoring his back leg and shaking when I found him."

"But you didn't see a car?"

"No."

"That's weird."

"Maybe it was just a graze. And when he ran off, they thought the dog was unhurt."

He watched as she gently squeezed Scottie's legs, one by one. The dog didn't whine; instead, he began to wiggle with excitement. Tru could see the concern on her face as she finally lowered Scottie to the ground. She watched the dog closely as he trotted off.

"He's not limping now," she remarked. From the corner of her eye, she could tell that the man was observing Scottie as well.

"Doesn't seem to be."

"Do you think I need to bring him to see the vet?"

"I don't know."

Scottie spotted another flock of seagulls. He broke into a flat-out run, leaping at one of them before veering away. Then, putting his nose to the ground, he headed in the direction of the cottage.

"He seems like he's doing okay," she murmured, more to herself than to him.

"Well, he certainly has a lot of energy."

You have no idea, she thought. "Thanks for checking on him and bringing him back to the beach."

"Glad to help. Before you go, you wouldn't happen to know if there's someplace nearby where I could get a cup of coffee, would you?"

"No. There are only houses in this direction. A little past the pier, you'll find a place called Clancy's. It's a restaurant and bar, but I don't think they open until lunch."

She understood his crestfallen expression. Mornings without coffee were terrible, and if she had magic powers, she'd ban the very thought of it. Scottie, meanwhile, was getting farther away, and she motioned toward him. "I should probably keep an eye on my dog."

"I was headed in the same direction before I got sidetracked," he said. He turned. "Do you mind if I walk with you?"

As soon as he asked, Hope felt a frisson of…something. His gaze, the deep cadence of his voice, his relaxed yet gracious manner set a vibration thrumming inside her like a plucked string. Startled, her first instinct was to simply decline. The old Hope, the Hope she'd always been, would have done so automatically. But something took over then, an instinct she didn't recognize.

"That would be fine," she answered instead.

Even in the moment, she wasn't sure why she agreed. Nor would she understand the reason years later. It would be easy to chalk it up to the worries plaguing her at the time, but she knew that wasn't entirely true. Instead, she came to believe that despite the fact that they'd only just met, he summoned something previously unknown in her, an urge both primal and foreign.

He nodded. If he was surprised by her response, she couldn't tell as they began to walk beside each other. He wasn't uncomfortably close, but he was close enough for her to note the way the tips of his thick, dark hair fluttered in the breeze. Scottie continued to explore ahead of them, and Hope felt the crunch of tiny seashells beneath her feet. On the back porch of a home, a light blue flag fluttered in the wind. Sunlight poured down, liquid and warm. Because they were otherwise alone on the beach, walking beside him felt strangely intimate, as if they were together on an empty stage.

"My name's Tru Walls, by the way," he finally said, raising his voice over the crash of the waves.

She looked over at him, noting the lines at the corners of his eyes, the kind that come from spending hours in the sun. "Tru? I don't think I've ever heard that name before."

"It's short for Truitt."

"Nice to meet you, Tru. I'm Hope Anderson."

"I think I saw you walking last night."

"Probably. Whenever I visit here, I bring Scottie out a few times a day. I didn't see you, though."

He lifted his chin in the direction of the pier. "I went in the other direction. I needed to stretch my legs. It was a long flight."

"Where did you fly in from?"

"Zimbabwe."

"Is that where you live?" Her face registered her surprise.

"All my life."

"Forgive my ignorance," Hope began, "but where in Africa is that?"

"In the south. It's bordered by South Africa, Botswana, Zambia, and Mozambique."

South Africa was always in the news, but the other three countries were only vaguely familiar to her. "You're a long way from home."

"I am."

"First time at Sunset Beach?"

"First time in the U.S. It's a different world here."

"How so?"

"Everything...the roads, the infrastructure, Wilmington, the traffic, the people...and I can't get over how green the landscape is."

Hope had no frame of reference for comparison, so she simply nodded. She watched as Tru tucked a hand in his pocket.

"And you?" he asked. "You mentioned that you're visiting?"

She nodded. "I live in Raleigh." Then, realizing he probably had no idea where that was, she added, "It's a couple of hours northwest. More inland...more trees, and no beach."

"Is it flat like it is around here?"

"Not at all. It has hills. It's also a sizable city, with lots of people and things to do. As you've probably noticed, it can be pretty quiet around here."

"I would have imagined that the beach would be more crowded."

"It can be in the summer, and there will probably be a few more people out and about this afternoon. But it's never really busy this time of year. It's more of a vacation spot. Anyone you do see probably lives on the island."

Hope pulled her hair back, trying to keep the strands from blowing in her face, but without an elastic band, it was pointless. Glancing over, she noticed a leather bracelet on his wrist. It was scuffed and worn, with faded stitching forming a design that she couldn't quite make out. But somehow, she thought, it seemed to suit him.

"I don't think I've ever met someone from Zimbabwe before." She squinted at him. "Are you here on vacation?"

He walked a few paces without answering, surprisingly graceful, even in the sand. "I'm here because I'm supposed to meet someone."

"Oh." His answer made her think it was probably a woman, and though it shouldn't bother her, she felt an unexpected flash of disappointment. *Ridiculous*, she chided herself as she pushed the thought away.

"How about you?" he asked, arching an eyebrow. "What brings you here?"

"A good friend of mine is getting married this Saturday in Wilmington. I'm one of the bridesmaids."

"Sounds like a nice weekend."

Except that Josh went to Las Vegas instead, so I won't have anyone to dance with. And I'll be asked a million questions about him and what's going on, none of which I really want to answer, even if I could. "A celebration for sure," she agreed. Then: "Can I ask you a question?"

"By all means."

"What's Zimbabwe like? I've never been to Africa."

"It depends where you are, I suppose."

"Is it like America?"

"So far, not in the slightest."

She smiled. Of course it wasn't. "Maybe this is a silly question, but have you ever seen a lion?"

"I see them almost every day."

"Like outside your window?" Hope's eyes widened.

"I'm a guide at a game reserve. Safaris."

"I've always wanted to go on safari..."

"Many of the people I guide describe it as the trip of a lifetime."

Hope tried and failed to imagine it. If she went, the animals would probably go into hiding, like they had at the zoo when she'd visited as a girl.

"How do you even get into something like that?"

"It's regulated by the government. There are classes, exams, an apprenticeship, and finally a license. After that, you start out spotting, and then eventually you become a guide."

"What do you mean by spotting?"

"Many of the animals are fairly adept at camouflage, so sometimes they're not too easy to find. The spotter searches for them, so that the guide can drive safely and answer questions."

She nodded, regarding him with growing curiosity. "How long have you been doing this?"

"A long time," he answered. Then, with a smile, he added, "More than twenty years."

"At the same place?"

"Many different camps."

"Aren't they all the same?"

"Every camp is different. Some are expensive, others less so. There are different concentrations of animals depending on where you are in the country. Some areas are wetter or drier, which affects species concentrations and migration and movement. Some camps advertise themselves as luxury camps and boast fantastic chefs; others offer only the basics—tents, cots, and cellophane-wrapped food. And some camps have better game management than others."

"How's the camp where you work now?"

"It's a luxury camp. Excellent accommodations and food, excellent game management, and a large variety of animals."

"You'd recommend it?"

"Certainly."

"It must be incredible seeing the animals every day. But I guess it's just another day at work for you."

"Not at all. Every day is new." He studied her, his blue

eyes penetrating yet warm. "How about you? What do you do?"

For whatever reason, she hadn't expected him to ask. "I'm a trauma nurse at a hospital."

"As in...gunshots?"

"Sometimes," she said. "Mainly car accidents."

By then, they were closing in on the place Tru was staying and he began a slow angle away from the compact sand.

"I'm staying at my parents' cottage over there," Hope volunteered, pointing to the place beside his. "Where are you?"

"Right next door. The big three-story."

"Oh," she said.

"Problem?"

"It's...big."

"It is." He laughed. "But it's not my house. The man I'm supposed to meet is letting me stay there. My guess is he owns it."

The *man* he was meeting, she noted. That made her feel better, though she reminded herself that there was no reason to care one way or another. "It's just that it blocks some of the late-afternoon light on our back deck. And to my dad especially, it's a bit of an eyesore."

"Do you know the owner?"

"I've never met him," she answered. "Why? Don't you?"

"No. Until a few weeks ago, I'd never heard of him."

She wanted to ask more, but assumed he was being circumspect for a reason. Scanning the beach, she spotted Scottie sniffing along the dunes up ahead, nearing the steps that led to the walkway and cottage. As usual, he was covered in sand.

Tru slowed, finally coming to a stop when he had reached his steps.

"I guess this is where we part."

"Thank you again for checking on Scottie. I'm so relieved he's okay."

"Me too. Still disappointed by the lack of coffee in this neighborhood, though." He gave a wry smile.

It had been a long time since she'd had a conversation like this, let alone with a man she'd just met—easy and unforced, without expectation. Realizing she didn't want it to end just yet, she nodded toward the cottage. "I brewed a pot before I left this morning. Would you like a cup?"

"I would hate to intrude."

"It's the least I can do. It's only me at the cottage, and I'll probably just end up throwing the rest of the pot away. Besides, you saved my dog."

"In that case, I'd appreciate a cup."

"Come on then," she said.

She led the way to the steps, then over the walkway to the deck of the cottage. Scottie was already at the gate, tail wagging, and darted for the back door as soon as she opened it. Tru peeked over at the house where he was staying, thinking she was right. It *was* a bit of an eyesore. The cottage, on the other hand, felt like a *home*, with white paint and blue shutters, and a planter box filled with flowers. Near the back door stood a wooden table surrounded by five chairs; in front of the windows, a pair of rockers flanked a small weather-beaten table. Though wind and rain and salt had taken their toll, the deck felt positively cozy.

Hope walked to the door. "I'll get your coffee, but Scottie has to stay on the deck for a minute. I need to towel him off, or I'll spend the rest of the afternoon sweeping," she said over her shoulder. "Go ahead and sit. It'll only take a minute."

The screen door banged shut behind her, and Tru took a seat at the table. Beyond the railing, the ocean was calm and inviting. Perhaps he would go for a swim later in the afternoon.

Through the window, he was able to see into the kitchen as Hope emerged from around a corner, a towel draped over her shoulder, and pulled two cups from the cabinet. She interested him. That she was beautiful there was no doubt, but it wasn't simply that. There was an air of vulnerability and loneliness behind her smile, as if she was wrestling with something troubling. Maybe even a few somethings.

He shifted in his seat, reminding himself that it wasn't his business. They were strangers and he was leaving after the weekend; aside from waving at each other from the back deck over the next few days, this might be the last time he saw or spoke to her.

He heard a tap at the door; through the screen, he saw her standing expectantly, holding two cups. Tru rose from his seat and opened it for her. She scooted around him and set both cups on the table.

"Do you need milk or sugar?"

"No, thank you," he said.

"Okay. Go ahead and start. Let me take care of Scottie."

Slipping the towel from her shoulder, she squatted beside the dog and began rubbing him briskly with the towel.

"You wouldn't believe how much sand gets into his fur," she said. "He's like a sand magnet."

"I'll bet he's good company."

"He's the best," she said, planting an affectionate kiss on the dog's snout. Scottie licked her face joyfully in return.

"How old is he?"

"He's four. My boyfriend, Josh, bought him for me."

Tru nodded. He should have assumed that she was seeing someone. He reached for his cup, not sure what to say, and decided not to ask anything more. He took a sip, thinking the coffee tasted different from the kind his family grew on the farm. Less smooth, somehow. But it was strong and hot, just what he needed.

When Hope finished with Scottie, she draped the towel over the railing to dry and walked back to the table. When she sat, her face fell half in shadow, lending her features a mysterious cast. She blew delicately on her coffee before taking a sip, the gesture strangely arresting.

"Tell me about the wedding," he finally said.

"Oh, gosh . . . that. It's just a wedding."

"You said it's for a good friend?"

"I've been friends with Ellen since college. We were in the same sorority—do they have sororities in Zimbabwe?" she interrupted herself. At his quizzical expression, she went on. "Sororities are a kind of all-women club at colleges and universities . . . you know, where a group of girls live and socialize together. Anyway, all the bridesmaids were in the same sorority, so it'll be a little reunion, too. Other than that, it's just a typical wedding. Photos, cake, a band at the reception, tossing the garter belt and all that. You know how weddings are."

"Aside from my own, I've never been to one."

"Oh . . . you're married?"

"Divorced. But the wedding wasn't anything like they do here in the U.S. We were married by an official of the court, and went straight from there to the airport. We spent our honeymoon in Paris."

"That sounds romantic."

"It was."

She liked the matter-of-factness of his answer, liked that he didn't feel the need to elaborate or romanticize it. "How do you know about American weddings, then?"

"I've seen a few movies. And I've had guests tell me about them. Safaris are popular honeymoon destinations. In any case, the weddings sound very complicated and stressful."

Ellen would definitely agree with that, Hope thought. Switching tacks, Hope asked, "What is it like to grow up in Zimbabwe?"

"I can only talk about my own experience. Zimbabwe is a big country. It's different for everyone."

"What was it like for you?"

He wasn't sure what or how much to tell her, so he kept it general. "My family owns a farm near Harare. It's been in the family for generations. So I grew up doing farm chores. My grandfather thought it would be good for me. I milked cows and collected eggs when I was young. In my teen years, I did heavier work, like repairs: fencing, roofs, irrigation, pumps, engines, anything that was broken. In addition to going to school."

"How did you end up guiding?"

He shrugged. "I felt at peace whenever I was in the bush. Whenever I had spare time, I'd venture out on my own. And when I finished school, I let my family know I would be leaving. So I did."

As he answered, he could feel her eyes on him. She offered a skeptical expression as she reached for her coffee again.

"Why do I have the sense that there's more to the story?"

"Because there's always more to the story."

She laughed, the sound surprisingly hearty and unself-conscious. "Fair enough. Tell me about some of the most exciting things you've seen on safari."

On familiar ground, Tru regaled her with the same stories he shared with guests whenever they asked. Now and then she had questions, but for the most part, she was content to listen. By the time he finished, the coffee was gone and the sun was scorching the back of his neck. He set the empty cup back on the table.

"Would you like more? There's a little left in the pot."

"One cup is plenty," he said. "And I've taken too much of your time already. But I did appreciate it. Thank you."

"It was the least I could do," she said. She rose as well, walking him to the gate. He pulled it open, keenly aware of her closeness. He started down the steps, but turned when he reached the walkway to offer a quick wave.

"Nice meeting you, Tru," she called out with a smile. Though he had no way to know for sure, he wondered whether she continued to watch him as he wound toward the beach. For some reason, it took a great deal of willpower to stop himself from glancing over his shoulder to find out.

AUTUMN AFTERNOONS

Back at the house, Tru found himself at loose ends. If he could, he'd call Andrew, but he wasn't comfortable with the thought of dialing from the house phone. Overseas charges were substantial, and besides, Andrew likely wouldn't be home yet. After school, he played soccer with his youth club; Tru always enjoyed watching him practice. Andrew lacked the innate athleticism that other kids on the team displayed, but he was a relaxed and natural leader, much like his mother.

Thinking about his son eventually made Tru retrieve his drawing materials, which he carried out to the back deck. Next door, he noticed that Hope had gone inside, although the towel she'd used on Scottie was still draped over the railing. Settling himself in the chair, he debated what he should sketch. Andrew had never seen the ocean, not in person, so Tru decided to try to capture the enormity of the sight before him, assuming that was even possible.

As always, he started with a general and faint outline of the scene—a diagonal point of view that included the shoreline, breaking waves, the pier, and a sea that stretched to the horizon. Drawing had always been a way to relax his mind, and as he sketched, he allowed it to wander. He thought about Hope and wondered what it was about her that had captured his interest. It was unusual for him to be so instantly taken with someone, but he told himself it didn't really matter. He'd come to North Carolina for other reasons, and he found his thoughts drifting to his family.

He hadn't seen or spoken to his stepfather, Rodney, or his half brothers, Allen and Alex, in almost two years. The reasons were rooted in history, and wealth had further compounded the estrangement. In addition to the Walls family name, Tru had inherited partial ownership of the farm and business empire. The profits were substantial, but in his daily life, he had little need for money. Whatever he earned from the farm was sent to an investment account in Switzerland that the Colonel had set up when Tru was still a toddler. The funds had been piling up for years, but Tru seldom checked the balance. From that account, he arranged for money to be sent regularly to Kim and he paid for Andrew's schooling, but aside from the outright purchase of the house in Bulawayo, that was it. He had already arranged to sign over a chunk of the money to Andrew when his son reached the age of thirty-five. He assumed that Andrew would find more use for it than he would.

Recently, his half brothers had started to become resentful about that, but theirs had always been a distant relationship, so it wasn't altogether unexpected. Tru was nine years older than the twins, and by the time they would have been old enough to remember Tru, he was already spending most of his time in the bush, as far away from the farm as possible.

He moved away for good when he was eighteen. In essence, they were, and always had been, strangers to each other.

Things with Rodney, on the other hand, were more complicated. Tru's equity in the business had been causing problems with Rodney ever since the Colonel had died, thirteen years ago, but in truth, the relationship had been broken far longer than that. To Tru's mind, it dated back to the fire, when Tru was eleven years old. Much of the compound had gone up in flames in 1959. Tru had barely escaped by jumping from a second-floor window. Rodney had carried Allen and Alex to safety, but Tru's mother, Evelyn, had never made it out.

Even before the fire, Rodney had never been supportive or affectionate with his stepson; he mostly tolerated Tru. In the aftermath, Rodney's attention became almost nonexistent. Between dealing with his grief, raising toddlers, and managing the farm, he was overwhelmed. In retrospect, Tru understood that. At the time, it hadn't been so easy, and the Colonel hadn't offered much in the way of support, either. After the death of his only child, he sank into a profound depression that seemed to lock him away in a vault of silence. He would sit near the blackened ruins of the compound, staring at the wreckage; when the debris was hauled off and construction began on the new houses, he stared without speaking at the ongoing work. Occasionally Tru went to sit with him, but the Colonel would mumble only a few words in acknowledgment. There were rumors, after all; rumors about his grandfather, the business, and the real reason for the fire. At the time, Tru knew nothing about them; he knew only that no one in his family seemed willing to speak to him or even offer so much as a hug. If it hadn't been for Tengwe and Anoona, Tru wasn't sure he would have survived the loss of his mother. The only thing he could really remember from that period was regularly crying himself to sleep and spending long hours wandering the property alone after school and his chores. He understood now that those had been his first steps on the journey that led him from the farm to living in the bush. Had his mother survived, he had no idea who he would have become.

But that wasn't the only change in the aftermath of his mother's death. After she passed, Tru had asked Tengwe to purchase some drawing paper and pencils. Because he recalled seeing his mother sketch, he began to do so as well. He had no training and little natural skill; it was months before he could re-create on paper something as simple as a tree with any semblance of realism. It was, however, a way to escape his own feelings and the quiet desperation always present at the farm.

He longed to draw his mother, but her features seemed to vanish more quickly than his skill developed. Everything he attempted struck him as wrong somehow, not the mother he remembered, even when Tengwe and Anoona protested otherwise. Some attempts were closer than others, but never once did he complete a drawing of his mother that he felt fully captured her. In the end, he threw the stack of sketches away, resigning himself to that additional loss, like the other losses in his life.

Like his father.

Growing up, it had sometimes felt to Tru as though the man had never existed. His mother had said little about him, even when Tru pressed; the Colonel refused to speak of him at all. Over time, Tru's curiosity waned to almost nothing. He could go years without thinking or wondering about the man. Then, out of the blue, a letter had arrived a few months ago at the camp in Hwange. It had originally been sent to the farm; Tengwe had forwarded it, but Tru hadn't bothered opening it right away. When he finally did, his initial instinct was to regard it as some sort of practical joke, despite the plane tickets. It was only when he scrutinized the faded photograph that he realized that the letter might be genuine.

The photo showed a young, handsome man with his arm around a much younger version of a woman who could only be Tru's mother. Evelyn was a teenager in the photograph— she had been nineteen when Tru was born—and it struck Tru as surreal that he was more than twice the age she'd been back then. Assuming, of course, that it actually was her.

But it was. In his heart, he knew it.

He didn't know how long he stared at it on that first evening, but over the next few days, he found himself continually reaching for it. It was the only photograph he had of his mother. All the others had been lost in the same fire that had killed her, and seeing her image after so many years triggered a flood of additional memories: the sight of her sketching on the back veranda; her face hovering above him as she tucked him into bed; the sight of her wearing a green dress as she stood in the kitchen; the feel of her hand in his as they walked toward a pond. He still wasn't sure whether any of those events were real or simply figments of his imagination.

Then, of course, there was the man in the photograph...

In the letter, he'd identified himself as Harry Beckham, an American. He claimed to have been born in 1914, and to have met Tru's mother in late 1946. He'd served in World War II as part of the U.S. Army Corps of Engineers, and after the war, he'd moved to Rhodesia, where he worked at the Bushtick Mine in Matabeleland. He'd met Tru's mother in Harare, and said that the two of them had fallen in love. He further claimed not to have known that she'd been pregnant when he moved back to America, but Tru wasn't sure he believed that. After all, if he hadn't even suspected that Tru's mum had been pregnant, why would he have searched for a long-lost child in the first place?

Tru supposed he would find out soon enough.

Tru continued to labor over the sketch for a couple of hours, stopping only when he thought he had something that Andrew might enjoy. He hoped it might make up for the week they wouldn't be together.

Heading inside, he toyed with the idea of going fishing. He enjoyed it and hadn't had much time for it in the past few years, but after sitting for much of the afternoon, he felt the urge to get his blood flowing. Maybe tomorrow, he thought, and instead changed into the only pair of shorts he owned. He found a closet full of beach towels, grabbed one, then went to the beach. Dropping the towel in the dry sand near the water's edge, he waded in, surprised by how warm the water was. He moved through the first set of mild breakers, then the next, and once he was beyond them, he was chest-deep in the water. Kicking off the bottom, he began to swim, hoping to make it to the pier and back.

It took a while to find his rhythm, despite the placid surface of the ocean. Because he hadn't swum any kind of distance in years, he found it slow going. He inched past one house and then another; by the fifth house, his muscles had begun to tire. When he reached the pier, exhaustion had set in, but he was nothing if not persistent. Instead of wading ashore, he turned and began the even slower swim back to where he'd started.

When he finally reached his house and went ashore, the muscles in his legs were shaking and he could barely move his arms. Nonetheless, he felt satisfied. At the camp, he was limited to calisthenics and the kind of explosive jumps that could be done in confined areas. He ran whenever possible—he would circle the interior perimeter of the guide camp for half an hour a few times a week, the most boring jog on the planet, he'd long ago decided—but on most days, he was able to do quite a bit of walking. In the camp where he worked, a guide could allow guests to leave the jeep and head into the bush, as long as the guide was armed. Sometimes that was the only way to get close enough to spot some of the rarer animals like black rhinos or cheetahs. For him, it was a way to stretch his legs; for the guests, it was usually the highlight of any game drive.

Once inside, he took a long shower, rinsed his shorts in the sink, and had a sandwich for lunch. After that, he wasn't quite sure what to do. It had been a long time since he'd had an afternoon with nothing whatsoever on the schedule, and it left him feeling unsettled. He picked up his sketchbook again and examined the drawing he'd done for Andrew, noticing some changes he wanted to make. It was always that way; Da Vinci once said that art is never finished but only abandoned, and that made perfect sense to Tru. He decided he'd work on it again tomorrow.

For now, he picked up his guitar and went to the back deck. The sand blazed white in the sun and the blue water stretching to the horizon was strangely calm beyond the breakers. Perfect. But as he tuned his guitar, he realized he had no desire to spend the rest of the day at the house. He could call for a car, but that seemed pointless. He had no idea where he would even want to go. Instead, he remembered that Hope had mentioned a restaurant a little way past the pier, and he decided that later tonight, he'd have dinner there.

Once the guitar was readied, he played for a while, running through most of the songs he'd ever learned. Like sketching, it allowed his mind to wander, and when his gaze eventually drifted to the cottage next door, his thoughts again landed on Hope. He wondered why, despite having a boyfriend and the wedding of a close friend only days away, she had come to Sunset Beach alone.

Hope found herself wishing that her hair and nail appointments had been scheduled for today instead of tomorrow morning, just so she'd have an excuse to get out of the house. Instead, she spent the morning going through a few of the closets at the cottage. Her mom had suggested that she take anything she wanted, with the unspoken caveat that Hope should try to anticipate her sisters' desires as well. Both Robin and Joanna would be coming down to the cottage in the next few weeks to help with the sorting, and all of them had been raised in a way that left little room for selfishness. Because Hope had only limited storage space at her condominium, she had no problem with keeping almost nothing for herself.

Still, going through a single box took more time than she'd anticipated. After disposing of the junk (which was most of it), she'd been left with a favorite pair of swim goggles, a tattered copy of *Where the Wild Things Are*, a Bugs Bunny key chain, a Winnie the Pooh stuffed animal, three completed coloring books, postcards from various places where the family had vacationed, and a locket with a photograph of Hope's mother. All those items made her smile for one reason or another and were worth keeping, and she suspected that her sisters would feel the same way. Most likely, anything kept would end up in another box tucked away in an attic somewhere. Which raised the question of why they were bothering to go through it all in the first place, but deep down, Hope already knew the answer. Throwing it all away didn't feel right. For some crazy reason, part of her wanted to know these things were still around.

She'd be the first to admit that she hadn't been thinking all that straight lately, starting with the idea of coming here ahead of the wedding. In hindsight, it seemed like a bad idea, but she'd already requested and received the vacation days, and what was the alternative? Visiting her parents and trying not to worry about her dad? Or staying in Raleigh, where she'd be equally alone, but surrounded by constant reminders of Josh? She supposed she could have taken a vacation somewhere else, but where would she have gone? The Bahamas? Key West? Paris? She would have been alone there, too, her dad would still be sick, Josh would still be in Las Vegas, and she would still have a wedding to attend this weekend.

Ah, yes…the wedding. Though she hated to admit it, there was a part of her that didn't want to go, and not only because she didn't relish explaining that Josh had ditched her. And it wasn't because of Ellen, either. She was genuinely happy for Ellen, and normally, she couldn't wait to see her closest friends. They knew everything about each other, and had stayed in touch regularly after graduation. They'd also all been bridesmaids in each other's weddings, starting with Jeannie and Linda. They'd both married a year after graduation and now had five kids between them. Sienna got married a couple years after that and now had four kids. Angie tied the knot when she was thirty, and had twin three-year-old girls. Susan had been married two years ago, and now—as of next Saturday, Ellen, too, would join the ranks of the married.

It hadn't surprised her when Susan had recently called to tell her that she was three months pregnant. But Ellen, too? Ellen, who'd met Colson for the first time *last December*? Ellen, who'd once sworn she'd never get married or have kids? Ellen, who'd lived life on the wild side until her late twenties, and used to commute to Atlantic City to spend weekends with her then-boyfriend, a cocaine dealer? Not only had Ellen been able to find someone willing to marry her—a churchgoing investment banker, no less—but two weeks ago, she'd confided to Hope that, like Susan, she was twelve weeks pregnant. Ellen and Susan would be having children at roughly the same time, and the realization made Hope suddenly feel very much on the verge of becoming an outsider in what was once the closest circle of friends. The rest of them were either in or about to enter a new phase of life, and Hope had no idea when, or even if, she'd ever join them. Especially when it came to having kids.

That scared her. For a long time, she'd believed that the whole "ticking biological clock" thing was a myth. Not the part where age made it increasingly difficult to have children—every woman knew about that. But it wasn't something she'd ever believed would pertain to her. Having children was one of those things she'd taken for granted, that it would simply happen when the time was right. She was wired that way and had been as long as she could remember; she couldn't imagine a future without children of her own, and it wasn't until college that she learned that not every woman felt the same way. When her freshman roommate Sandy told her otherwise—that she'd rather have a career than children—the concept was so foreign that she'd initially thought Sandy was kidding. Hope hadn't spoken to Sandy since graduation, but a couple of years ago, she'd bumped into her at the mall, with her new baby in tow. Hope guessed that Sandy had no memory of the conversation they'd had in the dorm that night, and Hope hadn't reminded her. But Hope had gone home and cried.

How was it that Sandy had a child, but Hope didn't? And her sisters, Robin and Joanna? And now, *all* of her closest friends were either already there or on their way? It made no sense to her. For as long as she could remember, she'd pictured herself pregnant, then holding her newborn infants, marveling at their growth and wondering whose traits they had inherited. Would they have her nose, or their dad's big feet? Or the red hair she'd inherited from her grandmother? Motherhood had always seemed foreordained.

But then, Hope had always been a planner. She'd had her life charted out by the age of fifteen: Get good grades, graduate from college, become a registered nurse by twenty-four, work hard at your job, and get your career going. Meanwhile, have some fun along the way—you're only young once, right? Hang out with your girlfriends and date some guys, without letting anything get too serious. Then, maybe as thirty was approaching, meet *the one*. Date him, fall in love, and get married. After a year or two, start having children. Two would be perfect, hopefully one of each sex, though if that last part didn't happen, she knew she wouldn't really be disappointed. As long as she had at least one girl, that is.

One by one, through her teens and twenties, she'd checked those things off. And then Josh came along right on schedule. In her wildest dreams, she never would have believed that six years later, she'd still be single and child-less, and she had trouble figuring out exactly where the plan had gone awry. Josh had told her that he wanted marriage and children as well, so what had they been doing all this time? Where had the six years gone?

One thing she knew for sure: Being thirty-six was a lot different than being thirty-five. She'd learned that on her birthday last April. Her family was there, Josh was there, and it should have been a happy event, but she'd taken one look at the cake and thought, *Wow, that's a LOT of candles!* Blowing them out had seemed to take an inordinately long time.

It wasn't the age thing that had bothered her. Nor was it that she was closer to forty than to thirty. In spirit she still felt closer to twenty-five. But the following day—as if God had wanted to smack her in the face with a not-so-gentle reminder—a pregnant thirty-six-year-old had entered the emergency room after slicing her finger while cutting an onion. There was a lot of blood, followed by a local anesthetic and stitches, and the lady had joked that she wouldn't have come in at all, except for the fact that hers was considered a *geriatric* pregnancy.

Hope had heard the term before when she'd been in nursing school, but as a trauma nurse in the ER, she saw few pregnant women and had forgotten about it.

"I hate that it's called a geriatric pregnancy," Hope remarked. "It's not as if you're *old*."

"No, but trust me. It's a lot different than being pregnant in my twenties." She smiled. "I have three boys, but we wanted to try for a girl."

"And?"

"It's another boy." She rolled her eyes. "How many kids do you have?"

"Oh," Hope had answered. "I don't have any. I'm not married."

"No worries. You still have time. How old are you? Twenty-eight?"

Hope forced a smile, thinking again about the term *geriatric pregnancy*. "Close enough," she responded.

Tired of her thoughts—and really, really tired of the pity party—Hope figured a distraction was in order. Since she hadn't bothered to pick up any groceries on her drive down and needed to get out of the house for a while, she first visited a roadside vegetable stand. It was just off the island and had been around for as long as she could remember. She filled a straw basket with zucchini, squash, lettuce, tomatoes, onions, and peppers, then drove to a neighboring island, where she purchased some Spanish mackerel. By the time she got back to the cottage, though, she realized she wasn't hungry.

After opening the windows, she put the food away, poured herself a glass of wine, and began sorting through more boxes. She tried to be selective (while keeping both Robin and Joanna in mind), condensing down to a small pile of keepsakes that she returned to a single box she stored in the closet. She brought the rest downstairs to the garbage cans, satisfied with her day's work. Scottie had followed her out, and she stayed with him at the front of the house, not wanting to chase him down the beach again.

Checking the clock, she fought the urge to call Josh. He was staying at Caesars Palace, but she reminded herself that if he wanted to talk to her, he knew the number of the cottage. *Instead*, she thought, *why not a little me time?* What she really needed was a nap—the lack of sleep the night before had caught up with her. She lay down on the living room couch...and the next thing she knew, it was midafternoon. Through the open windows, she could hear the faint sounds of someone playing the guitar and singing.

Peeking out the window, she caught a partial glimpse of Tru through the railings. She listened to the music for a few minutes while she tidied up the kitchen, and despite her gloomy thoughts of earlier, she couldn't help but smile. She couldn't even remember the last time she'd been attracted to someone right off the bat. And then she'd gone and invited him over for coffee! She still couldn't believe she'd done that.

After wiping the counters, Hope decided that a long bath was in order. She enjoyed a good bubble bath, but the rush of her daily life made showering easier, so baths were something of a luxury. After filling the tub, she soaked for a long time, feeling the tension slowly ebb from her body.

Afterward, she swaddled herself in a bathrobe and pulled a book from the shelf, an old Agatha Christie mystery. She remembered loving the books as a teenager, so why not? Taking a seat on the couch, she settled into the story. It was easy reading, but the mystery was just as good as what she found on television these days, and she got halfway through the book before finally putting it aside.

By then, the sun was beginning to dip at the horizon, and she realized she was hungry. She hadn't eaten all day, but she found she wasn't in the mood to cook. She wanted to keep the relaxing flow of the afternoon going. Throwing on some jeans, sandals, and a sleeveless blouse, she did a quick pass with her makeup and pulled her hair back into a messy ponytail. She fed Scottie and let him out in the front yard—he was visibly disappointed when he registered that he wouldn't be going with her—and locked the front door. Then, she left the house via the back deck, strode down the walkway, and descended the steps to the beach. Whenever their family had come to Sunset Beach, they'd always eaten at Clancy's at least once, and keeping up the tradition felt right on a night like tonight.

DINNER ON THE DECK

Clancy's was a few minutes' walk past the pier, and Tru liked the place even before he climbed up to the main deck from the beach. He could hear strains of music intermingled with conversation and laughter. At the top of the stairs was a wooden arch decorated with white Christmas lights and faded lettering indicating the restaurant's name.

The deck was illuminated by clutches of tiki torches, the flames rippling in the breeze. Peeling bar tables and mismatched stools near the railings framed a cluster of wooden tables in the center, half of them unoccupied. The interior had more seating; the kitchen was located to the left and the sparsely populated bar area housed a juke-box, which Tru noted with interest. There was a fireplace as well with a cannonball on the mantel, and the wall surrounding it was decorated with maritime items—an ancient wooden wheel, a tribute to Blackbeard, and nautical flags. As Tru surveyed his surroundings, a waitress in her midfifties emerged through a set of swinging doors, carrying a tray of food.

"Take a seat anywhere, inside or out," she called out. "I'll bring you a menu."

The night was too gorgeous to waste inside, so Tru took a seat at one of the bar tables near the railing, facing the ocean. The moon was hovering just over the horizon, making the water glitter, and he was struck again by the contrast between this place and the world he knew, even if there were fundamental similarities. At night, the bush was dark and mysterious, rife with hidden dangers; the sea struck him as much the same. Though he could swim during the day, the fear of doing so at night resounded within him on some elemental level.

The waitress dropped off a menu and hustled back toward the kitchen. From the jukebox, a song came on that he didn't recognize. He was used to that. Often, when riding with guests, he heard them referencing movies and television shows he'd never heard of, and the same went with bands and songs. He knew the Beatles—who didn't?—and he favored their songs when playing the guitar, along with a bit of Bob Dylan, Bob Marley, Johnny Cash, Kris Kristofferson, the Eagles, and Elvis Presley mixed in whenever the mood struck. The song from the jukebox had a memorable hook, though it was a little too synthesizer-driven for his taste.

He skimmed the menu, pleasantly surprised by the selection of seafood, in addition to the expected burgers and fries. Unfortunately, most of the seafood was deep-fried. He whittled his decision down to a choice between grilled tuna and pan-fried grouper before folding the menu and turning his attention to the ocean again.

Minutes later, the waitress brought out a tray of drinks, stopping at some nearby tables before retreating inside without so much as a glance in his direction. He gave a mental shrug; he had nowhere to go and all night to get there.

Sensing movement near the gate, he lifted his gaze and was surprised to see Hope stepping onto the deck. They had probably been on the beach at the same time, and for an instant, he wondered whether she'd seen him leave and followed him. He dismissed the thought quickly, wondering why it had come to him at all. He turned toward the water again, not wanting her to catch him staring, but he found himself replaying their visit earlier that morning.

Her smile, he realized. He'd really liked the way she smiled.

Hope was amazed at how unchanged the place seemed. It was one of the reasons her dad liked Clancy's so much—he used to tell her that the more the world changed, the more comfortable Clancy's felt—but she knew he really liked to come because Clancy's served the best lemon meringue pie in the world. Clancy's mother had supposedly perfected the recipe decades earlier, and had won blue ribbons at six consecutive state fairs, as well as allegedly inspiring the recipe at Marie Callender's, a restaurant chain in California. Whatever the truth, Hope had to admit that a slice of the pie was often the perfect way to end an evening at the beach. There was something about the mixture of sweet and tang that was always just right.

She looked around the deck. In all their years coming to the place, she'd never eaten inside, and the thought didn't occur to her now. Near the railings on the right, three of the bar tables were occupied; on the left, more were open.

She started automatically in that direction, suddenly pausing when she recognized Tru.

Seeing him alone at the table made her wonder about his reason for coming to Sunset Beach. He'd mentioned that he didn't know the man he was supposed to meet, but the trip from Zimbabwe was a long one, and even she knew that Sunset Beach was hardly a destination for international tourists. She wondered who was important enough to make him come all this way.

Just then, he opened his hands in greeting. She hesitated, thought, *I have to at least say hello*, and walked toward his table. As she drew near, she noticed again the scuffed leather bracelet and the way his shirt was unbuttoned at the top; it was easy to imagine him heading into the bush in just such attire.

"Hi, Tru. I didn't expect to see you here."

"Likewise."

She expected him to say more, but he didn't. Instead, his eyes held hers a beat too long and she felt an unexpected twinge of nervousness. He was obviously more at ease with the silence between them than she was, and she tossed her ponytail over her shoulder, trying to exude more calm than she felt. "How was the rest of your day?" she asked.

"Relatively uneventful. I went for a swim. You?"

"Did a little grocery shopping and puttered around the house. I think I heard you playing the guitar earlier."

"I hope it wasn't a nuisance."

"Not at all," she said. "I enjoyed what you were playing."

"That's good, since you'll likely hear the same songs over and over."

She surveyed the other tables, then nodded at his menu. "Have you been waiting long?"

"Not too long. The waitress seems busy."

"Service has always been a little slow here. Friendly, but slow. Like everything else in this part of the world."

"It does have its charms." He gestured at the seat across from him. "Would you like to join me?"

As soon as he asked, she recognized it for the telling moment it was. Offering a neighbor a cup of coffee after he'd rescued her dog was one thing; having dinner with him was something else entirely. Spontaneous or not, this had the makings of a date, and she suspected that Tru knew precisely what was going through her mind. But she didn't answer right away. Instead, she studied him in the flickering light. She remembered their walk and their conversation on her deck; she thought about Josh and Las Vegas and the argument that had resulted in her being at the beach alone.

"I'd like that," she finally said, realizing how sincerely she meant it. He stood as she pulled out her stool, then helped her adjust its position. By the time he returned to his own seat, she felt like someone else entirely. The thought of what she was doing left her slightly off-kilter, and she reached for the menu, as if it would ground her. "May I?"

"By all means."

She opened the menu, feeling his gaze on her. "What are you having?" she asked, thinking small talk would tame her butterflies.

"Either the tuna or the grouper. I was going to ask the waitress which one is better, but maybe you know?"

"The tuna is always delicious. It's what my mom orders when she comes here. They have a deal with a few of the fishermen around here, so it's fresh every day."

"Tuna it is," he concurred.

"That's what I should do. The crab cakes are really delicious, too. But they're fried."

"So?"

"They're not good for me. Or my thighs."

"Seems to me that you don't have anything to worry
about. You look lovely."

She said nothing to that. Instead, she felt the blood rise
in her cheeks, aware that another line had just been crossed.
As flattered as she was, it definitely felt like a date now.
There was no way on earth she could have foreseen any
of this, and she tried to concentrate on the menu, but the
words seemed to jump around. She finally set it aside.

"I assume you decided on the crab cakes?" he asked.

"How did you know?"

"Habit and tradition often render change undesirable."

His response brought to mind an upper-class Englishman
ensconced in a wood-paneled library at his country estate—
an image utterly incongruous with the man sitting across
from her.

"You certainly have a unique turn of phrase," she remarked with a smile.

"I do?"

"You can definitely tell you're not American."

He seemed amused by that. "How's Scottie doing? Still
moving around?"

"He's back to his rambunctious self. But I think he was
mad at me for not bringing him out to the beach again. Or
at least disappointed."

"He does seem to enjoy chasing the birds."

"As long as he doesn't catch them. If he did, he probably
wouldn't know what to do."

The waitress approached, seeming less harried than she'd

been earlier. "Have you two decided what you'd like to drink?" she asked.

Tru looked over at Hope, and she nodded. "I believe we're ready to order," he said. He gave the waitress their food orders and asked if the restaurant had any local beers on tap.

"Sorry, sweetheart," the waitress answered. "Nothing fancy here, and nothing on tap. Just Budweiser, Miller, and Coors, but the bottles are ice cold."

"I'll try a Coors, then," he said.

"And you?" she asked, turning to Hope.

It had been years since she'd had a beer, but for some reason, it sounded strangely appealing right now. And she definitely needed something to ease her anxiety. "I'll have the same," she said, and the waitress nodded, leaving them alone at the table. Hope reached for her napkin and set it in her lap.

"How long have you been playing the guitar?" she asked.

"I started when I was apprenticing to become a guide. One of the men I was working with used to play at night when we were at the camp. He offered to give me some lessons. The rest I just picked up over the years. Do you play?"

"No. I took a few piano lessons when I was a kid, but that's it. My sister can play, though."

"You have a sister?"

"Two," she said. "Robin and Joanna."

"Do you see them often?"

She nodded. "We try. The whole family lives in Raleigh, but it's harder these days to get everyone together except on holidays or birthdays. Both Robin and Joanna are married and they work, and their kids keep them constantly on the go."

"My son, Andrew, is the same way."

The waitress dropped off the two bottles of beer from a tray filled with other drinks. Hope tilted her head in surprise.

"I didn't know you had a son."

"He's ten. Because of my work schedule, he lives with his mother most of the time."

"Your work schedule?"

"I work for six weeks straight, then go home for two weeks."

"That has to be hard for both of you."

"Sometimes it is," he agreed. "At the same time, it's all he's ever known, so I tell myself that he's used to it. And we have a lot of fun when we're together. He wasn't pleased when he learned that I would be coming here for a week."

"Have you spoken with him since you've been here?"

"No, but I'm planning to call him tomorrow."

"What's he like?"

"Curious. Bright. Handsome. Kind. But I'm biased." He grinned and took a sip of his beer.

"You should be. He's your son. Does he want to become a guide one day, too?"

"He says he does, and he seems to enjoy spending time in the bush as much as I do. But then again, he also says he wants to drive race cars. And be a veterinarian. And maybe a mad scientist."

She smiled. "What do you think?"

"He'll make his own decision in the end, like we all do. Being a guide means leading an unconventional life, and it's not for everyone. It's also one of the reasons my marriage ended. I just wasn't around enough. Kim deserved better."

"It seems like you and your ex get along well."

"We do. But she's easy to get along with, and she's a marvelous mother."

Hope reached for her beer, impressed by the way he spoke about his ex, thinking it said as much about him as it did about her.

"When do you fly back?"

"Monday morning. And you leave?"

"Sometime on Sunday. I have to work on Monday. When is your meeting?"

"On Saturday afternoon." He took a drink before slowly lowering the bottle to the table. "I'm supposed to meet my father."

"Do you mean visit?"

"No," he answered. "I mean meet for the first time. According to the letter I received, he moved from Zimbabwe before I was born, and he learned of my existence only a short time ago."

Hope opened her lips, then closed them again. After a moment, she ventured, "I can't imagine not knowing my father. Your mind must be going a hundred miles an hour."

"I admit it's an unusual circumstance."

Hope shook her head, still trying to grasp what he'd told her. "I wouldn't know how to start that conversation. Or even what to ask him."

"I do." For the first time, Tru glanced off to the side. When he spoke again, his voice was almost lost in the sound of the rolling waves. "I'd like to ask him about my mother."

She hadn't expected that and pondered what he could mean. She thought she saw a flash of sadness in his expression, but when he faced her again, it was gone.

"It seems we both have memorable weekends ahead," he observed.

His desire to change the subject was obvious and she played along, despite her growing curiosity. "I just hope it doesn't rain. Ellen would probably burst into tears."

"You mentioned you're a bridesmaid?"

"I am. And thankfully, the dress is actually pretty stylish."

"Dress?"

"The bridesmaids wear matching dresses, picked out by the bride. And sometimes the bride doesn't have the greatest sense of style."

"You sound like you speak from experience."

"This is the eighth time I've been a bridesmaid." She sighed. "Six friends and both my sisters. I've liked maybe two of the dresses."

"What happens if you don't like the dress?"

"Nothing. Except you'll probably hate the photos for the rest of your life. If I ever get married, I might pick ugly dresses just to get back at some of them."

He laughed, and she realized she liked the sound of it—deep and rumbly, like the beginnings of an earthquake.

"You wouldn't do that."

"I might. One of the dresses was lime green. With puffy shoulders. That one was actually for my sister Robin's wedding. Joanna and I still tease her about it."

"How long has she been married?"

"Nine years," she said. "Her husband, Mark, is an insurance broker, and he's kind of quiet, but very nice. And they've got three boys. Joanna has been married to Jim for seven years. He's an attorney, and they have two little girls."

"Sounds like you're all very close."

"We are," she said. "And we live near each other, too. Of course, depending on the traffic, it can still take twenty minutes to get to each other's houses. It's probably nothing like where you're from."

"The big cities like Harare and Bulawayo have traffic issues, too. You'd be surprised."

She tried to imagine the cities but couldn't.

"I'm embarrassed to admit it, but when I think of Zimbabwe, all I can picture are those nature shows on cable. Elephants and giraffes, things like that. What you see every day. I know there are cities there, but anything I imagine is probably wrong."

"They're like all cities, I suppose. There are nice neighborhoods, and others where you probably shouldn't go."

"Do you feel culture shock going from the bush to the city?"

"Every single time. It still takes me a day or two to get used to the noise and traffic and number of people. Part of that, though, is because I was raised on a farm."

"Your mom was a farmer?"

"My grandfather."

"How does a kid who grew up on the farm end up being a guide?"

"That's a long and complicated story."

"The good ones usually are. Care to share?"

As she asked, the waitress arrived with their meals. Tru had finished his beer and ordered a second one; Hope followed his lead. The food smelled delicious, and this time, the waitress was prompt with the drinks, returning with two more beers before either had taken a bite. Tru raised his bottle, indicating that she should do the same.

"To enchanted evenings," he said simply before clinking his bottle to hers.

Maybe it was the formality of a toast amid the informality

of Clancy's, but she realized that at some point, her nervousness had slipped away without her even noticing it. She suspected it had to do with Tru's authenticity, and it reinforced her impression that too many people spent their lives performing a role they thought they were supposed to play, as opposed to simply being who they were.

"Back to your question. I don't mind speaking on the subject, but I wonder if it's appropriate for dinner. Perhaps later?"

"Sure." She shrugged. She sliced off a piece of crab cake and took a bite. Amazing, as always. Noticing Tru had sampled his tuna, she asked, "How is it?"

"It's flavorful," he said. "Yours?"

"It's going to be hard not to eat both of them. But I have to get into the dress this weekend."

"And it is one of the stylish ones."

She was flattered that he seemed to remember everything she told him. Over dinner, they settled into a conversation replete with familiar stories. She told him a little about Ellen, describing some of her friend's devil-may-care exploits while whitewashing the worst parts of her past, like the drug-dealing ex. She mentioned her other sorority sisters as well, the talk eventually drifting to Hope's family. She told him what it had been like to grow up with teachers for parents, both of whom insisted that their children learn how to schedule and complete their homework on their own, without help. She described running cross-country and track, expressing her admiration for the deft way her dad had handled coaching all of his daughters. She reminisced about baking cookies with her mom. She talked about her work, too—the fierce energy of her days in the emergency room, and the patients and families who touched her heart. Though there were times when images of Josh broke into her thoughts, they were surprisingly few and far between.

As they talked, the stars slowly spread throughout the sky. Breakers sparkled in the moonlight, and the breeze picked up slightly, carrying the briny scent of the sea. The tiki torches sputtered in the breeze, casting an orange glow over the tables while other patrons drifted in and out. The ambiance grew quieter, more subdued as the evening progressed, conversations interrupted only by muted laughter and the same songs cycling from the jukebox.

After their plates were cleared, the waitress came by with two slices of lemon meringue pie, and it took Tru only a single bite to understand that she hadn't been exaggerating when touting its virtues. While they lingered over dessert, he did most of the talking. He spoke about the various camps where he'd worked and told her about his friend Romy, and the way Romy would sometimes badger him to play his guitar after their long day was over. He told her a bit more about his divorce from Kim, and spoke for a long time about Andrew. She could tell by the longing in his voice that Tru already missed him, and it made her think again how much she wanted a child of her own.

She sensed in Tru a comfort level with who he was and the life he'd chosen, but it was balanced by a genuine uncertainty as to whether he was good enough as a father. She supposed that was normal, but his honesty about all of it seemed to deepen the intimacy between them. She wasn't used to that, especially with a stranger. More than once, she found herself unconsciously leaning across the table in order to hear him better, only to pull herself upright when she realized what she was doing. Later, when he laughingly recounted how terrified he'd been when they'd first brought Andrew home from the hospital, she felt an unexpected surge of warmth toward him. That he was handsome there was no question, but for a moment it was easy for her to imagine their dinner conversation as the start of a lifetime of unending conversations between them.

Feeling foolish, she dismissed the thought. They were temporary neighbors, nothing more. But the feeling of warmth persisted, and she was conscious of blushing more than usual as the evening wore on.

When the check arrived, Tru reached for it automatically. Hope offered to split it, but Tru shook his head, simply saying, "Please. Allow me." By then, a ball of clouds had formed in the eastern sky, partially obscuring the moon. But they continued to talk as the last of the tables cleared out. When they finally rose from their seats, Hope glanced at Tru, surprised by how relaxed she felt. They meandered to the gate, Hope watching as he held it open for her, suddenly certain that dinner with Tru was the perfect way to cap off one of the more surprising days of her life.

A WALK IN THE DARK

After interacting with thousands of guests over the years, Tru had become adept at reading people. When Hope reached the beach and turned toward him, he noticed an aura of contentment that had been lacking when they'd first locked eyes in the restaurant. He'd sensed caution and uncertainty then, maybe even worry, and though it would have been easy for him to conclude their initial pleasantries in a way that left no hard feelings, he hadn't. For some reason, he'd suspected that eating alone wouldn't help her overcome whatever demons she was wrestling with.

"What are you thinking about?" she inquired, her drawl sounding melodic to his ears. "You had a faraway look there for a moment."

"I was thinking about our conversation."

"I probably talked too much."

"Not at all." Reprising their morning routine, they walked the beach side by side, the pace even more leisurely now. "I enjoyed learning about your life."

"I don't know why. It's not all that exciting."

Because you interest me, he thought, but he didn't say that. Instead, he zeroed in on what she hadn't mentioned all night. "What's your boyfriend like?"

By her expression, he knew she was thrown by the question. "How did you know I had a boyfriend?"

"You mentioned that he gave you Scottie as a gift."

"Oh...that's right. I did say that, didn't I?" She pursed her lips for a second. "What do you want to know?"

"Anything you want to tell."

She felt her sandals sinking into the sand. "His name is Josh, and he's an orthopedic surgeon. He's smart and successful and...he's a nice guy."

"How long have you been dating?"

"Six years."

"Sounds serious."

"Yeah," she agreed, though to his ears, it sounded almost like she was trying to convince herself.

"I assume he's coming to the wedding?"

She walked a few paces before answering. "Actually, he isn't. He was supposed to, but he decided to go to Las Vegas with some friends instead." She offered a half smile, one that betrayed her unhappiness. "Right now, we're kind of on the outs, but we'll figure it out, I'm sure."

Which explained why she'd said nothing about him at dinner. Still..."I'm sorry to hear that. And for bringing it up."

As she nodded, Tru noticed something skittering in the sand directly in front of him. "What was that?" he asked.

"That's a ghost crab," she said, sounding relieved by the distraction. "They come out at night from their burrows in the sand. But they're harmless."

"Are there a lot of them?"

"Between here and the house, it wouldn't surprise me if we saw a hundred of them."

"Good to know." Ahead of them lay the pier, looking forlorn and deserted in the darkness. Offshore, Tru noticed lights from a distant fishing trawler, a deep span of black water separating it from the beach.

"Can I ask you a personal question now?"

"Of course," he answered.

"Why do you want to ask your father about your mother? Does it have anything to do with the reason you became a guide?"

He smiled at her perceptiveness. "As a matter of fact, it does." He tucked a hand in his pocket, wondering where to start before deciding to just come out with it. "I want to ask my father about my mother because I realize I've never known who she really was. What she enjoyed, what made her happy or sad, what she dreamed about. I was only eleven years old when she died."

"That's terrible," she murmured. "You were so young."

"So was she," he countered. "She was still a teenager when she had me. Had her pregnancy occurred a couple of years later, it probably would have been more of a scandal. But it wasn't long after the war, and she wasn't the only young lady to have fallen for a former soldier after the war ended. More than that, we were kind of cut off from the rest of civilization because of where we lived, so supposedly, no one aside from the workers at the farm even knew about me for a long while. My grandfather preferred to keep it quiet. People eventually found out, but by then it was old news. Besides, my mother was still young and beautiful, and as the daughter of a wealthy man she was considered quite desirable. But as I said, I don't feel as though I knew her. Her name was Evelyn, but I never heard them talk about her, or even speak her name after she died."

"Them?"

"My grandfather. And Rodney, my stepfather."

"Why not?"

Tru watched another ghost crab scurry past. "Well...I'll have to provide some context and history to answer that question properly." He sighed as she looked at him expectantly. "Back when I was still a young boy, there was another farm that bordered ours, with lots of good, fertile land and ready access to water. At that time, tobacco was quickly becoming the most profitable crop to farm, and my grandfather was intent on controlling as much of the production as he could. He was ruthless when it came to business. The neighbor discovered just how ruthless when he turned down my grandfather's offer to buy his farm, and my grandfather diverted a lot of the water from the neighbor's land to his own."

"That sounds illegal."

"It probably was, but my grandfather knew the right people in the government, so he got away with it. And while that made things immeasurably more difficult for the neighbor, the neighbor's property manager was something of a genius. It was also common knowledge that he was interested in my mother. So my grandfather eventually made the property manager an offer he couldn't refuse—an ownership stake in our farm and daily proximity to my mother—and he came to work for us. His name was Rodney."

"The man who became your stepfather."

Tru nodded. "After he came on, our tobacco yield doubled almost immediately. At the same time, when the neighbor's farm began to fail, my grandfather offered the neighbor a loan when no one else would. It only postponed the inevitable, and in the end, my grandfather foreclosed, which meant he got all the property for next to nothing. He then diverted the water back to its original flow pattern, making him even richer than he already was. All of that took a few years, and in the meantime, my mother fell for Rodney's charms. They got married and had twins—Allen and Alex, my half brothers. Everything had worked out just the way my grandfather and Rodney had planned...but not long after that, our family compound went up in flames. I jumped out of a second-story window, and Rodney rescued the twins, but my mother never made it out."

He heard her inhale. "Your mom died in a fire?"

"The investigators suspected arson."

"The neighbor," she said.

"Those were the rumors. I didn't hear them until a few years later, but I think my grandfather and Rodney knew, and they felt guilty about what happened. After all, they may well have been indirectly responsible for my mother's death. After that, it was like a hush fell over her memory, and neither Rodney nor my grandfather seemed to want anything to do with me, so I started to go my own way."

"I can't imagine how hard that was. It must have been an incredibly sad and lonely time for you."

"It was."

"And the neighbor got away with it?"

Tru stopped to pick up a seashell, a partially broken conch he examined before tossing it aside.

"The neighbor died in a house fire a year after my mother died. At the time, he was living in a shack in Harare, completely destitute. But I didn't find out about that until years later. My grandfather mentioned it in passing one night when he'd been drinking. He said the man got what he deserved. By then, I was already guiding."

Glancing at Hope, he watched her put the pieces together.

"Did anyone ever suspect your grandfather?"

"I'm sure they did. But if you were white and wealthy in Rhodesia, justice could be purchased. Maybe not as much these days, but back then, it could. My grandfather died a free man. These days, Rodney and my half brothers run the farm, and I keep my distance from them as much as possible."

He watched as Hope shook her head, trying to absorb it all.

"Wow," she said. "I don't think I've ever heard a story like that...I can understand why you left. And why you didn't tell me earlier. It's a lot to think about."

"It is," he agreed.

"Are you certain the man you're supposed to meet this weekend is your actual father?"

"No, but I think there's a pretty good chance." He told her about the letter and the photograph he'd received along with the plane tickets.

"Does the photo resemble your mom?"

"From what I can recall, but...I suppose I can't be one hundred percent sure. All the photographs of her were lost in the fire, and I didn't want to ask Rodney about it."

She appraised him carefully, with new respect.

"You've had a hard life already."

"In some ways." He shrugged. "But I also have Andrew."

"Did you ever think about having another child? When you were married?"

"Kim wanted more, but I ended up contracting measles, which left me sterile, so I couldn't."

"Was that a factor in the divorce?"

He shook his head. "No. We were just two different people. We probably shouldn't have married in the first place, but she was pregnant, and I knew what it was like to grow up without a father. I didn't want that for Andrew."

"I know you said you don't remember much about your mom, but is there anything you do remember?"

"I remember that she used to sit on the back veranda and draw. But the only reason I remember that is because I started to sketch, too, not long after she passed away."

"You draw?"

"When I'm not playing the guitar."

"Are your drawings any good?"

"Andrew likes them."

"Do you have any here?"

"I started one this morning. There are others, too, in my sketchbook."

"I'd like to see them. If you wouldn't mind."

By then, the pier was long behind them and they were drawing closer to both the cottage and the home where he was staying. Beside him, Hope had grown quiet, and he knew she was digesting everything he'd told her. It wasn't like him to share so much; usually he volunteered little about his past, and he wondered what it was about tonight that had made him so voluble.

But deep down, he already knew that his reaction had everything to do with the woman walking beside him. As they reached the steps that led up to the cottage walkway, he realized that he'd wanted her to know who he really was, if only because he felt as though he already knew her.

After all he'd told her about his upbringing, it didn't feel right to end the conversation so abruptly. She motioned toward the cottage. "Would you like to come up and have a glass of wine? It's such a pretty night, and I was thinking of sitting on the deck for a little while."

"A glass of wine sounds nice," he said.

Hope led the way and when they reached the back deck, she pointed at a pair of rocking chairs near the window. "Is chardonnay okay? I opened a bottle earlier today."

"Anything is fine."

"I'll be back in a minute," she said. *What am I doing?* she wondered as she went inside, leaving the door cracked. Never in her life had she invited a man up for a nightcap, and she hoped she wasn't sending mixed signals or giving him the wrong impression. The thought of what *he* might be thinking left her feeling unusually light-headed.

Scottie had followed her into the house and was eager to greet her, tail wagging. She stooped over to pet him.

"It's not that big of a deal, is it?" she whispered. "He knows I was just being neighborly, right? And it's not like I invited him inside."

Scottie stared at her with sleepy eyes.

"You're not helping."

She pulled two long-stemmed glasses from the cupboard and added wine, filling them both halfway. She thought about turning on the outdoor lights, but decided that would be too bright. Candles would be perfect, but that would definitely send the wrong message. Instead, she turned on the kitchen light, its diffused glow spilling onto the porch. Better.

Glasses in hand, she nudged the door open with her foot. Scottie dashed out ahead of her and raced to the gate, ready to head to the beach.

"Not now, Scottie. We'll go tomorrow, okay?"

Scottie ignored her as usual while Hope approached the rockers. When she handed Tru his glass, their fingers brushed, sending a little shock up her arm.

"Thank you," he said.

"You're welcome," she murmured, still feeling the after-effects of his touch.

Scottie continued to stand near the gate as she took her seat, as if to remind her of her real purpose in life. Hope was glad for the distraction.

"I told you we'll go out tomorrow. Why don't you lie down instead?"

Scottie stared up at her, his tail wagging expectantly. "I don't think he understands me," she said to Tru. "Either that, or he's trying to get me to change my mind."

Tru smiled. "He's a cute dog."

"Except when he's running off and getting hit by cars. Right, Scottie?"

His tail wagged harder at the sound of his name.

"I had a dog once," Tru said. "He wasn't around long, but he was good company while I had him."

"What happened to him?"

"You probably don't want to know."

"Just tell me."

"He was killed and eaten by a leopard. I found what was left of him in the tree branches."

She stared at him. "You're right. I didn't want to know."

"Different worlds."

"You're not kidding," she responded with an amused shake of her head. For a long while, they merely sipped their wine, neither of them saying anything. A moth began to dance near the kitchen window; a windsock fluttered in the gentle breeze. Waves rolled ashore, the sound like shaken pebbles in a jar. Though he kept his gaze on the ocean, she had the sense that he was watching her as well. His eyes, she thought, seemed to notice everything.

"Will you miss it here?" he finally asked.

"What do you mean?"

"When your parents sell the cottage. I saw the sign out front when I was dropped off yesterday."

Of course he did. "Yes, I'm going to miss it. I think everyone will miss being able to come here. It's been in the family a long time, and I never once imagined that it wouldn't be."

"Why are your parents selling?"

As soon as he asked, she felt her worries resurface. "My dad is sick," she said. "He has ALS. Do you know what that is?" When Tru shook his head, she explained, and added that there was only so much the government and insurance would cover. "They're selling what they can, so they'll have money to modify their house or pay for in-home care."

She rotated her glass in her fingers before going on. "The worst part is the uncertainty...I'm scared for my mom. I don't know what she'll do without him. Right now, she seems to be pretending that nothing is wrong with my dad at all, but I worry that it's only going to make it even worse for her later. My dad, on the other hand, seems at peace with the diagnosis, but maybe he's just pretending, too, so that all of us will feel better about it. Sometimes it feels like I'm the only one worrying."

Tru said nothing. Instead, he leaned back in his rocker, studying her.

"You're thinking about what I said," Hope ventured.

"Yes," he admitted.

"And?"

His voice was quiet. "I know it's hard, but worrying doesn't help them or you. Winston Churchill once described worry as a thin stream of fear trickling through the mind that, if encouraged, cuts a channel into which all other thoughts are drained."

She was impressed. "Churchill?"

"One of my grandfather's heroes. He used to quote the man all the time. But Churchill made a good point."

"Is that how you are with Andrew? Worry free?"

"You know by now I'm not."

Despite herself, she laughed. "At least you're honest about it."

"Sometimes it's easiest to be honest with strangers."

She knew he was talking about her as much as he was about himself. Glancing past him, down the beach, she noticed that all the other homes were darkened, as though Sunset Beach were a ghost town. She took a sip of her wine, feeling a sense of peace coursing through her limbs and radiating outward like the glow of a lamp.

"I can see why you're going to miss this place," he said into the silence. "It's quite peaceful."

She felt her mind drift to the past. "Our family used to spend most of our summers here. When we were young, my sisters and I spent almost all of our time in the water. I learned to surf over there near the pier. I never got really good at it, but I was okay. I spent hours floating out there, waiting for good swell. And I saw some amazing things—sharks, dolphins, even a couple of whales. None of them were very close, but one time, when I was around twelve or so, I saw what I thought was a floating log, until it surfaced just a few feet away. I saw its face and whiskers and my whole body froze. I was too terrified to even scream because I didn't know how long it had been there, or what it was. It looked like a hippopotamus, or maybe a walrus. But once I realized that it didn't intend to hurt me, I just began to... watch it. I even paddled to keep up with it. In the end, I must have stayed out there for a couple of hours. It's still one of the most amazing things ever to happen to me."

"What was it?"

"It was a manatee. They're much more common in Florida. Every now and then there are sightings off this coast, but I've never seen another one. My sister Robin still doesn't believe me. She says I was making it up to get attention."

Tru smiled. "I believe you. And I like that story."

"I figured you might. Since it featured an animal. But there's another really neat thing that you should see while you're here. Before it rains."

"What's that?"

"You should visit Kindred Spirit tomorrow. It's past the pier and on the next island, but you can walk there at low tide. When you see the American flag, start angling toward the dunes. You can't miss it."

"I'm still not sure what it is."

"It's better if it surprises you. You'll know what to do."

"I don't understand."

"You will."

She could tell by his expression that she'd aroused his curiosity. "I was planning to go fishing tomorrow. As long as I can find some bait, that is."

"They'll have bait at the pier shop, but you can do both," she assured him. "I think low tide is around four in the afternoon."

"I'll think about it. What's on your agenda tomorrow?"

"Hair and nails for the wedding. And I want to find a new pair of shoes. Girl stuff."

He nodded before taking another sip of wine, and another simple calm descended. They rocked in easy synchronicity for a while, admiring the glorious night sky. But when she caught herself stifling a yawn, she knew it was time for him to go. By then, he'd finished his wine, and again, he seemed to know exactly what she was thinking.

"I should probably head back," he said. "It's been a long day. Thank you for the wine."

She knew it was the right thing, but nonetheless felt a faint stab of disappointment as well. "Thank you for dinner."

He handed her his glass before making his way toward the gate. She left the glasses on the table and trailed behind him. At the gate, he paused and turned. She could almost feel the energy emanating from him, but when he spoke, his voice was soft.

"You're an incredible woman, Hope," he said. "And I trust that things will work out with you and Josh. He's a lucky man."

His words caught her off guard, but she knew he'd meant them in a kind way, without judgment or expectation.

"We'll be fine, I'm sure," she said, as much to herself as to him.

Pulling open the gate, he started down the steps. Hope followed him, stopping at the halfway point. Crossing her arms, she watched as he reached the walkway and headed for the beach. When he was a quarter of the way there, he turned and waved. She waved back, and when he was a bit farther away, she finally retraced her steps to the deck. She grabbed the glasses and brought them to the sink before padding to the bedroom.

She undressed and stood before the mirror. Her first thought was that she really needed to lose a few pounds, but overall, she was content with her appearance. Of course, it would have been great to have the kind of lithe body that graced fitness magazines, but she just wasn't built that way, and never had been. Even as a girl, she'd always found herself wishing that she were a few inches taller, or even as tall as either of her sisters.

And yet, as she stared at her reflection, she thought about the way that Tru had looked at her, his interest in whatever she was saying, and the compliments he'd given her about her appearance. She missed basking in a man's obvious attraction to her, without recognizing it as simply a prelude to sex. Even as she tried to sort through her feelings, she knew it was a dangerous way of thinking.

Turning from the mirror, she went to the bathroom and washed her face. After removing the elastic band she'd used for her ponytail, she ran a brush through her hair so it wouldn't be knotted in the morning. Moving to her suitcase, she pulled out a pair of pajamas before hesitating. Tossing them back into her suitcase, she went to the closet and retrieved an extra blanket instead.

She hated being cold at night, and slipping naked beneath the covers, she closed her eyes, feeling sensual and strangely content.

SUNRISE AND SURPRISES

Tru ambled past Hope's cottage the following morning, carrying the tackle box, with a fishing pole over his shoulder. He looked over, noting that the paint had begun to peel on a lot of the trim and some of the railings were rotting away, but thinking again that it suited him better than the house where he was staying. That one was too big and definitely too modern, and he still couldn't figure out how to work the coffee machine. Even a single cup would have been nice, but he supposed it simply wasn't meant to be.

It was an hour past dawn, and he wondered whether Hope was awake. In the morning glare, it was impossible to tell if any lights were on, but there was no sign of her on the deck. He thought about her boyfriend and shook his head, wondering what the man was thinking. Despite a life spent mostly in the bush, even Tru knew that the wedding of a close friend pretty much mandated attendance on the boyfriend's part. It didn't matter how well they were getting along, or even if they were temporarily on the outs, as she'd put it.

Despite himself, he found himself imagining how she

looked in the morning before getting herself ready for the day. Even with hair askew and puffy eyes, she'd still be beautiful. Some things just couldn't be hidden. When she smiled, there was a gentle light about her, and it was easy to get lost in that accent of hers. There was something soft and rolling to it, like a lullaby, and when she'd been recounting stories about Ellen or telling him about the manatee, he'd felt like he could have listened to her forever.

Despite an overcast sky, the morning was warmer than it had been the day before, and the humidity had increased. The breeze, too, had picked up, all of which meant that Hope had been right about the possibility of storms this weekend. In the days leading up to rain in Zimbabwe, the air had a pregnant charge that felt much the same.

There were already half a dozen men fishing from the pier by the time he started toward the steps, and he watched as one began to reel something in. It was too far away to make out any detail, but he took it as a good sign. He doubted whether he'd keep anything he caught; there was too much food in the refrigerator as it was. Nor was he in the mood to clean anything, especially since the knife in the tackle box seemed dull. But catching something was always a thrill.

Entering the shop, he saw shelves filled with snacks and drinks crowding the center aisles; along the back wall was a grill that offered hot food. Assorted fishing gear was perched on racks and hung on pegs; near the door was a cooler, with a sign advertising bait. Tru plucked out a couple of containers of shrimp and brought them to the register. There was a fee to fish from the pier as well, and after receiving his change, Tru strolled out the door, past a pay phone, and down the pier. Despite the overcast sky, the sun had broken through momentarily, glinting hard off the water.

Most of the people were clustered near the end, and assuming they knew more than he did, he took up a spot in their vicinity. Unlike the tackle box, the fishing pole was in like-new condition, and after baiting and weighting the line, he cast out into the water.

In the corner of the pier a radio was playing, something country-western. Strangely, Andrew was a fan of Garth Brooks and George Strait, though Tru had no idea how he'd ever encountered their songs. When Andrew had mentioned their names a few months back, Tru had stared at him blankly, at which point Andrew had insisted that Tru listen to "Friends in Low Places." It was catchy, he had to admit, but nothing could touch Tru's loyalty to the Beatles.

Whether consciously or subconsciously, Tru had selected the side of the pier that allowed him a view of Hope's cottage in the distance. He reflected on their dinner and walk, realizing that she'd made him feel at ease the entire evening. For all their heady attraction, he'd seldom felt that way with Kim; all too often, he'd felt as though he was disappointing her. And even though they were now friends, there were times that he still felt as though he was disappointing her, especially when it came to the time he spent with Andrew.

He'd also been taken with the way Hope had spoken about her friends and family. It was clear that she genuinely cared for all of them. She was naturally empathetic, not just sympathetic, and people like that struck him as rare. He'd sensed it even when they'd spoken about Andrew.

Thinking about his son, he now wished he had postponed leaving for the trip, given that he wouldn't see his father until Saturday afternoon. It was odd that the man hadn't called to explain, but it irritated Tru only with regard to Andrew. He had awakened in the morning missing his son, and resolved to give Andrew a call from the pay phone he'd passed. It would have to be collect and the charges would be substantial, but Kim would let him reimburse her when he returned. With the time difference, and knowing Andrew was in school and had homework, Tru figured he still had a couple of hours to wait. He was already looking forward to his flight home on Monday.

Except...

Raising his eyes toward Hope's cottage again, he smiled when he saw her trailing after Scottie as he trotted down the walkway, then the steps. At the beach, she bent over, releasing Scottie from the leash, and the dog took off running. There were no seagulls nearby, but he'd find them; of that Tru had no doubt. As he watched, he wondered whether Hope was thinking about him, and hoped that she'd enjoyed their evening together as much as he had.

She drew farther from the pier with every step, her image growing smaller. He watched her anyway, until he registered a light movement on his line. When he felt a tug, he jerked the tip of the rod upward, sinking the hook, and all at once, the pull on the line intensified. He lowered the tip and began winding the reel, keeping just enough tension on the line, and was struck again by how strong fish were, no matter their size. They were all muscle. But he played the game, knowing the fish would eventually tire.

Continuing to work the reel, he watched as a strange-looking fish eventually emerged from the water at the end of his line. He swung it to the pier, having no idea what to make of it. It was flat and oval, with two eyes on its back. Using the toe of his boot to keep it from flapping, he plucked a glove and pair of pliers from the toolbox and began to remove the hook, trying not to damage the fish's mouth. As he was working, he heard a voice beside him.

"That's a helluva flounder. Big enough to keep, too."

Tru glanced up and saw an older man with a baseball cap, wearing clothes that were several sizes too large. He had a gap where his front teeth should have been and his accent, much heavier than Hope's, was difficult to understand.

"Is that what it is?"

"Don't tell me you ain't never seen a flounder before."

"This is a first."

The man squinted at him. "Where you from?"

Wondering whether the man had ever heard of Zimbabwe, he simply said, "Africa."

"Africa! You don't look like you're from Africa."

By then Tru had removed the hook, and setting the pliers aside, he grabbed the fish and was about to toss it over when he heard the man speak up.

"Whatcha doin'?"

"I was going to let it go."

"Can I have it? I ain't had much luck yesterday or this morning. I'd sure appreciate some flounder for dinner."

Tru debated before shrugging. "Sure."

The man reached over and took the fish, crossing back to the other side of the pier, where it vanished into a small cooler.

"Thank you," the man called out.

"You're welcome."

Tru readied his line again, casting out a second time. By then, Hope was nothing but a smudge in the distance.

He recognized her anyway, and for a long time, he couldn't take his eyes off her.

Hope kept watch over Scottie, calling for the dog to come whenever he approached the dune, not that he ever seemed to listen. Hoping that Scottie would suddenly begin to obey was an exercise in futility. Of course, it fit perfectly with how her morning was already going.

Immediately after waking, she'd heard the phone begin to ring in the kitchen. Hope had to wrap the blanket around herself and stubbed her toe on the corner as she'd raced to answer it. She'd thought it might be Josh, but she remembered the time difference in the same instant she heard Ellen crying on the other end. Sobbing, actually—at first Hope had no idea what Ellen was trying to tell her. It was all Ellen could do to choke out a few words here and there. Hope initially believed that the wedding had been called off, and it took a while for her to decipher that Ellen was crying about the weather. Between sobs, Ellen informed Hope that it was supposed to start raining later today, and that storms were virtually certain over the weekend.

It struck Hope as a bit of an overreaction, but Ellen remained inconsolable, no matter what she told her. Not that Hope had the chance to do much talking. The phone call was more like listening to a weepy forty-minute monologue about the unfairness of life. As her friend went on and on, Hope leaned against the counter with her legs crossed and toe still throbbing, absently wondering if Ellen would even notice if she set the phone down to use the bathroom. She really, really had to pee, and by the time she was finally able to get Ellen off the phone, she had to ditch the blanket and hobble as fast as she could.

After that, as though some deity had it out for both Tru

and Hope, her coffee maker went on the blink. The light came on but the water wouldn't heat, and Hope debated whether to boil some water and pour it through the grounds. By then, however, Scottie was at the door and she knew that if she didn't get him outside soon, she would have a mess to clean up. So, throwing on some clothes, she brought her dog to the beach, hoping to salvage the morning with a relaxing walk. But Scottie made that impossible. On two different occasions, he ran to the top of the dune and up someone's walkway—either trying to find that cat again or purposely attempting to give her a heart attack—and she had to scramble after him. She supposed she could put the leash back on, but Scottie would likely alternate between trying to pull her arm off and sulking, and she wasn't in the mood for either.

Despite all that...

While on the phone, she'd seen Tru walk past her house on the way to the pier with his fishing gear and couldn't help smiling. She still had trouble believing she'd actually had dinner with him. Her thoughts drifted back to their conversation...she was surprised by how pleasant the evening had been, and how effortlessly they'd seemed to get along.

She wondered whether he'd take her advice and visit Kindred Spirit after he finished fishing. With storms on the way, tomorrow would probably be too late, but that went for her as well. After her appointments, she guessed she might have some extra time to swing by the mailbox, and as she walked the beach, she made the decision to do just that.

But she had to get going or she'd be late. She had a hair appointment in Wilmington at nine and a pedicure at eleven. She also wanted to see if she could find an appropriate pair of shoes to wear to the wedding—the burgundy pumps that Ellen had picked out for the bridesmaids pinched her feet terribly, and she'd decided she couldn't spend the whole night in agony. Traffic would probably be heavy, and cutting the walk short, she called to Scottie before turning around. Not long after, Scottie barreled past her with his tongue hanging out. As she watched him run, she glanced toward the pier. She could see a cluster of people, but they were nothing but shadows, and she wondered whether Tru was having any luck.

Back at the cottage, she dried Scottie with a towel, then took a quick shower. Afterward, she dressed in jeans, a blouse, and sandals. She'd worn pretty much the same outfit the day before, but when she glanced in the mirror, she couldn't help feeling that she looked different—prettier, maybe, or even more desirable—and she understood that she was seeing herself as a stranger might see her. The way Tru had seen her last night, as they'd sat across the table from each other.

With that realization came another decision. Hope rummaged through the drawer beneath the phone, finding everything she needed. After scribbling the note, she left through the back door and descended to the beach. Taking the steps and using the walkway at the house next door, she tacked the note next to the latch of the gate, where Tru couldn't help but find it.

She returned the way she'd come and grabbed her handbag as she headed out the door. As she got in her car, she let out a deep breath, wondering what was going to happen next.

Tru wasn't sure what Hope had done.

He'd seen her emerge onto the back deck, maybe forty minutes after she'd returned from her walk with Scottie, and then make her way to the house where he was staying. He felt a pang of disappointment at the thought that she'd gone to see him when he wasn't there, but at the gate, she'd stopped. He supposed she might have been debating whether or not to proceed to the back door, but she was only there for a few seconds before she retraced her steps and vanished inside her parents' cottage. He hadn't seen her since.

Strange.

His thoughts remained on her. It would have been easy to chalk his feelings up to infatuation, maybe desperation. Kim, no doubt, would agree with that. Since the divorce, his ex would occasionally ask him whether he'd met any-one. When he would reply that he hadn't, she'd jokingly suggest that he was so out of practice that he'd probably end up falling head over heels in love with the first woman who so much as glanced at him.

That wasn't what was going on here. He wasn't infatu-ated with Hope, nor was he desperate, but he admitted to himself that he found her arresting. Ironically, it had some-thing to do with Kim. Early on, he'd realized that Kim knew exactly how attractive she was and that she'd spent a life-time learning to use it to her advantage. Hope seemed to be the opposite, even though she was equally beautiful, and it spoke to him in the same intuitive way as when he finished a drawing and thought, *That's exactly the way it should be.*

He knew that it wasn't appropriate to think such things, if only because nothing good could come of it. Not only was he leaving on Monday, but Hope would return to her life on Sunday, a life that included the man she thought she'd marry, even if they were having difficulties at present. Nor, with their respective weekends on tap, was he sure he'd even see Hope again.

Feeling another tug on the line, he played the game, timed it right, and set the hook. After a struggle that surprised him, he ended up pulling in a fish different from the flounder, but one he still didn't recognize. The older man in the ball cap wandered back toward him, watching as Tru began to remove the hook.

"That's a helluva whiting," the man said.

"Whiting?"

"English Whiting. Sea mullet. Big enough to keep, too. Sure would be nice to cook it up. If you were planning to throw it back, I mean."

Tru handed over the fish, watching as it vanished into the cooler again.

He didn't have much luck the rest of the morning, but by then it was time to call Andrew. He packed up his things, walked to the shop, and got some change, then went to the pay phone. It took half a minute and a lot of coins to get through to an international operator, but eventually he heard the familiar ring as the call was placed.

When Kim answered, she agreed to accept the charges, and Andrew came on the line. His son had all sorts of questions about America, most of which had to do with various movies he'd seen. He seemed disappointed to learn that there weren't endless shootouts on the streets, people in cowboy hats, or movie stars on every corner. After that, the conversation settled into something more normal and Tru listened as Andrew caught him up on what he'd been doing in the past few days. The sound of his voice made Tru ache

at the thought that the two of them were half a world apart.
For his part, Tru told Andrew about the beach and described
the two fish he'd caught; he also told him about Scottie, and
how Tru had gone to help him. They spoke longer than Tru
had anticipated—nearly twenty minutes—before Tru heard
Kim reminding Andrew that he still had homework to do.
She popped on the line after Andrew.

"He misses you," she said.

"I know. I miss him, too."

"Have you seen your father yet?"

"No," he answered. He told her about the meeting
planned for Saturday afternoon. When he finished, Kim
cleared her throat. "What was that I heard about a dog? It
was hit by a car?"

"It wasn't that serious," Tru said before repeating the
story. He made the mistake of mentioning Hope by name,
and Kim immediately latched onto that.

"Hope?"

"Yes."

"A woman?"

"Obviously."

"I'm assuming that you two hit it off."

"Why would you assume that?"

"Because you know her name, which means that the two
of you spent some time in conversation. Which is something you never do anymore. Tell me about her."

"There's not much to tell."

"Did the two of you go out?"

"Why is that important?"

Instead of answering, Kim laughed. "I can't believe it!
You've finally met a woman, and in America of all places!
Has she ever been to Zimbabwe?"

"No..."

"I want to hear all about her. In exchange, I won't ask you to reimburse me for the call..."

Kim stayed on the line for ten minutes, and though Tru did his best to downplay his feelings about Hope, he could almost hear Kim smiling on the other end. By the time he hung up, he was disconcerted by the call, and he took his time on the walk back up the beach. Beneath a belt of clouds that were turning the color of lead, he wondered how Kim could have deduced as much as she had so quickly. Even if he accepted the idea that she knew him better than almost anyone, it struck him as uncanny.

Women were indeed the mysterious sex.

A short while later, as he mounted the steps to the back deck, he was startled by the sight of a piece of white paper tacked near the latch. Realizing that Hope must have left it for him—and that was the reason she'd come by—he removed the tack and read the note.

Hi there! I'm heading out to Kindred Spirit today. If you'd like to join me, meet me on the beach at three.

He raised an eyebrow. Definitely the mysterious sex.

Inside the house, he found a pen and wrote a response. Remembering that she'd said she had some appointments, he left through the front door, walked to her place, and tucked the note into the door jamb next to the knob of her front door. Her car, he noticed, wasn't in the drive.

Back at the house, he did a workout and then had a bite to eat. As he sat at the table, he gazed out the window at a sky that was slowly growing more ominous, hoping that the rain would hold off, at least until the evening.

Ellen had recommended not only the salon in Wilmington, but the stylist, Claire, as well. As Hope took a seat, she eyed the reflection of a woman with multiple piercings in her ears, a black studded dog collar, and black hair with purple streaks. She wore tight black pants and a black sleeveless top, completing the ensemble. Silently, Hope wondered what Ellen had been thinking.

It turned out that Claire had worked in Raleigh before moving to Wilmington earlier this year, and Ellen had been a loyal customer. Hope still wasn't sure, but saying a little prayer to herself, she settled back in the chair. After asking her questions about the length and style she was interested in, Claire kept up a steady stream of chatter. When Hope gasped at the sight of nearly three inches of hair being lopped off, Claire promised that Hope would be thrilled before going on with whatever she'd been talking about in the first place.

Hope was nervous throughout the transformation, but after the highlights, blow dry, and style, she had to admit that Claire had talent. Hope's naturally auburn hair now carried some lighter tints, as though she'd spent most of the summer in the sun, and the cut itself seemed to frame her face in a way that Hope had never envisioned possible. She left Claire an extra-generous tip on the way out and crossed the street to the nail salon, opening the door just as her appointment was set to begin. The nail technician, a middle-aged Vietnamese woman, spoke little English, so Claire pointed out a burgundy-rose color that would match the bridesmaid dress and read a magazine while her toes were being done.

Afterward, Hope swung by Wal-Mart to pick up a new coffee maker. She chose the least expensive model. It seemed pointless, since they were selling the cottage, but a cup of coffee was part of Hope's morning routine, and she figured she'd just wrap it up on Saturday to give to Ellen as a wedding gift, with a note saying it was slightly used. *Just kidding.* But the thought made her giggle. She then spent some time scouting the nearby shops and was thrilled to find a pair of comfortable strappy heels that matched her bridesmaid dress. Though they were a bit expensive, she felt lucky to find a suitable pair, given her last-minute efforts. She also splurged on some beaded white sandals to replace the scuffed-up ones she was wearing. Popping into the clothing boutique next door, she browsed the racks. A little retail therapy never hurt anyone, after all, and she ended up purchasing a flower-patterned sundress that happened to be on sale. There was a small scoop in the front, a cinch at the waist, and the hemline reached just above her knees. It wasn't the kind of dress she usually bought—to be honest, she seldom if ever bought dresses—but it was fun and feminine, and she couldn't say no, even if she had no idea where or when she'd ever wear it.

The return trip was easier, with less traffic and a series of lucky breaks when it came to hitting green lights. On the highway, she passed through low-country farmland before eventually reaching the turnoff to Sunset Beach. A few minutes later she pulled into the drive. Gathering her purchases, she climbed the steps to the front door and saw a scrap of paper near the doorknob. Pulling it free, she recognized it as the note she'd written to Tru earlier. Her first thought was that he'd simply returned it to her without comment, which confused her, and it wasn't until she flipped it over that she realized he'd written something in response.

I'll be on the beach at three. I look forward to warm conversation and learning the mystery surrounding Kindred Spirit; I'm anticipating surprise with you as my guide.

She blinked, thinking that the man knew how to write a note. The wording struck her as vaguely romantic, which only deepened the flush she experienced at the thought that he'd actually agreed to join her.

When she opened the door, Scottie circled her legs, his tail wagging. She grabbed the old coffee maker and tossed it in the outdoor garbage can while Scottie did his business, then set up the new machine in its place. She put the other bags in the bedroom and, noting the time, saw that she had an hour to get ready. With her hair already done, that simply entailed grabbing a light jacket from her suitcase and setting it within easy reach until she was ready to go.

Which meant she had nothing else to do, other than to alternate between trying to relax on the couch and rising regularly to check her appearance in the mirror, fully conscious of how slowly time seemed to be moving.

A LOVE LETTER

At ten minutes to three, Tru left the house and proceeded down the walkway toward the beach, noting that the temperature had cooled markedly since the morning. The sky was gray and a steady breeze was churning up the ocean. Foam blew down the beach, rolling like tumbleweeds in the westerns he'd sometimes watched on television as a child.

He heard Hope before he saw her. She was shouting at Scottie not to pull so hard. As she descended to the beach, he noticed that she'd donned a light jacket, and her auburn hair not only was shorter, but seemed to glint in places. He watched as Scottie dragged her toward him.

"Hey there," she said when close. "How was your day?"

"Quiet," Tru answered, thinking her normally turquoise eyes now reflected the gray of the sky, lending them an almost ethereal quality. "I went fishing earlier."

"I know. I saw you going that way this morning. Any luck?"

"A bit," he said. "How about you? Did you accomplish all you'd hoped?"

"I did, but I feel like I've been rushing around ever since I woke up."

"Your hair is lovely, by the way."

"Thank you. She cut more than I thought she would, but I'm glad you still recognize me." She zipped her jacket before bending over to release Scottie from the leash. "Do you think you'll need a coat? It's kind of chilly out here, and we'll be walking for a while."

"I'll be all right."

"It must be all that Zimbabwean blood coursing through your veins."

As soon as Scottie was free, he took off running, sand flying from his feet. The two of them began to follow.

"I know you probably think he's out of control," she said, "but I've taken him to obedience classes. He's too stubborn to learn."

"I'll take your word for it."

"You don't believe me?"

"Why wouldn't I?"

"I'm not sure. I'm thinking that maybe you figure I'm just a pushover when it comes to my dog."

"I'm not sure there's a safe way for me to respond to that comment."

She laughed. "Probably not. Did you get the chance to speak with Andrew?"

"I did. But I'm fairly certain that I miss him more than he misses me."

"I think that's typical for kids, isn't it? Whenever I went off to camp, I was having too much fun to even have time to think about my parents."

"Good to know," he said. He glanced over at her. "Did you ever think about having children?"

"All the time," she admitted. "I can't imagine not having children."

"Yeah?"

"I guess I'm just into the whole marriage and family thing. I mean, I enjoy my job, but that's not what life is about for me. I can remember when my sister had her first baby, and she let me hold her, and I just...melted. Like I knew my purpose in life. But then again, I've always felt that way." Her eyes glowed. "When I was a little girl, I used to walk around with a sofa cushion stuffed under my shirt, pretending I was pregnant." She laughed at the memory. "I've always pictured myself as a mother...somehow, the idea of growing a person within you, bringing it into the world and loving it with a kind of primal intensity feels...*profound* to me. I don't get to church that often anymore, but my feelings about this are as close to spiritual as I get, I suppose."

He watched as she tucked a strand of hair behind her ear, as though trying to push away a painful truth, her vulnerability making him long to put his arms around her.

"But then, things don't always work out the way that we imagine they will, do they?" The question was rhetorical, so he didn't answer. After a few steps, Hope went on. "I know that life isn't fair, and I've heard that old saying about how man plans and God laughs, but I never expected to be single at my age. It's like my life is on hold somehow. It seemed like everything was on track. I'd met this wonderful man, we were making plans, and then...nothing. We're exactly where we were six years ago. We don't live together, we're not married or even engaged. We're just dating." She shook her head. "I'm sorry. You probably have no interest in hearing about any of this."

"That's not true."

"Why would you care?"

Because I care about you, he thought. Instead, he said: "Because sometimes, all a person needs is for someone else to listen."

She seemed to contemplate that as they walked through the sand. Scottie was far ahead, already past the pier, chasing one flock of birds after another, as energetic as always.

"I probably shouldn't have said anything," she remarked with a defeated shrug. "I'm just disappointed in Josh right now and it makes me wonder what the future holds for us. Or even if there's going to be a future. But that's just my anger talking. If you'd asked me when things were good between us, I'd have gone on and on about how wonderful he is."

When she trailed off, Tru glanced over at her. "Do you know if he wants to be married? Or have kids?"

"That's the thing...he says he does. Or he used to, anyway. We haven't talked about it much recently, and when I finally tried to bring it up again, the discussion went south real fast. That's why he's not here. Because we ended up in this huge argument, and now instead of coming to the wedding with me, he's in Las Vegas with his buddies."

Tru winced. Even in Zimbabwe, people knew about Las Vegas. Meanwhile, Hope continued. "I don't know. Maybe it's me. I probably could have handled it better, and I know I'm making him sound completely selfish. But he isn't. It's just, sometimes, I think he hasn't finished growing up yet."

"How old is he?"

"Almost forty. How old are you, by the way?"

"Forty-two."

"When did you finally feel like an adult?"

"When I was eighteen and left the farm."

"That doesn't come as a shock. With all you went through, you had no choice but to grow up."

By then they'd reached the pier, and Tru noticed that many of the pilings were no longer submerged. Low tide, just as she'd told him.

"What do you intend to do?" he asked.

"I don't know," she said. "Right now, I'm guessing that in the end, we'll get back together and try to pick up from where we left off."

"Is that what you want?"

"I love him," she conceded. "And he loves me. I know he's being a bit of a jerk right now, but most of the time, he's...really great."

Though he'd expected the words, there was part of him that wished she hadn't said them. "Of that, I have no doubt."

"Why would you say that?"

"Because," he responded, "you've chosen to stay with him for six years. And from what I know about you, you would never have done so unless he had numerous admirable traits."

She stopped to pick up a colorful seashell, but it turned out to be broken. "I like the way you phrase things. You often sound very British. I've never heard anyone described as having 'numerous admirable traits.'"

"That's a pity."

She tossed the shell aside and laughed. "You want to know what I think?"

"What's that?"

"I think Kim might have made a mistake by letting you go."

"That's kind of you to say. But she didn't. I'm not sure I was ever cut out to be a husband."

"Does that mean you'll never get married again?"

"I haven't given the matter any thought. Between work and spending time with Andrew, meeting someone is rather low on my list of priorities."

"What are the women like in Zimbabwe?"

"In my world, you mean? Single women?"

"Sure."

"Few and far between. Most of the women I meet are already married and they're at the lodge with their husbands."

"Maybe you should move to another country."

"Zimbabwe is my home. And Andrew is there. I could never leave him."

"No," she said. "You can't."

"How about you? Have you ever considered moving from the United States?"

"Never," she said. "And it's certainly not possible now, since my dad is sick. But even in the future, I'm not sure that I could. My family's here, my friends are here. But I do hope to make it to Africa one day. And go on safari."

"If you do, keep your guard up around the guides. Some of them can be extremely charming."

"Yeah, I know." She playfully nudged his shoulder with hers. "Are you ready for Kindred Spirit?"

"I still don't know what it is."

"It's a mailbox on the beach," she said.

"To whom does the mailbox belong?"

She shrugged. "To anyone, I guess. And everyone."

"Am I supposed to write a letter?"

"If you'd like," she said. "The first time I went, I did."

"When was that?"

She considered the question. "Maybe five years ago?"

"I assumed you'd been going there since you were young."

"It hasn't been around that long. I think my dad told me that it went up in 1983, but I could be wrong about that. I've only been there a few times. Including the day after Christmas last year, which was kind of crazy."

"Why?"

"Because it snowed fifteen inches. It's the only time I've ever seen snow on the beach. When we returned home, we built a snowman near the steps. I think there's a photo of it in the cottage somewhere."

"I've never seen snow."

"Ever?"

"It doesn't snow in Zimbabwe, and I've only been to Europe in the summers."

"It rarely snows in Raleigh, but my parents used to bring us skiing at Snowshoe in West Virginia during the winter."

"Are you any good?"

"I'm all right. I never liked to go too fast. I'm not a risk taker. I just want to have fun."

Up ahead, he saw clouds flickering on the distant horizon. "Is that lightning?"

"Probably."

"Does that mean we should turn back?"

"It's out to sea," she said. "The storm will be coming from the northwest."

"Are you sure?"

"Pretty sure," she said. "I'm willing to risk it if you are."

"All right, then," he said with a nod, and they continued on, the pier growing ever smaller behind them. Sunset Beach eventually came to an end, with Bird Island directly ahead. They had to skirt the dune to keep their feet from getting wet, and Tru found his thoughts drifting back to the way she'd playfully bumped against him. It seemed as though he could still feel the sensation, a tingling up and down his arm.

"It's a mailbox," Tru said.

They'd reached Kindred Spirit, and Hope watched as Tru simply stared at it.

"I already told you that."

"I thought it might be a metaphor."

"Nope," she said. "It's real."

"Who takes care of it?"

"I have no idea. My dad could probably tell you, but I assume it's a local. Come on."

As she walked toward the mailbox, she glanced at Tru, noting again the small dimple in his chin and his wind-blown hair. Over his shoulder, she saw Scottie sniffing near the dune, his tongue hanging out, tired from the endless quest to keep birds in the air. "You'll probably take this idea back with you to Zimbabwe, and you'll put up a mailbox in the middle of the bush. How neat would that be?"

He shook his head. "The termites would eat the post in less than a month. Besides, it's not as though anyone could put a letter in it, or sit around reading it. Too dangerous."

"Do you ever go out into the bush alone?"

"Only if I'm armed. And only when I can predict that I'll be safe, because I know what animals are in the vicinity."

"What are the most dangerous animals?"

"That depends on the time and the location and the mood of the animal," he answered. "Generally, if you're in or around the water, crocodiles and hippos. In the bush during daylight, elephants, especially if they're in heat.

In the bush at night, lions. And black mambas anytime. That's a snake. Very poisonous. The bite is nearly always fatal."

"We have water moccasins in North Carolina. Copperheads, too. A kid came into the emergency room once after being bitten. But we had antivenin at the hospital, and he recovered. And how did we get on this subject again?"

"You suggested that I put a mailbox in the middle of the bush."

"Oh yeah," she said. By then, she had her hand on the handle. "Are you ready for this?"

"Is there a protocol?"

"Of course there is," she said, "First you do ten jumping jacks, then sing 'Auld Lang Syne,' and you're supposed to bring red velvet cake as an offering, which you place on the bench."

When he stared at her, she giggled. "Gotcha. No, there's no protocol. You just…read what's in the mailbox. And if you want to, you can write something."

Hope pulled it open and removed the entire stack of mail that rested inside, bringing it with her to the bench. When she set it beside her, Tru took a seat next to her, close enough that she could feel the heat from his body.

"How about I read first, and then just pass them to you?"

"I'll follow your lead," he answered. "Proceed."

She rolled her eyes. "Proceed," she repeated. "It's fine if you just say 'okay,' you know."

"Okay."

"I hope there's a good one. I've read some amazing letters when I've been here."

"Tell me about the one you remember most."

She took a few seconds to consider it. "I read about this

man who was searching for a woman he'd met briefly at a restaurant. They were at the bar and they spoke for a few minutes before her friends arrived and she went to her table. But he knew she was the one for him. There was this beautiful line in there about stars colliding, sending shimmers of light through his soul. And anyway, this guy was writing because he hoped that someone knew who she was and would let her know that he wanted to see her again. He even left his name and phone number."

"He'd barely spoken to her? He sounds obsessive."

"You had to read the way he wrote it," she said. "It was very romantic. Sometimes a person just knows."

He watched as she lifted a postcard from the top of the stack, one displaying the USS *North Carolina*, a World War II battleship. When she was finished reading it, she handed it to him without comment.

Tru scanned it before turning toward her. "It's a shopping list for someone planning a barbecue."

"I know."

"I'm not sure why I'd be interested in this."

"You don't have to be," she said. "That's why this is exciting. Because we're hoping to find that diamond in the rough, and who knows," she said, lifting a letter from the stack, "maybe this is it."

Tru set the postcard aside, and when she was finished with the letter, she handed it to him. It was from a young girl, a poem about her parents, and it reminded him of something Andrew might have written when he was younger. As he read, he felt Hope's leg move against his, and by the time he finished, Hope was handing him a sheaf of pages torn from a notebook. He wondered if she realized that they were touching, or if she was simply lost in the words of anonymous writers and didn't even notice. Now and then, he saw her glance up to make sure that Scottie was still nearby; because there were no birds, he'd plopped himself down a bit closer to the water's edge.

There was another postcard, and a handful of photographs with comments on the back. That was followed by a letter from a father to his children, with whom he seldom spoke. In the letter, there was more bitterness and blame than sadness about the broken relationship. Tru wondered whether the man took any responsibility for what had happened.

As he set it aside, Hope was still reading the next letter in the stack. In the silence, he spotted a pelican skimming low over the water, just past the breakers. Beyond them, the sea continued to darken, becoming almost black near the horizon. Broken seashells littered the smooth, hard sand, left behind by the receding tide. Hope's hair was lifting slightly in the breeze; in the graying light, she seemed to be the only element of color.

She had yet to hand him another letter, and only then did he realize that she was reading the one in her hand a second time. He heard her sniff.

"Wow," she finally said.

"Did he write about stars colliding and sending shimmers of light through his soul?"

"No. And on second thought, you're probably right. That other guy was definitely obsessive."

He laughed as she handed over the letter. She didn't reach for another one, instead keeping her gaze on him.

"You're not going to watch me read it, are you?" he asked.

"I have a better idea," she said. "Why don't you read it aloud?"

The suggestion caught him off guard, but he took the letter, feeling her hand brush against his. He thought how relaxed they already seemed to be with each other, and how easy it would be to fall for someone like her. And that maybe, just maybe, he was already falling, and there was nothing he could do to stop it.

In the silence, he felt her move closer. He could smell her hair, the scent clean and sweet, as fresh as flowers, and he fought the urge to put his arm around her. Instead, he took a deep breath and, lowering his gaze, began to read the shaky scrawl.

Dear Lena,

The sands in the hourglass have fallen without mercy throughout my life, but I try to remind myself of the blessed years that we shared—especially now, when I am drowning in riptides of sorrow and loss.

I wonder who I am without you. Even when I was old and tired, it was you who helped me face the day. I sometimes felt as though you could read my mind. You seemed to always know what I wanted and needed. Even though we had our struggles at times, I can think back on the more than half a century we spent together and know that I was the lucky one. You inspired and fascinated me, and I walked just a bit taller because you were by my side. Every time I held you, I felt as though I needed nothing else. I would trade anything to hold you just one more time.

I want to smell your hair, and sit at the dinner table with you. I want to watch as you cook the fried chicken that always made my mouth water, the meal the doctor warned me against eating. I want to see you slip your arms into the blue sweater I bought you for your birthday, the one you usually wore in the evenings, when you settled beside me in the den. I want to sit with our children and grandchildren, and Emma, our one and only great-grandchild. How can I be this old? I think when I hug her, but when I listen for you to tease me about it, I never hear your voice. And it always breaks my heart.

I'm not good at this. Spending my days alone. I miss your knowing smile, and I miss the sound of your voice. Sometimes I imagine that I can still hear you calling to me from the garden, but when I go to the window, there are nothing but cardinals, the ones you made me hang the bird feeder for.

I keep it filled for you. I know you'd want me to do that. You always enjoyed watching those birds. I never understood why, until the man at the pet store mentioned that cardinals mate for life.

I don't know if that's true, but I want to believe it. And as I watch them, just as you used to, I think to myself that you have always been my cardinal, and I have always been yours. I miss you so much.

Happy Anniversary.
Joe

When he finished, Tru continued to stare at the page, more affected by the words than he wanted to admit. He knew that Hope was watching him, and when he turned toward her, he was struck by the open, unguarded nature of her beauty.

"That letter," she said quietly, "is the reason I like to come to Kindred Spirit."

Folding the page, he put it back in the envelope and set it atop the small stack beside him. Even as he watched her reach toward the unread pile, he had the feeling that the remaining messages would be anticlimactic, and they were. Most were heartfelt and earnest, but there was nothing that struck a chord in the same way Joe's letter had. Even as they rose from the bench and refilled the mailbox, he wondered about the man: where he lived, what he was doing, and considering his obvious age, how he'd been able to make his way to this isolated stretch of beach on a mostly inaccessible island.

They started back toward the house, sometimes making idle conversation but mainly content to remain silent as they walked. Their ease made Tru think about Joe and Lena again, a relationship rooted in comfort and trust and a lasting desire to be together. He wondered whether Hope was thinking the same thing.

Up ahead, Scottie was zigzagging from the dunes to the water's edge and back again. The clouds continued to darken, shape-shifting in the wind, and a few minutes later, it started to sprinkle. The tide had come in and they had to step onto the dune to keep the waves from washing over them, but Tru quickly realized that it was pointless to attempt to stay dry. There were two flashes of lightning followed by two booms of thunder, and the world suddenly dimmed. The sprinkle turned to rain and then became a downpour.

Hope squealed and started to run, but with the pier still in the distance, she eventually slowed to a walk again. Turning around, she held up her hands.

"I guess I was wrong about how much time we had, huh?" she called out. "Sorry!"

"Not a worry," he answered, walking toward her. "It's wet, but not terribly cold."

"Not just wet," she said. "Soaking wet. And it's been an adventure, right?"

In the downpour, he saw a smudge of mascara on her cheek, a hint of imperfection on a woman who otherwise struck him as nearly perfect in every way. He wondered why she'd come into his life, and how he could have come to care for her as deeply as he already did. All his thoughts revolved around her. He didn't reflect on his life in Zimbabwe or the reason he'd come to North Carolina; instead, he marveled at her beauty and replayed the time they'd spent together, a reel of vivid images. It was a tidal wave of sensation and emotion, and he suddenly felt that every step he'd taken in his life had been on a path leading to her, as if she were his ultimate destination.

Hope seemed frozen in place. He guessed she knew what he was feeling, and he wondered whether she felt the same. He couldn't tell, but she didn't move even when he reached out, finally placing a hand on her hip.

For a long time, they stood that way, the energy passing back and forth between them through that single, simple touch. He stared at her and she stared back, the moment seeming to last forever before he finally inched forward. He tilted his head, his face slowly drawing toward hers, before feeling Hope place a gentle hand on his chest.

"Tru..." she whispered.

Her voice was enough to stop him from going further. He knew he should step back, make space between them, but he felt powerless to move.

Nor did she step back. Instead, they faced each other in the downpour, and Tru felt the old instincts rising up, instincts he couldn't control. With sudden clarity he understood that he'd fallen in love—and perhaps even that he'd been waiting for someone just like her all his life.

Hope stared at Tru, her mind racing, trying to ignore the gentle strength she felt in his hand. Trying to ignore the desire and longing she sensed in his touch. Part of her knew she wanted him to kiss her, even as another part, the stronger part, warned her against it, causing her to put a hand between them.

She wasn't ready for this...

Finally, reluctantly, she averted her gaze, sensing both his disappointment and his acceptance. When at long last, he stepped back, she finally felt like she could breathe again, even though his hand remained on her hip.

"We should probably be getting back," she murmured.

He nodded and as he slid his hand from her hip, she reached for it, intending to give it a squeeze. He happened to rotate his hand at the same time, and their fingers interlocked as if choreographed. The next thing she knew, they were holding hands as they walked side by side.

The sensation was heady, even though she knew holding hands meant nothing in the grand scheme of things. She vaguely remembered doing the same thing with Tony, the boy she'd kissed at the cottage, when they'd gone to the movies the following day. Back then, that simple gesture had probably impressed her as a sign of maturity, as if she were finally growing up, but here and now, it struck her as one of the most intimate things that had ever happened to her. His touch carried with it the possibility of even greater intimacy later, and she focused on keeping Scottie in sight to avoid thinking too deeply about it.

Eventually they passed Clancy's and then the pier; not too long after that, they'd reached the steps of the cottage. It was only when she stopped that Tru let go of her hand. As she stared at him, she knew she wasn't yet ready to end their time together.

"Would you like to have dinner tonight? At the cottage? I picked up some fresh fish the other day at the market."

"Yes," he said. "Very much."

MOMENTS OF TRUTH

As soon as she opened the door to her cottage, Scottie raced inside, paused, then shook himself vigorously, sending a fine spray of water over everything in the vicinity. Hope rushed to get a towel, but Scottie shook again before she could reach him. She grimaced. After she was dry, she would have to wipe down the furniture and walls. But first, a bath.

They had arranged to meet in an hour and a half, so there was plenty of time. She started the water in the tub, peeled out of her wet clothing, and tossed it into the dryer. By the time she returned, the tub was half-full, and she added some bubbles. Realizing something was missing, she wrapped a towel around herself, went to the kitchen, and poured a glass of wine from the bottle she'd opened the day before. On her way back to the bathroom, she grabbed candles and a book of matches from the cabinet.

She lit the candles before slipping into the hot, soapy water, and took a long sip of wine. Leaning her head back, she thought the experience seemed different than it had the day before, more luxurious somehow. As she relaxed, she replayed that moment on the beach when Tru had almost kissed her. Even though she had ultimately stopped him, there'd been a dreamlike quality to all of it, and she wanted to relive it. It wasn't just about feeling attractive again; there was something graceful and unforced about her connection with Tru, something almost peaceful. Until meeting him, she'd had no idea how much she'd been craving something exactly like that.

What she didn't know was whether that feeling was new or had been buried in her subconscious all along, lost among her worries and frustrations and the anger she felt at Josh. All she knew for sure was that the emotional turbulence of the last few months had left her with little energy to take care of herself. Periods of peace or simple relaxation were rare these days; sadly, she realized that she wasn't even excited about seeing her friends this weekend. Somewhere along the way, she'd lost her spark.

Spending time with Tru had awakened her to the fact that she didn't want to be the person she'd recently become. She wanted to be the person she remembered herself to be— someone who embraced life, an enthusiast for both the ordinary and extraordinary. Not in the future, but starting now.

She shaved her legs and soaked a little while longer before the water finally began to cool. After toweling off, she reached for the lotion on the counter. She spread it over her legs and breasts and belly, relishing the silky feeling as her skin came to life.

Pulling out the new sundress, she slipped it on, along with her new sandals. She thought about putting on a bra but decided it wasn't necessary. Feeling scandalous but not wanting to think about what it might mean for later, she didn't reach for a pair of panties, either.

She dried and styled her hair, trying to remember exactly how Claire had done it. When she was satisfied, she started with her makeup. For eye shadow, she selected a dusting of aqua, hoping it would accent the color of her eyes. She dabbed on a bit of perfume and chose a pair of crystal drop earrings that Robin had given her for her birthday.

Afterward, she stood in front of the mirror. She adjusted the straps of her sundress and primped her hair until she was satisfied. There were times when she was somewhat critical about her appearance, but tonight, she couldn't help but be pleased with the way she looked.

She carried what was left of her glass of wine back to the kitchen. Beyond the windows, the world continued to darken. Instead of starting the dinner preparations, she mopped up the remainder of Scottie's mess in the entranceway and did a quick run-through of the family room, straightening up the pillows and putting the novel she'd been reading back on the shelf. She switched on some lamps in the living room, using the dimmer to get the ambiance right. She turned on the radio and adjusted the tuner until she found a station offering classic jazz. Perfect.

In the kitchen, she opened another bottle of wine but put it in the refrigerator to cool. Then, pulling out some yellow squash, zucchini, and onions, she brought them to the counter and diced them before setting them aside. The salad came next—tomatoes, cucumbers, carrots, and romaine lettuce, which she'd just finished tossing in a wooden bowl when she heard a knock at the front door.

The sound kicked up butterflies in her stomach.

"Come in!" she called out as she moved to the sink. "It's open!"

The sound of rain suddenly intensified as the door opened, then quickly receded again.

"Give me just a minute, would you?"

"Take your time," his voice echoed in the hallway.

She rinsed and dried her hands, then retrieved the wine. As she poured it into glasses, it occurred to her that she should probably set out snacks. There wasn't much in the cabinets, but in the refrigerator she found some kalamata olives. Good enough. She dumped a handful into a small ceramic bowl and placed it on the dining room table. Then, after turning on the light above the stove, she turned off the overhead light and picked up the glasses. She took a deep breath before heading around the corner to the family room.

He'd squatted low to show some affection to Scottie, his back to her. He was dressed in a long-sleeved blue shirt and she noted the way his jeans stretched tight around his thighs and his butt. She stopped in midstride and all she could do was stare. It was just about the sexiest thing she'd ever seen.

He must have heard her, because he finally stood and turned with an automatic smile before registering the sight of her. His eyes widened as he absorbed the way she looked, his mouth slightly ajar. He seemed immobilized, struggling and failing to find his voice.

"You're...indescribably beautiful," he finally whispered. "Truly."

He was in love with her, she realized with sudden force. Despite herself, she basked in the sensation, somehow certain that the two of them had been moving toward this moment all along. More than that, she knew now that she'd wanted this to happen, because she understood that she was undeniably in love with him, too.

When Tru finally lowered his gaze, Hope moved to his side and handed him a glass of wine.

"Thank you," he said, taking in her appearance again. "I would have worn a jacket if I'd known. And if I'd packed one."

"You look perfect," she said, knowing that she wouldn't have wanted him dressed any other way. "It's a different wine from last night. I hope it's okay."

"I'm not particular," he said. "I'm sure it's fine."

"I haven't started cooking yet. I wasn't sure if you were ready to eat."

"It's up to you."

"I put out some olives if you want to nibble on something."

"All right."

"They're on the dining room table."

She knew they were skirting the edge of things, but with her emotions in upheaval, it was all she could do not to spill her wine. With a deep breath, she started toward the dining area. Beyond the window, the horizon flickered as though hiding a strobe light in its depths.

She pulled out a chair and took a seat. Tru did the same, both of them facing the window. Her throat felt dry and she took a sip of wine, thinking that their actions were unconsciously mirroring each other's. When Tru lowered his glass to the table, the fingers of both his hands remained on the stem. She knew he was as nervous as she was, which she found strangely comforting.

"I'm glad you came with me today."

"Me too," he said.

"I'm glad you're here."

"Where else would I be?"

The phone rang.

The receiver was on the wall, near Tru, but for a few beats, they just continued to watch each other. Only when it rang a second time did Hope turn toward the sound. Part of her was inclined to let the answering machine get it, but then she thought of her parents. Rising, she stepped past Tru and lifted the receiver.

"Hey there," Josh said. "It's me."

Her stomach tightened. She had no desire to talk to him. Not with Tru here, not now.

"Hi," she said tightly.

"I wasn't sure I'd catch you. I thought you might be out somewhere."

She heard him slur his words and realized he'd been drinking.

"I'm here."

"I just came in from the pool for a few minutes. It's pretty hot out there. How are you?"

Tru sat unmoving and silent at the table. He was so near...

Noting the way his shirt hugged his body, she sensed the muscles beneath the fabric, remembering the feel of his hand on her hip.

"I'm fine," she said, trying to sound nonchalant. "You?"

"I'm doing great," he said. "I won some money last night playing blackjack."

"Good for you."

"How's the cottage? Good weather at the beach?"

"It's raining right now, and it's supposed to last through the weekend."

"I'll bet Ellen's upset, huh?"

"Yes," Hope answered, and for an awkward moment there was silence on both ends.

"Are you sure you're okay?" he asked. She could almost see his frown. "You seem quiet."

"I told you I'm fine."

"It seems like you're still angry with me."

"What do you think?" She fought to keep her irritation under control.

"Don't you think you might be overreacting?"

"I'd rather not talk about it on the phone," she said.

"Why not?"

"Because this is something we should do face-to-face."

"I don't know why you're acting like this," he said.

"Then maybe you don't know me at all."

"Oh, come on. Don't be so melodramatic..." She could hear the ice clink in his glass as he took a drink.

"I think I should go," she said, cutting him off. "Bye."

She could hear Josh continuing to argue even as she hung up the receiver.

Hope stared at the phone for a moment before letting her hand fall to her side. "I'm sorry about that," she told Tru, sighing. "I probably shouldn't have answered in the first place."

"Do you want to talk about it?"

"No."

On the radio, one song ended and another began. The music was plaintive, restless, and she watched as Tru rose from the table. He was so very close now; she could feel her back pressing against the wall as he stared at her.

She met his gaze without wavering. He moved even closer.

She knew what was happening. No words were needed. She thought again that none of this could be real, but as his body pressed up against hers, it suddenly felt more real than anything she'd ever known.

She could still stop this. Maybe she should stop it. In a few days, he'd be half a world away, and the physical and emotional bond between them was destined to be broken. He would be hurt and she would be hurt, and yet—

She couldn't stop herself. Not anymore.

Rain sheeted against the windows and the clouds continued to flicker. Tru slipped his arm around her back, his eyes never leaving hers. His thumbs traced small circles and the fabric of her dress was thin and light enough for her to feel as if she had nothing on at all. She wondered whether he could tell she wasn't wearing any panties, and felt herself growing wet.

He pulled her tightly against him, the heat of his body imprinting on her own. With a soft escape of breath, she put her arms around his neck. She could hear the music, and they began to rotate in a slow circle, his body swaying ever so slightly. He smiled then, as if inviting her into his world, and the last of her defenses began to crumble. She knew she wanted this. When she felt his breath on her neck, she trembled.

He kissed her gently on her earlobes and her cheek, leaving traces of moisture, and when his lips finally met hers, she felt him restraining himself, as if giving her one last chance to end it. The realization was exhilarating, almost liberating, and when he buried his hands in her hair, she parted her mouth. She heard a soft moan, barely recognizing it as her own, as their tongues came together. He ran his hands over her back and her arms and then her belly, the sensation like a trail of tiny electric shocks. He traced a finger beneath the swell of her breasts and her nipples hardened.

She could feel her body against his. She brought a hand to his cheek and ran her fingertips over the stubble as he moved back to her neck, nibbling softly while she caressed his chest. Finally, taking his hand, she led him to the bedroom.

In the bedroom mirror, she saw him watching her as she found the candles and matches and lit them, placing one candle on the end table and the other on the bureau. The dim light made shadows dance along the walls, and when Hope turned, their eyes met and all they could do was drink in the sight of each other.

She sensed his desire and allowed herself to soak it in before finally taking a step toward him. He did the same, the world between them shrinking, and when they kissed, she relished the moisture and warmth of his tongue. Untucking his shirt, she unbuttoned it slowly, and when it hung open, she traced her fingernail over his stomach and his hip bone. His body was hard and lithe, the muscles of his stomach visible, and she pulled the shirt over his shoulders, allowing it to fall to the floor.

Her mouth moved to his neck, and she bit gently at it as she reached for his belt. She unbuckled it, then undid the button on his jeans. As she began to slide the zipper down, she felt his hands begin to move over her breasts. Tugging at his pants, she slid them down and Tru stepped back. He untied his boots and slipped them off, his socks after that. Then came the jeans, and finally his boxers.

He stood naked before her, his body perfect, like an ancient statue carved from marble. Hope lifted one foot to the bed, then the other, deliberately removing her sandals with tantalizing slowness. Tru moved toward her, taking her in his arms again. His tongue flickered against her earlobe as he reached for the strap of her sundress. He slid it over one shoulder, then repeated the process with the other strap. The dress fell from her body, crumpling at her feet, their naked bodies coming together. His skin was hot against hers as he ran his finger gently down her spine. She exhaled as his hand drifted even lower, and in a single motion, he scooped her up, kissing her as he carried her to the bed.

Moving onto the bed beside her, he caressed her breasts and her belly. She nibbled softly on his lower lip even as her fingers pressed hard into his back, feeling beautiful in the candlelight, feeling desired in his arms. He slowly ran his tongue between her breasts and over her belly before coming back up. The next time, his mouth went even lower, and she knotted her fingers in his hair while his tongue teased and aroused her. It went on and on until she couldn't take it anymore and she finally pulled him back to her, clinging to him, drawing him even closer.

He moved atop her then, radiating heat, and reaching for her hand, he kissed her fingertips one by one. He kissed her cheek and her nose, and then her mouth again, and when he finally entered her, she arched her back and moaned, knowing that she wanted him more than she'd ever wanted another man.

They moved together, both of them fully attuned to the other's needs, each of them trying to please the other, and she felt her body shiver with growing urgency. When the massive wave of pleasure crested over her, she cried out, but as soon as the feeling passed, it began to build again. She climaxed over and over, an endless sequence of pleasure, and when he finally climaxed as well, Hope was exhausted, her body wet with perspiration. She was breathing hard as Tru held her. Even then, his hands never stopped moving over her skin, and as the candles burned lower, she let herself drift on the tide of what they had just shared.

Later, they made love again, this time more slowly, but with the same intensity. She climaxed even more power-fully than she had before and was shaking with exhaustion by the time he finished. She felt utterly spent, but as the storm outside continued to rage, unbelievably, she felt her desire begin to build again. A third time wasn't possible, she thought, but it was, and only after she climaxed again was she was finally able to fall into a dreamless sleep.

In the morning, Hope woke to gray light streaming through the windows and the aroma of coffee drifting from the kitchen. She grabbed a robe from the bathroom and padded down the hallway, conscious of a ravenous hunger. Only then did she remember that they hadn't eaten the night before.

Tru was at the table, and she noticed that he'd already set out scrambled eggs and sliced fruit. He was dressed in the same clothing he'd worn the night before. When he saw her, he stood from the table and wrapped his arms around her.

"Good morning," he said.

"You, too," she said. "Don't kiss me, though. I haven't brushed my teeth yet."

"I hope you don't mind that I made breakfast."

"It's perfect," she said, admiring the spread. "How long have you been awake?"

"A couple of hours."

"You didn't sleep?"

"I slept enough." He shrugged. "And I figured out how to work your coffee maker. Can I pour you a cup?"

"Definitely," she said. She kissed him on the cheek and took a seat before scooping some eggs and fruit onto her plate. Beyond the glass, she noticed that the rain had stopped, but if the sky was any indication, the respite was only temporary.

Tru returned with her cup and set it beside her. "There's milk and sugar on the table," he said.

"I'm impressed you found everything."

"I am, too," he said, sitting beside her.

She thought about how much she cared about him and how natural the morning already felt. "Aside from making breakfast, what have you been doing?"

"I went next door and brought back some towels. A few other things, too."

"Why did you need towels?"

"I wanted to dry off the chairs out on the deck," he said.

"They're just going to get wet again."

"I know," he said. "But I'm hoping I have some time before that happens."

She studied him as she reached for her coffee. "You're being very mysterious about all this. What's going on?"

Reaching for her hand, he kissed the back of it. "I love you," he said simply.

Hearing the words aloud made her feel suddenly dizzy, and she knew she felt exactly the same way about him.

"I love you, too," she murmured.

"Then will you do something for me?"

"Anything."

"After breakfast, will you sit outside for me?"

"Why?"

"I want to draw you," he answered.

Startled, Hope nodded her assent.

After breakfast, she led the way outside, and Tru motioned to the chair. She took a seat, feeling strangely self-conscious, both hands cradling her cup of coffee.

"Should I put this down?" she asked, nodding at her cup.

"It doesn't matter."

"How do you want me to pose?"

He opened the sketchbook. "Just be yourself and pretend I'm not here."

It wasn't easy. No one had ever drawn her likeness before. She crossed one leg over the other, then tried again with the other leg. But what to do with the coffee? Again she debated setting the cup aside, but she took a sip instead. She leaned forward, then tried leaning back. She turned toward the house where Tru was staying, then toward the ocean, then back to Tru. Nothing felt right, but she noticed that he was staring at her with quiet concentration.

"How am I supposed to pretend you're not here with you looking at me like that?"

"I don't know," he said with a laugh. "I've never been on the other side."

"Some help you are," she teased, and tucked a leg beneath her, trying to get comfortable. *Better*, she thought. Thankfully, Scottie had followed them out and she decided to focus on him as he lay curled beneath the kitchen window.

By then, Tru had descended into silence, and she watched him pick up the pencil. His eyes flickered from her to the sketch and back again, and she noted the confident movement of his hand as he drew and smudged with practiced ease. Occasionally he would squint or furrow his brow, and she knew he wasn't even aware of it. Somehow, that flash of nakedness beneath his assured demeanor made her want him even more.

When the clouds began to darken again, they both knew it was time to stop.

"Would you like to see it? It's not finished, but there's enough to show the general idea."

"Maybe after I shower," she demurred, rising from her seat. Tru collected the pad and the pencils, and halting just inside the doorway, he kissed her tenderly. He pulled her close and she leaned into him, inhaling his scent, wondering again at the mysterious forces that had brought them together.

TOGETHER

After her shower, Hope sat beside Tru on the couch as he showed her his drawing of her, as well as others in his sketchbook. She took her time admiring them. Later, when the rain tapered off, they ventured out for lunch at a café on Ocean Isle Beach, while the storm rose to a fury beyond the windows.

When she finally had to start getting ready for the rehearsal dinner, Tru sat on the edge of the bed, his gaze steady in her direction. There was something about watching a woman put on makeup that he'd always found sexy, and he sensed that she enjoyed having him as an audience.

At the door, when it was time for her to leave, they kissed for a long time. He held her close, imprinting her body upon his, and stood on the front porch, waving as she pulled away. She'd asked him to take Scottie out later, and said he was welcome to stay at the cottage if he wished.

He made a quick trip next door to pick up a steak and some side items, and prepared the meal in Hope's kitchen. As he ate, he tried to imagine Hope among her friends, wondering whether they would be able to see in her face all that had happened in the last few days.

He spent some time adding further detail to the drawing of her that he'd started earlier, stopping only when he was finally satisfied. Still not ready to put the pencils aside, however, he started another drawing of the two of them standing on the beach, facing each other in profile. She didn't need to be there for that; it was enough to imagine the scene, and the work went quickly. By the time he stopped for the night, hours had passed, and he felt Hope's absence like an ache.

She made it back to the cottage by midnight. They made love, but she was still exhausted from the night before, and soon after, he heard her breathing change as she fell asleep in his arms. For him, sleep was elusive. Their time together here would be ending soon, yet he knew she was the woman with whom he wanted to spend the rest of his life.

He stared at the ceiling, trying desperately to reconcile those two realities.

In the morning, Tru was quieter than usual. Instead of speaking, he held her for a long time in bed, and she felt her entire being resound with the depths of her feelings for him.

But it frightened her, in the same way she suspected that it frightened Tru. What she wanted was for all this, these last few days, to last forever while time stopped everywhere else. But the clock seemed to be ticking louder with every passing minute.

It was still raining moderately when they got out of bed, but they decided to take another walk on the beach nonetheless. Hope found rain jackets in the closet, and they brought Scottie out. They held hands as they walked, and by unspoken agreement, they paused at the spot where they'd met for the very first time. He kissed her and when she pulled back, he took her hands in his.

"I think I wanted all of this to happen from the moment I met you."

"What part? Sleeping with me or falling in love?"

"Both," he admitted. "When did you know?"

"I think I knew we might sleep together when we had wine on the porch after dinner. I didn't know I'd fall for you until the night you came over for dinner." She squeezed his hand. "I'm sorry about turning away when you tried to kiss me the first time."

"Don't be."

They started the trek back, stopping in at the house where Tru was staying. On the answering machine was a message from his father, saying that he hoped to arrive at the house between two and three. Which would work out perfectly, Hope thought. She'd be leaving around then for the wedding. Even though the ceremony started at six, she had to be there early for photographs.

Tru gave her a quick tour of the house while Scottie explored on his own, and she had to admit it was more tasteful than she'd imagined it would be. Despite her initial prejudice, she could imagine renting the place with her friends for a week and having a fantastic time. When they got to the master bathroom, Hope gestured at the huge whirlpool tub.

"Shall we?" she suggested. The next thing she knew, they'd disrobed, tossing their clothes and jackets in the dryer. Once submerged in the foaming water, she leaned back against Tru, sighing as he gently moved the washcloth over her breasts and belly, her arms and legs.

They had an early lunch in bathrobes while their clothes continued to dry. Afterward, Hope slipped back into her dryer-warmed outfit, and the two of them sat at the table talking until it was time for her to return to the cottage and start getting ready.

Like the day before, he watched from his spot on the bed as she styled her hair and put on her makeup. The bridesmaid dress and new shoes came next, and when she was finished she did a quick pirouette for him.

"Okay?"

"Stunning," he said, his admiring gaze underscoring his sincerity. "I'm sorely tempted to kiss you, but I don't want to mess up your lipstick."

"I'll risk it," she said, leaning over to kiss him. "If you weren't supposed to meet your father today, I'd ask you to join me."

"I would have had to purchase appropriate attire."

"I'll bet you're incredibly handsome in a suit." She patted his chest and perched next to him on the bed. "Are you nervous about meeting your father?"

"Not really."

"What if he doesn't remember much about your mom?"

"Then I imagine our meeting will be a short one."

"You're really not interested in who he is? What he's like? Where he's been all these years?"

"Not particularly."

"I don't know how you can remain so detached about all this. It seems to me that he might want a relationship of some sort with you. Even a minor one."

"I've considered that, but I doubt that's true."

"But he flew you out here."

"And at the same time, I've yet to see him. If he wanted a relationship, I suspect he would have come by earlier in the week."

"Then why do you think he wanted you to come?"

"I think," Tru finally answered, "he wants to tell me why he left my mother."

A few minutes later, Tru walked Hope to her car, holding two umbrellas so that she wouldn't get wet.

"I know it sounds silly, but I think I'm going to miss you," she said.

"Me too," he responded.

"Will you tell me what happens with your father?"

"Of course. And I'll make sure to get Scottie out for a walk, too."

"I don't know what time I'll be back. It might be late. You're welcome to wait at the cottage for me. I won't be hurt if you're already asleep when I get in."

"Have a good time."

"Thank you," she said, slipping behind the wheel.

Though she gave him a cheery wave as she backed out, for some reason he felt a touch of foreboding as she vanished from sight, making him wonder why the feeling had arisen in the first place.

FATHER TIME

Deciding it was probably best to leave Scottie at the cottage, Tru gathered his sketchbook and pencils and went back to the house, awaiting the visit from his father.

He continued with the drawing of him and Hope, the work coming easily. Soon, he progressed to the point where he began focusing on the finer details, an unconscious signal that the sketch was approaching completion. Lost in his work, it took him a moment to realize that someone was knocking.

His father.

Rising from the table, he crossed through the living room. He paused when he grasped the knob, readying himself. Upon opening the door, he saw the face of his father for the very first time. To his surprise, he recognized some of his own features in the old man who stood before him, the same dark blue eyes and a small dimple in the chin. His father's hair was thinning and what little remained had turned white, with only faint streaks of gray. He was stooped slightly, pale, and on the frail side; the jacket he was wearing seemed to envelop him, as though it had been purchased for someone much larger. Over the sound of the storm, Tru could hear him wheezing.

"Hello, Tru," he finally said, the words labored. In one hand he held an umbrella, and Tru noticed a briefcase on the porch.

"Hello, Harry."

"May I come in?"

"Of course."

His father bent to pick up his briefcase and froze, wincing. Tru reached for it.

"Can I get that for you?"

"Please," Harry answered. "The older I get, the farther away the ground seems."

"Come in."

Tru retrieved the briefcase as his father stepped past him, slowly shuffling into the living room and toward the windows. Tru joined him, standing by his side, watching his father in his peripheral vision.

"It's quite a storm here," Harry said, "but it's even worse inland. It took forever to get here because there was so much water on the highway. My driver had to make more than a few detours."

Because it was more of a comment than a question, Tru said nothing. Instead, he studied his father, thinking that it was akin to seeing the future. *This*, Tru thought, *is what I will eventually look like if I live as long as he has.*

"Has the house been satisfactory?"

"It's big," Tru responded, recalling the way Hope had first described it. "But yes. It's a beautiful home."

"I had it built a few years ago. My wife wanted a place at the beach, but we've hardly ever used it." He took two long, wheezy breaths before going on. "Was there enough food in the refrigerator?"

"Too much," Tru answered. "There's probably going to be a lot left over when I leave."

"That's fine. I'll have the cleaning service take care of it. I'm just glad it arrived in time. I'd forgotten about it until you were already in the air, but there was little I could do. I was in the ICU and they don't allow phone calls, so I asked my daughter to handle the details. She made arrangements with the property manager to receive the delivery."

The words continued to roll through his mind even after his father finished speaking. *Wife, ICU, daughter*...Tru found it hard to concentrate. Hope had been right in predicting that the meeting would feel a bit surreal.

"I see" was all Tru could think to say.

"I'd also like to apologize for not setting you up with a rental car instead of having a driver pick you up. It might have been more convenient for you."

"It didn't bother me. I wouldn't have known where to go. You said you were in the ICU?"

"I was released from the hospital yesterday. My kids tried to talk me out of coming, but I couldn't miss this chance to meet you."

"Would you like to sit?" Tru asked.

"I think I probably should."

They crossed to the dining room table and Harry seemed to collapse into a chair. In the gray light streaming through the windows, he looked even more depleted than when he'd arrived.

Tru took a seat beside him. "May I ask why you were in the ICU?"

"Lung cancer. Stage four."

"I don't know much about cancer."

"It's terminal," Harry said. "The doctors give me a couple of months, maybe less. Maybe a little more. It's in God's hands, I suppose. I've known since the spring."

Tru felt a twinge of sadness at that, though it was the kind associated with learning bad news about a stranger, not family. "I'm sorry to hear that."

"Appreciated," he said. Despite the information he'd shared, Harry smiled. "I don't have any regrets. I've had a good life, and unlike a lot of people, I've been given the chance to say goodbye. Or even, in your case, hello." He pulled a handkerchief from his jacket pocket and coughed into it. When he finished, he took a couple of labored, wet-sounding breaths. "I want to thank you for making the trip here," he added. "When I sent the ticket, I wasn't sure you would agree to come."

"Initially, I wasn't, either."

"But you were curious."

"Yes," Tru admitted.

"I was, too," he said. "Ever since I learned that you existed. I didn't know about you until last year."

"And yet you waited to meet me."

"Yes."

"Why?"

"I didn't want to complicate your life. Or mine."

It was an honest answer, but Tru wasn't quite sure what to make of it.

"How did you find out about me?"

"That's a long story, but I'll do my best to be brief. Frank Jessup, a man I knew from way back, happened to be in town. I hadn't seen him in almost forty years, but we'd kept in minimal contact since then. Christmas cards, the occasional letter, but no more than that. Anyway, when we were having lunch, he made a reference to your mother, and mentioned that there were rumors she'd had a son less than a year after I left the country. He didn't say it was mine, but I think he wondered about it. After the conversation, I wondered, too, so I hired an investigator and he went to work. Which took time. There are still a lot of people afraid to speak about your grandfather, even though he's not around any longer, and we both know the country has gone to hell, so records are sketchy. But long story short, the guy was good and I eventually sent someone to the lodge in Hwange. He took photographs of you, and when I saw them, I knew right away. You have my eyes, but you got your facial structure from your mother."

Harry turned toward the window, letting the silence hang. Tru thought about something the man had said only moments before.

"What did you mean when you said that you didn't want to complicate my life?" Tru asked.

It was a few beats before his father answered.

"People talk about truth like it's the solution to all of life's problems. I've been around long enough to know that isn't the case, and that sometimes truth can do more harm than good."

Tru said nothing. He knew his father was building to a point.

"That's what I've been considering. Ever since I realized that you'd agreed to come, I've been asking myself the question of how much I should tell you. There are some... aspects to the past that might be painful for you, and parts that, in retrospect, you might wish I hadn't told you. So I suppose what I say next is up to you. Do you want the whole truth, or selected parts of it? Remember, though, I'm not the one who's going to live with the knowledge for years to come. My regrets will be much more short-lived. For obvious reasons."

Tru brought his hands together, considering the question. The opaque references and careful phrasing made him curious, but the warning gave him pause. How much did he really want to know? Instead of answering right away, he rose from the table.

"I'm getting some water. Would you like a glass?"

"I'll have hot tea, if it's not a problem."

"Not at all," Tru said. He found a teakettle in one of the cabinets, filled it with water, and set it on the burner. In yet another cabinet he found packets of tea. He filled his glass with water, took a drink, then refilled it. It didn't take long for the kettle to whistle, and he prepared the cup and brought it to the table. He took his seat again.

Through all of that, his father said nothing. Like Tru, the man didn't seem inclined to fill the silence with small talk. Interesting.

"Have you made up your mind yet?" his father asked.

"No," Tru answered.

"Is there anything you do want to know?"

I want to know about my mother, he thought again. But sitting beside the old man at the table led to an entirely different question instead.

"First, tell me about you," he said.

His father scratched at an age spot on his cheek. "All right," he said. "I was born in 1914, in Colorado, in a sod house, if you can believe that. Three older sisters. In my teens, the Depression hit and times were tough, but my mother was a teacher, and she always stressed education. I went to the University of Colorado, and picked up a couple of degrees. After that, I joined the army. I think I mentioned in my letter that I was in the Corps of Engineers, right?"

Tru nodded.

"At first, most of my work was stateside, but then the war came. I spent time in North Africa, Italy, and then finally Europe. Mainly demolition at first, but by late 1944 and the spring of 1945, it was primarily bridge building, under Montgomery. The Allies were moving quickly into Germany by then, and there were a lot of water barriers, including the Rhine. Anyway, throughout the war, I grew friendly with one of the engineers from the British side. He'd grown up in Rhodesia and had a lot of contacts. He told me about the mining and the minerals, just waiting to be tapped, so after the war, I followed him there. He helped me find a job at the Bushtick mine. I worked there for a few years and met your mother."

He took a sip of tea, but Tru knew he was also debating how much to say.

"After that, I returned to the States. I went to work for Exxon, and met my wife, Lucy, at the company Christmas party. She was the sister of one of the executives, and we hit it off. Started dating, got married, had children. I worked in a lot of different countries over the years, some safe, others not so much. Lucy and the kids either joined me there or stayed in the States while I did my time overseas. The perfect company family, so to speak, which aided my career. I rose through the ranks and worked there right up until retirement. Finished as one of the vice presidents and made a fortune along the way. We moved to North Carolina eleven years ago. Lucy had grown up here and wanted to go home."

Tru scrutinized him, thinking of the new family—and life—that his father had created after his time in Africa. "How many children did you have?"

"Three. Two boys and a girl. All of them now in their thirties. My wife and I will celebrate forty years this November. If I make it that long."

Tru took a sip of water. "Is there anything you want to know about me?"

"I think I have a pretty good idea about you. The investigator filled me in."

"So you know I have a son. Your grandson."

"Yes."

"Do you have any desire to meet him?"

"Yes," he answered. "But it's probably not a good idea. I'm a stranger and I'm dying. I don't see how it would do him any good."

Tru thought he was probably right about that. But...

"For me, though, you felt differently. Same reality, but you drew a different conclusion."

"You're my son."

Tru took a sip from his water glass. "Tell me about my mother," he finally said.

His father lowered his chin, the words coming more softly. "She was beautiful," he said. "One of the most beautiful women I've ever seen. She was a good deal younger than I was, but she was...intelligent and mature for her age. She could speak at length about poetry and art, things I knew nothing about, with passion and expertise. And she had the most wonderful laugh, the kind that just draws you right in. I think I fell in love with her the first night I met her. She was...extraordinary."

He wiped his mouth with the handkerchief again. "We

spent a lot of the next year together—she was at the university, and the mine had a laboratory there. We saw each other whenever we could. I was working long hours, of course, but we'd make the time. I remember that she used to carry with her this book of poetry by Yeats, and I can't tell you how many times we read those poems aloud to each other." He paused, his breath coming unsteadily. "She fancied tomatoes. Had them with every meal we ever ate together. Always sprinkled with a bit of sugar. She adored butterflies, and she thought Humphrey Bogart in *Casablanca* was the sexiest man she'd ever seen. I began smoking even before I joined the army, but after she told me about Bogart, I began to hold the cigarette the same way he did in that movie. Between the forefinger and thumb."

He rotated the teacup, seemingly lost in thought.

"I taught her to drive a car, you know. She didn't know how until we met, and I remember thinking that was strange, especially since she grew up on a farm. And over time, I began to sense something else about her. Beneath the surface, as smart and mature as she was, I noticed a deep-seated insecurity, even though it made no sense to me. To me, she had everything and was everything I'd ever wanted. But the more I got to know her, the more secretive I realized she really was. For a long time, I knew little about her father or the power he wielded. She hardly ever spoke about him. But toward the end of our relationship, she would often make me promise to take her with me when I returned to the States, and the way she begged sometimes made me think that her desire had more to do with escaping her circumstances than how she felt about me. Nor would she ever introduce me to her father, or let me visit the farm. We always had to meet in out-of-the-way places.

And strangely, she never referred to him as her father or her dad. He was always the Colonel. And all of those things eventually made me wonder."

"Wonder what?"

"I think this is where you need to ask yourself again how much you really want to know. Last chance."

Tru closed his lips and nodded. "Go on."

"When she finally began to open up about your grandfather, she would describe two different people entirely. In one version, she adored him and stressed how much they needed each other, but the next time she spoke of him, she would tell me that she hated him. She would say that he was evil, that she wanted to get as far away from him as possible and never wanted to see him again. I don't know the full details of what went on in that house when she was growing up, nor am I sure I want to know. What I do know is that when her father found out about me, your mother panicked. She showed up at my place, hysterical and babbling that we had to leave the country right then, because the Colonel was furious—there wasn't even time to gather my things. I couldn't calm her down, but when she realized that I wasn't going to do what she asked, she ran off. That was the last I ever saw of her. At the time, I didn't know she was pregnant. Maybe if she'd told me, things would have been different. I like to think that I would have gone after her and helped her get away. But I never got the chance."

He brought his hands together, squeezing as though hoping for strength.

"They showed up at my house that night, after I'd gone to sleep. A group of men. They roughed me up pretty good and put a hood over my head before tossing me into the trunk of a car. They drove me to some kind of dwelling with a cellar, and after being dragged from the car, the next thing I knew, I was tumbling down a set of stairs. I was knocked unconscious, and when I woke, I could smell the dank and mold. I'd been handcuffed to some pipes. Which hurt like hell, because my shoulder had been dislocated in the fall."

He took a few long breaths, as if gathering his strength for a final push.

"When they finally took the hood off, a flashlight was shined in my eyes. I couldn't see a thing. But he was there. The Colonel. He told me that I had two choices: I could either leave Rhodesia the following morning, or I could die in the cellar, handcuffed to the pipes, without food or water."

He turned toward Tru. "I'd been in war. I'd seen terrible things. I'd been shot—got myself a Purple Heart—and there'd been times when I wondered how I'd survive. But I'd never been more scared than in that moment, because I knew he was a stone-cold killer. You could hear it in his voice. The following day, I got in my car and didn't stop driving until I reached South Africa. I caught a flight back to the States. I never saw or spoke to your mother again."

He swallowed.

"I've spent my life knowing that I was a coward for doing what I did. For leaving her with him. For vanishing completely from her life. And not a day has gone by when I haven't regretted it. I mean...I love my wife, but I've never felt for her the deep, burning passion that I felt with your mother. I left Evelyn with that man, and I know in my heart that it's the worst thing I've ever done. You should also know that I didn't come here for your forgiveness. Some things can't be forgiven. But I want you to know that if I'd known about you, things would have been different. I understand those are only words and that you don't know me, but it's the truth. And I'm sorry for the way everything turned out."

Tru said nothing, realizing that it wasn't difficult to reconcile the story he'd just heard with the grandfather he'd known. It left him disgusted, but more than that, he felt it give rise to a piercing sorrow for his mother, and pity for the man who was sitting beside him at the table.

His father motioned toward the briefcase. "Would you mind handing me that?"

Tru reached for the briefcase and placed it on the table, watching as his father opened the lid.

"I also wanted to give you some things," he said. "I put them in my trunk on the day I left Rhodesia, and over the years, I completely forgot about them. But when I saw your photograph, I had one of my sons find the trunk in the attic and bring it down. In the event you didn't visit, I was planning to send them to you."

Inside the briefcase was an envelope, set atop a stack of drawing paper that had yellowed at the edges. His father handed Tru the envelope.

"One of my friends back then was a photographer, and he used to bring his camera with him everywhere. There are a couple of shots of the two of us, but most of them are of your mother. He tried to convince her to become a model."

Tru slid the photographs from the envelope. There were eight in total; the first he examined showed his mother and father seated together in front of a river, both of them laughing. The second was also of the two of them, staring at each other in profile, similar to the drawing he'd been working on of Hope and himself. The others were all of his mother in various poses and outfits, with clean backgrounds, a photographic style common in the late 1940s. His throat tightened at the sight of her, and he felt a sense of sudden loss he hadn't expected.

His father handed over the drawings next. The first was a self-portrait of his mother staring at a reflection of herself in the mirror. Despite her beauty, her darkly shadowed expression gave her a haunted quality. The next was a drawing of his mother from behind. She was draped in a sheet and gazing over her shoulder, making Tru wonder whether she had used a similar photograph as inspiration. There were three more self-portraits and several landscape scenes similar to those that Tru created for Andrew. One of them, however, depicted the family's main house before the fire, with imposing columns gracing the veranda. He realized that he'd forgotten how it had looked then.

When Tru finally set the drawings aside, his father cleared his throat.

"I thought she was good enough to open a studio, but she wasn't interested in that. She said that she drew because she wanted to lose herself in the process. At the time, I wasn't sure what that meant, but I spent many afternoons watching as she sketched. She had a charming habit of licking her lips whenever she was working, and she was never completely satisfied with the results. In her mind, none of the drawings were ever finished."

Tru took a sip of water, thinking. "Was she happy?" he finally asked.

His father held Tru's gaze. "I don't know how to answer that. I like to think she was happy when we were together. But..."

His father trailed off and Tru mulled the implications of what his father had told him earlier, the words still left unspoken. About what had really happened in that house when his mother was growing up.

"If it's all right with you, I'd like to ask you a question," his father said.

"Yes?"

"Is there anything you want from me?"

"I'm not sure I understand the question."

"Would you like to keep a line of communication open? Or would you prefer that I vanish after I leave here today? I've already told you that I don't have much time left, but after all these years, I thought it best for you to be able to make the decision."

Tru stared at the old man seated next to him, considering it.

"Yes," he finally answered, surprising himself. "I'd like to be able to speak with you again."

"All right." His father nodded. "How about my other kids?" he asked. "Or my wife? Would you like to speak with them?"

Tru thought about it before finally shaking his head. "No," he said. "Unless they'd like to speak with me. We're strangers, and like you, I suppose I have no desire to add further complications to any of our lives."

His father offered a half smile at that. "Fair enough. But I do have a favor to ask of you. Feel free to say no, of course."

"What is it?"

"Do you happen to have a photograph of my grandson that I could see?"

His father stayed for another forty minutes. He said that his wife and children supported his decision to make contact with Tru—despite their confusion about a relation they'd never met, someone sprung from a past that predated any of them. When he added that the drive back to Charlotte was a long one and that he had no desire to worry them further, Tru knew it was his father's way of saying that it was time for him to go. Tru toted the briefcase and held the umbrella over his father as they descended the stairs to the car that had been waiting in the driveway.

Tru watched the car as it pulled away, then walked to the cottage to let Scottie out. Despite the storm, he wanted to walk the beach, needing open space and time to think.

It had been a surprising encounter, to say the least. Never had he imagined his father as a family man, someone married to the same woman for decades. Or that he'd fled the country in fear for his life because of Tru's grandfather. As he pushed through the sand, Tru couldn't shake a mounting feeling of revulsion for the most dominant male figure of his childhood.

There was also the family he'd never known about—half siblings, three of them—and though he'd declined to meet them, he did wonder about them. Who were they? What were they like? He doubted that any of them had felt the need to leave home the moment they'd turned eighteen as he had; their lives had surely been nothing like his. For a while he tried to picture what his own life would have looked like had his mother and father found a way to be together, but it felt too far-fetched and he soon gave up.

Staring out at the churning surf, he thought to himself that there were still too many unanswered questions, too many things he would never learn. Even about his mother. All he knew was that her short life had been even more tragic than he'd imagined, and if his father had brought her any joy at all, he was glad for that.

Tru found himself wishing that this meeting with his father had happened years earlier, when they would have had
more time to get to know each other. But some things were
not meant to be, and as the sun began to set, he turned
back toward the house. He walked slowly, absently keeping
his eye on Scottie, weighed down by the afternoon's revelations and an ineffable sense of regret. It was nearly dark by
the time he got back to the house. He left Scottie on the
back porch while he showered and put on some dry clothing, then gathered up the photographs and drawings that
his father had left.

At Hope's place, he took a seat at the kitchen table, examining the images. He wished that Hope were with him;
she would know how to help him make sense of things, and
without her, he felt on edge. To soothe himself, he returned
to work on the drawing of the two of them while the rain
continued to fall. Beyond the windows, lightning flickered,
mirroring his own roiling emotions, and he thought of the
odd parallels between himself and his father.

Harry had left his mother in Africa and returned to
America; in a couple of days, Tru would return to Africa,
leaving Hope here in the States. His father and mother
couldn't find a way to be together, but Tru wanted to believe
that he and Hope could be different. He wanted the two of
them to make a life together, and as he continued to sketch,
he wondered how to make that happen.

Exhausted, Tru didn't realize Hope had returned from the
wedding until he felt her slip into the bed beside him. It
was past midnight and she'd already undressed, her skin hot

to the touch. Without a word, she began to kiss him. He responded with caresses of his own, and when they began to make love, he tasted the salty tang of her tears. But he said nothing. It was all he could do to not cry himself at the thought of what the next day might bring. Afterward, she curled into him, and he held her as she fell asleep with her head on his chest.

Tru listened to the sound of her breathing, hoping it would settle him, but it didn't. Instead, he lay in the dark and stared at the ceiling, feeling strangely and entirely alone.

NO MORE TOMORROWS

Tru woke at dawn, just as the morning light began to stream through the window, and reached for Hope, only to realize that the bed was empty. Propping himself up on his elbow, he wiped the sleep from his eyes, surprised and a little disappointed. He'd wanted to spend the morning lingering in bed with Hope, whispering and making love, staving off the reality that this would be their final day together.

Rising from the bed, Tru threw on the jeans and shirt he'd been wearing the day before. On the pillowcase he saw smudges of mascara, a remnant of last night's tears, and felt a wave of panic at the thought of losing Hope. He wanted another day, another week, another year with her. He wanted a lifetime of years, and he was willing to do whatever she needed so they could stay together forever.

He mentally rehearsed what he would say to Hope as he headed toward the kitchen. He smelled coffee, but to his surprise Hope wasn't there. He poured himself a cup and continued his search, poking his head into the dining room and family room to no avail. He finally traced her whereabouts to the back porch, where he could see her beyond the window, sitting in a rocker. The rain had stopped, and as she stared toward the ocean, Tru thought again that she was the most beautiful woman he'd ever seen.

He paused only slightly before pushing the door open.

Hope turned at the sound. Though she offered up a tentative smile, her eyes were rimmed with red. The exquisite sadness of her expression made him wonder how long she'd been alone with her thoughts, replaying the impossibilities of their situation.

"Good morning," she said, her voice soft.

"Good morning."

When they kissed, he felt a hesitancy from her he hadn't expected, and it suddenly rendered moot all the speeches he had rehearsed. He had the sense that even if he said the words, she was no longer ready to hear them. Something had shifted, he realized with foreboding, even if he wasn't sure what.

"I didn't wake you, did I?" she asked.

"No," he answered. "I didn't hear you leave the bedroom."

"I tried to be quiet." The words sounded rote.

"I'm surprised you're even awake, since you got in so late."

"Sleeping in wasn't meant to be, I guess." He watched as she took a sip of coffee before going on. "Did you sleep okay?"

"Not really," he admitted.

"I didn't, either. I've been awake since four." She motioned with her cup toward the rocker. "I dried your seat, but you might want to give it another wipe just to make sure."

"All right."

Grabbing the towel she'd left on the seat, he ran it over the wooden planks before perching on the edge of the rocker. His insides were roiling. For the first time in days, the sky showed patches of blue, though a quilt of white clouds still trailed out over the water, the tail end of the storm receding in the distance. Hope turned back toward the ocean, as though unable to face him, saying nothing.

"Was it raining when you woke up?" he asked into the silence. Small talk, he knew, but he wasn't sure what else to do.

She shook her head. "No. It stopped sometime last night. Probably not long after I got home."

He angled his rocker toward hers, waiting to see if she would do the same with hers. She didn't. Nor did she speak. He cleared his throat. "How was the wedding?"

"It was beautiful," she said, still refusing to look at him. "Ellen was glowing, and a lot less stressed than I thought she would be. Especially considering her phone call the other day."

"The rain wasn't a problem?"

"They ended up holding the ceremony on the porch. People had to stand shoulder to shoulder, but that made it more intimate, somehow. And the reception went off without a hitch. The food, the band, the cake... It was a lot of fun for everyone."

"I'm glad it went well."

She seemed lost in thought for a moment before finally turning to face him. "How did it go with your father? I've been wondering about that since I left yesterday."

"It was..." Tru hesitated, searching for the right word. "Interesting."

"How is he? What's he like?"

"He's not what I imagined."

"How so?"

"I suppose I was expecting more of a roguish figure. But he's not like that at all. He's in his midseventies and he's been married for almost forty years to the same woman. He has three adult children, and worked for one of the big oil companies. He reminded me of many of the guests from America who visit the lodge."

"Did he tell you what happened between him and your mother?"

Tru nodded, then started at the beginning. For the first time that morning, Hope seemed to emerge from her shell, escaping in the moment the prison of her dark thoughts. Mesmerized by his account, she couldn't hide her shock when he finished.

"And he was sure your grandfather was the one who kidnapped him?" she asked. "He'd never met him, so it wasn't as though he could recognize the voice."

"It was my grandfather," Tru said. "There's no doubt in my mind. Just as there wasn't any in his."

"That's . . . terrible."

"My grandfather could be a terrible man."

"How do you feel about it?" Hope probed, her voice gentle.

"It was a long time ago."

"That's not much of an answer."

"It's also the truth."

"Does it make you think any differently about your father?"

"In a way," he said. "I'd always assumed he just ran off without a care for my mother. But I was wrong."

"Would you mind sharing the photographs and the drawings?"

Tru went back inside and fetched them from the end table. Handing her the stack, he took a seat in his rocker again and watched as Hope began to examine them.

"Your mother was very beautiful," she commented.

"Yes, she was."

"You can tell she was in love with him. And that he felt the same about her."

Tru nodded, his thoughts focused more on Hope than the events of the day before. He was trying to memorize everything about the way she looked, every quirk and gesture. When she finished with the photographs, she lifted the first of the drawings, the one of his mother staring at her reflection in the mirror.

"She was very talented," she said. "But I think your work is better."

"She was still young. And she had more natural ability than I do."

When she finished examining the stack of drawings, she took another sip of coffee, finishing the cup.

"I know you just woke up, but are you up for a walk on the beach?" she ventured. "I have to take Scottie out soon."

"Sure," he said. "Let me get my boots."

By the time he was ready, Scottie was already standing next to the gate, his tail wagging. Tru opened the gate, allowing Hope to lead the way, and once on the beach, Scottie took off, racing toward a flock of birds. They followed slowly, the morning cooler than it had been on previous days. For a while, neither one of them seemed to want to break the silence. When Tru slipped his hand into hers, she seemed to hesitate before her hand finally relaxed. Her defenses were going up, and it registered as an ache.

They walked in silence for a long time, Hope glancing at

him only now and then; mostly she seemed to be focusing on something in the distance or out over the water. As it had been most of the week, the beach was empty and quiet. There were no boats, and even the gulls and terns seemed to have taken flight. Confirming his earlier feelings of dread, he now sensed with certainty that something had happened, that there was something she was afraid to tell him. He had a strong premonition that whatever was on her mind would both surprise and hurt him, and he felt his heart sink. Desperate, he thought again about all he wanted to tell her, but before he could speak the words, she raised her gaze to his.

"I'm sorry I'm so quiet," she offered, forcing a smile. "I'm not very good company this morning."

"It's all right," he said. "You had a late night."

"It's not that," she said. "It's..." She trailed off, and Tru felt a touch of spray from the waves. It left him damp and chilled.

She cleared her throat. "I want you to know I had no idea what was going to happen."

"I'm not sure what you're talking about."

Her voice became softer, her fingers tightening in his grip. "Josh showed up at the wedding."

Tru felt his stomach tighten but said nothing. Hope went on.

"After the phone call the other night, he booked a flight to Wilmington. I guess he hadn't liked the way I sounded. He arrived right before the ceremony...He just showed up and could tell I wasn't happy about it." She took a few steps, watching the sand in front of her. "It wasn't too hard to avoid him at first. After the ceremony, the bridal party had to sit for a lot of photographs, and I was seated with Ellen at the main table. I stuck with my girlfriends for most of the evening, but toward the end of the reception, I went outside to cool off, and he found me." She drew a long breath, as if summoning the words she needed. "He apologized, said he wanted to talk, and..."

As she spoke, Tru felt everything beginning to slip away. "And?" he prompted gently.

She stopped walking and turned to face him. "When he showed up, all I could think about was this week and how much it's meant to me. Last week, I didn't even know you existed, so part of me can't help but wonder whether I'm crazy. Because I know that I love you."

Tru swallowed, noting that her eyes were bright with tears.

"Even now, when I'm here with you, all I can think is how right this feels. And I don't want to leave you."

"Then stay with me," he pleaded. "We'll figure something out."

"It's not that simple, Tru. I love Josh, too. I know that must be painful for you to hear, and the truth is that I don't feel the same way about him that I do for you." Her eyes beseeched him. "You're both so different..." She seemed to be grasping for something out of her reach. "I feel like I'm at war with myself—like two different people, who want completely different things. But..."

When she appeared unable to continue, Tru gripped her arms.

"I can't imagine a life without you, Hope, and I don't want one. I want you, and only you, forever. Could you really give up what we have without regret?"

She stood frozen, her face a mask of anguish. "No. I know there's part of me that will regret it forever."

He stared at her, trying to read her, already knowing what she was trying to tell him. "You're not going to tell him about us, are you?"

"I don't want to hurt him..."

"And yet you're willing to keep secrets from him?"

He regretted the words as soon as they came out. "That's not fair," she cried, shaking off his touch. "Do you think I want to be in this position? I didn't come here to make my life even more complicated than it already was. I didn't come here because I wanted to fall in love with another man. But no matter what I decide, someone is going to be hurt, and I never, ever wanted that."

"You're right," he murmured. "I shouldn't have said it. It wasn't fair, and I apologize."

Her shoulders slumped, her anger slowly giving way to confusion again. "Josh seemed different this time. Scared. Serious..." she mused, almost to herself. "I just don't know..."

It was now or never, Tru suddenly realized, and he reached for her hand again. "I wanted to talk to you earlier about this, but last night when I couldn't sleep, I did a lot of thinking. About you and me. About us. And maybe you're not quite ready to hear it, but..." He swallowed, his eyes on hers. "I want you to come with me to Zimbabwe. I know it's asking a lot, but you could meet Andrew and we could make a life there. If you don't like that I'm in the bush so much, I can find something else to do."

Hope blinked without speaking, trying to absorb what he was saying. She opened her mouth to respond, then closed it again, even as she released his hand. She turned, facing the ocean, before finally shaking her head.

"I don't want you to change who you are for me," Hope insisted. "Guiding is important to you—"

"You're more important," he said, hearing the desperation in his voice. Feeling the future, all his hopes, begin to recede. "I love you. Don't you love me?"

"Of course I do."

"Then before you say no, can you at least think about it?"

"I have," she said, so quietly he almost couldn't make out her voice over the sound of the surf. "Yesterday, when I was coming back from the wedding, I thought about exactly that. Just...running off to Africa with you. Leaving, without a second thought. And part of me longed to do that. I imagined explaining the situation to my parents, sure that they'd give me their blessing. But..."

She raised her eyes to his, her expression drawn in anguish. "How can I leave my dad, knowing he has only a few years left? I'll need to spend these last years with him, for me as much as him. Because I know I'll never forgive myself if I don't. And my mom is going to need me, even if she thinks that she won't."

"I could fly you back home as often as you want. Once a month if that's what you need. Or even more. Money's not an issue."

"Tru..."

He felt a surge of panic. "What if I move here?" he offered. "To North Carolina?"

"What about Andrew?"

"I'd fly back every month. I'll see him more than I do now. Whatever you need from me, I'll do it."

She stared at him in agony, her hand clenched in his.

"But what if you can't?" she asked. The words were almost a whisper. "What if there's something that I need that you can never give me?"

At her words, he flinched as if he had been slapped. All

at once, he understood what she'd been trying so hard not to tell him. That to be with him meant closing the door to having children of her own. Hadn't she told him about her lifelong dream? Her treasured image of holding the baby she had just given birth to, of creating a human life with the man she treasured? More than anything, she wanted to be a mother—she wanted to give birth to a child—and it was the one thing he could not give her. In her face, the silent plea for forgiveness was as pronounced as her pain.

He turned away, unable to face her. He'd always believed that anything was possible when it came to love, that any obstacle could be overcome. Wasn't that a truth that nearly everyone took for granted? As he struggled with the implacability of what Hope had just said, she hugged her arms to her body.

"It makes me hate myself," she cried, her voice cracking. "That there's this part of me that needs to have a baby. I wish I could imagine a life without a child, but I can't. I know it would be possible to adopt, and now there's even amazing medical technology, but..." She shook her head and let out a long breath. "It just wouldn't be the same. I hate that this is true for me, but it is."

For a long time neither of them spoke, both of them staring at the waves. Finally, Hope said in a ragged voice, "I never want to think to myself that I gave up my dream for you. I never want to have a reason to resent you...the thought terrifies me." She shook her head. "I know how selfish I sound, how much I'm hurting you. But please don't ask me to go with you, because I will."

He reached for her hand and brought it to his lips, kissing it. "You're not selfish," he said.

"But you despise me."

"Never."

He drew her into his arms, pulling her close. "I'll always love you. There's nothing you can ever do or say that will take that away."

Hope shook her head, trying and failing to keep the tears from spilling out.

"There's something else," she said, her voice thick as she began to cry in earnest. "Something I haven't told you."

Inwardly, he braced himself. Somehow he knew what she was going to say.

"Josh asked me to marry him last night," Hope said. "He told me he's ready to start a family."

Tru said nothing. Instead, feeling dizzy, he slumped in her arms, as if his limbs had turned to lead. Though he wanted to console her, he felt a numbness spreading through him.

"I'm sorry, Tru," she said. "I didn't know how to tell you last night. But I haven't given him an answer yet. I want you to know that. And I want you to understand that I had no idea he was going to ask me."

He swallowed, trying to keep his own emotions in check. "Does it really matter that you didn't expect him to ask?"

"I don't know," she said. "Right now, I don't feel like I understand anything. All I know is that I never wanted it to end like this. I never wanted to hurt you."

A physical ache seemed to flow through him, beginning in his chest and radiating outward until even his fingertips throbbed.

"I can't force you to stay with me," he whispered. "As much as I want to, I can't. Nor will I try, even if it means that I'll never see you again. But I would like to ask something of you."

"Anything," she whispered.

He swallowed. "Will you try to remember me?"

She made a strangled noise, and he knew she couldn't speak. Instead, she pressed her lips closed and nodded. Tru pulled her closer, feeling her collapse into him, as if her legs would no longer support her. When she began to sob, Tru felt himself crumbling. Beyond them, the waves marched on, indifferent to the world slowing to a stop between them.

He wanted her and only her, forever. But that wasn't possible. Not anymore, for despite the love they felt for each other, Tru already knew what Hope's answer to Josh was going to be.

Back at the cottage, Hope cleared any items from the refrigerator that might spoil and put them in a garbage bag. When she headed to the shower, Tru brought the bag to the bins outside. His head was spinning and by the time he returned to the kitchen, he heard the shower running in the bathroom. He rummaged through drawers until he located paper and a pen. Ravaged, he tried to order his feelings by putting words on the page. There was so much he wanted to say.

When he was finished, he returned to his father's house and retrieved two drawings. He put those, along with the letter, into the glove compartment of her car, knowing that by the time she discovered them, their time together would already be in the past.

When Hope finally emerged, she was carrying her suitcase. Dressed in jeans, a white blouse, and the sandals she'd picked up a few days earlier, she was heartbreakingly beautiful. He was sitting at the table again, and after turning out all the lights, Hope went to sit on his lap. She put her arms around him, and for a long time they simply held each other. When she pulled back, her expression was subdued.

"I should probably get going," she finally said.

"I know," he whispered.

She got up, and after putting Scottie on a leash, she moved slowly to the door.

It was time. Tru picked up her suitcase, along with the box of mementos she'd collected earlier in the week. He followed her out the front door, pausing beside her as she locked the door and inhaling the wildflower scent of the shampoo she used.

He loaded her things into the trunk while she put Scottie in the back seat. After closing the doors, she approached him slowly. He held her again, neither of them able to speak. When finally she pulled back, he tried a smile, even though everything was breaking inside.

"If you ever plan on taking a safari, make sure you let me know. I can tell you which lodges you should visit. It doesn't have to be in Zimbabwe. I have contacts all over the region. You can always reach me through the lodge at Hwange."

"All right," she said in an unsteady voice.

"And if you just want to talk or see me, I'll make that happen. Airlines make the world a much smaller place. If you need me, I'll come. All right?"

She nodded, unable to meet his eyes as she adjusted the purse strap on her shoulder. He wanted to beg her to come with him; he wanted to tell her that a love like theirs would never be replicated. He could feel the words forming, but they stayed inside him.

He kissed her, softly, gently, one last time, then opened the door for her. When she was behind the wheel, he pushed the door shut, his hopes and dreams shattering at the sound. He heard the engine fire up and saw her roll down the window.

She reached out, taking his hand in hers.

"I'll never forget you," she said. And then all at once, she let go. She put the car in reverse and began to back out of the driveway. Tru followed as if in a trance.

A ray of sunlight broke from the clouds, illuminating her car like a spotlight as it finally started rolling forward. Away from him. She didn't glance in his direction. He continued to follow, drawn into the street.

By then, her car was already growing smaller in the distance. It was fifty yards away, then even more, her image no longer visible through the rear window, but Tru continued to watch it. He felt hollowed out, a hull.

The brake lights flashed once, and then suddenly steadied, glowing red. The car came to a halt, and he saw the driver's-side door open. Hope stepped out and turned to face him. She seemed so far away and when she blew him a final, tender kiss, he couldn't bring himself to return the gesture. She waited for a moment, then got back in the car, the door closing behind her. The car started rolling forward again.

"Come back to me," he whispered, watching as she reached the corner that led to the main road off the island.

But she couldn't hear him. Ahead of him, the car slowed but didn't stop. No longer able to watch, Tru bent over double, his hands on his knees. Beneath him, the asphalt bore the inkblot stain of his tears.

When he looked up again, the car had vanished completely and the road was deserted.

AFTERMATH

Hope would never remember the drive back to Raleigh. Nor would she remember much about her lunch with Josh that Sunday afternoon. He had called her numerous times since the wedding, leaving messages at her apartment, begging her to meet him. Reluctantly, she agreed to meet him at a local café, but while Josh was talking to her across the table, all she could think about was the way Tru had stood in the road, watching her go. Abruptly, she told Josh that she needed a few days to think about things and left the restaurant before the food even arrived, feeling his stunned gaze on her as she hurried out.

He appeared at her apartment a few hours later and they spoke on her doorstep. He apologized again, Hope managing to mask her turmoil. After agreeing to meet with him on Thursday, she closed the door and leaned against it, utterly spent. She lay on the sofa in her living room, intending to doze for a short while, but somehow slept until the following morning. Her first thought upon waking was that Tru was already on his way back to Zimbabwe, the gulf between them increasing by the minute.

It was all she could do to function at work. She moved on autopilot, and with the exception of a teenage girl who'd been in a horrific car accident, she remembered none of the patients. If the other nurses noticed how detached she seemed to be, they didn't say anything.

On Wednesday, she planned to visit her parents after work. Her mom had left a message on her answering machine a couple of days earlier saying that she'd be making stew, and Hope decided to pick up a blueberry pie from a local bakery on her way over. The only problem was that the bakery only accepted cash, and in her daze of the last few days, she'd forgotten to go to the bank. Remembering that she kept some money in the glove compartment for emergencies, she returned to the car and opened it up. As she rummaged for the cash, she knocked some of the contents to the floor, and it was only while cleaning up that she recognized the drawing of herself that Tru had completed.

Seeing it in the car took her breath away. She knew he must have placed it in her glove compartment the morning she'd left. She stared at the image, her hands beginning to tremble, before remembering that she still had to pay for the pie. She carefully set the drawing on the passenger seat, then hurried back inside to complete her purchase.

Back in the car, she didn't start the ignition. Instead, she reached for the drawing again. Examining the image of herself, she recognized a woman hopelessly in love with the man who'd drawn her, and she felt an intense longing to be held by him just one more time. She wanted to breathe in the scent of him, feel the coarse scratch of his stubble, stare into the face of the man who intuitively understood her in a way that no one ever had before. To be with the man who'd stolen her heart.

Lowering it to her lap, she noticed another sheet of drawing paper in the open glove compartment. It was carefully folded; on top of it lay an envelope with her name on it. She picked them up with shaking hands.

Unfolding the drawing first, she saw the two of them standing on the beach, gazing at each other in profile. The sight left her breathless, and she was only vaguely aware that a car had pulled into the spot next to her, the radio blaring. She stared at the image of Tru, flooded with longing. She forced herself to put it aside.

The envelope felt heavy in her hands. She didn't want to open it, not here. She should wait until later, when she was back at her place, when she was alone.

But the letter was calling to her, and lifting the seal, she pulled it out and began to read.

Dear Hope,

I'm not sure whether you want to read this, but in my confusion, I am grasping at straws. Along with this letter, you'll find two drawings. Maybe you've already seen them. You might recognize the first one. I worked on the second one while you were at the rehearsal dinner and the wedding. I have a feeling that I'll complete more drawings of you when I get home, but I'd like to keep those, if it's all right with you. If not, please let me know. I can either send them to you, or dispose of them, and will not attempt another one. I hope that you believe that I am, and will always be, someone that you can trust.

I want you to know that while imagining a life without

you is unbearable, I understand your reasons. I saw your radiant expression when you spoke of having children, and I will never forget it. I know how agonizing this choice has been for you. It's been devastating for me, but I can't find it in my heart to blame you. After all, I have a son, and I can't imagine life without him.

After you leave, I suspect I'll walk the beach as I have every day since I arrived, but nothing will be the same. For with every step I take, I'll find myself thinking about you. I will feel you beside me, and within me. You have already become part of me, after all, and I know with certainty that this will never change.

I never expected to feel this way. How could I? For most of my life, and with the exception of my son, I've always felt as though I were meant to be alone. I'm not implying that I've lived the life of a hermit, because I haven't, and you already know that my job requires a certain level of social agreeableness. But I was never a person who felt incomplete without someone lying beside me in bed; I never felt as though I was only half of something better. Until you came along. And when you did, I understood that I'd been fooling myself, and that I'd really been missing you, all these long years.

I don't know what that means for my future. I do know that I'm not going to be the same person I used to be, because that's no longer possible. I'm not naive enough to believe that memories will suffice, and in quiet moments, I may reach for drawing paper and try to capture whatever remains. I hope you will not deny me that.

I wish that things could have been different for us, but fate seems to have had other plans. Still, you need to know this: The love I feel for you is real, and all the sadness that now comes with it is a price I would pay a thousand times over. For knowing you, and loving you, even for a short while, has given my life a different kind of meaning, and I know it always will.

I'm not asking the same of you. I know what's coming next for you, the new life that you'll be living, and there's no room for a third person there. I accept that. The Chinese philosopher Lao-tzu once said that being loved deeply by someone gives you strength, and loving someone deeply gives you courage. I understand now what he meant. Because you came into my life, I can face the oncoming years with the kind of courage that I never knew I had. Loving you has made me more than I was.

You know where I am and where I'll be if you ever want to contact me. It might take time. I've already mentioned that the world moves more slowly in the bush. And some items never reach their destination. But I firmly believe that you and I shared something special enough that if you reach out to me, the universe will somehow let me know. It's because of you, after all, that I now believe in miracles. With us, I want to believe that anything will always be possible.

Loving you,
Tru

Hope read the letter a second time, then once more, before finally returning it to the envelope. She pictured Tru writing the letter as he'd sat in her kitchen, and though she wanted to read it again, she doubted she would be able to make it to her parents' if she did.

She stowed the drawings and the letter in the glove compartment but didn't start the car right away. Instead, she leaned back against the headrest, trying to calm her raging emotions. Finally, after what seemed like forever, she forced herself to get on the road.

Her legs were unsteady as she walked to the door of her parents' home. She forced a smile as she stepped through inside, watching as her dad struggled to rise from his recliner to greet her. The aroma from the kitchen filled the house, but Hope couldn't muster an appetite.

At the table, she shared a few stories from the wedding. Asked about the rest of the week, she made no mention of Tru. Nor did she tell her parents that Josh had proposed.

After dessert, she retreated to the front porch, claiming a need for fresh air.

By then, the sky was full of stars, and when she heard the screen door creak open, she saw her dad framed in the lights from the living room. He smiled and touched her shoulder as he shuffled carefully to the seat next to hers. He carried a cup of decaffeinated coffee with him, and after he settled in, he took a sip.

"Your mom still makes the best beef stew I've ever tasted."

"It was very good tonight," Hope agreed.

"Are you feeling okay? You seemed a little quiet at dinner."

She tucked a leg up beneath her. "Yeah. I guess I'm still recovering from the weekend."

He placed the cup on the table between them. In the corner of the porch, a moth was dancing around the light, and crickets had begun their evening call.

"I heard that Josh showed up at the wedding." When she turned toward him, he shrugged. "Your mom told me."

"How did she find out?"

"I'm not sure," he answered. "I'm assuming someone told her."

"Yes," Hope said, "he was there."

"And the two of you spoke?"

"A little," she said. Until last week, she couldn't have imagined keeping the marriage proposal secret from her dad, but in the close, muggy air of that September evening, she couldn't form the words. Instead she said, "We're going to have dinner tomorrow night."

He looked over at his daughter, his soft eyes trying to read her. "I hope it goes well," he said. "Whatever that means to you."

"Me too."

"He has some explaining to do, if you ask me."

"I know," she answered. Inside, she heard the grandfather clock chime. Earlier in the day, she had taken a dusty atlas down from the shelf at home and calculated the time difference with Zimbabwe. Counting forward, she figured out that it was now the middle of the night there. She assumed that Tru was in Bulawayo with Andrew, and wondered what they had planned when they woke for the day. Would he take Andrew into the bush to see the animals, or would they kick a ball back and forth, or simply go for a walk? She wondered whether Tru was still thinking about her, in the same way she couldn't stop thinking about him. In the silence, the words from his letter tried to force their way to the surface.

She knew her dad was waiting for her to speak. In the past, whenever she'd had problems or concerns, she'd gone to him. He had a way of listening that always comforted her. Naturally empathetic, he seldom offered advice. He would instead ask what she thought she should do, silently encouraging her to trust her own instincts and judgment.

But now, after reading what Tru had written, she couldn't help thinking that she'd made a terrible mistake. As she sat beside her father, her final morning with Tru began to replay in slow motion. She remembered the way Tru had looked when he'd stepped onto the deck, the feel of his hand in hers as they strolled down the beach. She recalled his stricken expression when she'd told him of Josh's proposal.

Those weren't the most piercing memories, however. Instead, she thought about the way he'd begged her to come with him to Zimbabwe; she saw him bent over double as she made that final turn, away from a possible life together.

She knew she could change things. It wasn't too late. She could book a flight to Zimbabwe tomorrow and go to him; she'd say that she knew now that the two of them were destined to grow old together. They could make love in a foreign locale, and she would become someone new, whose life she had only fantasized about.

She wanted to say those things to her dad. She wanted to tell him everything. She wanted him to say that her happiness was all that mattered to him, but before she could speak, she felt a lick of breeze, and all at once, she pictured Tru sitting beside her at Kindred Spirit, the wind ruffling his thick hair.

She'd done the right thing, hadn't she?

Hadn't she?

The crickets continued to sing, the night settling heavily, with an almost suffocating weight. Moonlight threaded the branches of the trees. On the street, a car passed by, the windows down and radio playing. She remembered the jazz music on the radio when Tru had held her in the kitchen.

"I forgot to ask you," her dad finally said, "and I know it

was storming most of the week. But did you ever make it to Kindred Spirit?"

At his words, the dam suddenly burst and Hope choked out a cry, which quickly gave way to sobbing.

"What did I say?" he asked in a panic, but she could barely hear him. "What's wrong? Talk to me, sweetheart..."

She shook her head, unable to answer. In a haze, she felt her father put a hand on her knee. Even without opening her eyes, she knew he was staring at her with alarm and concern. But all she could think about was Tru, and there was nothing she could do to stop the tears.

Part II

PART II

SANDS IN THE HOURGLASS

October 2014

Memories *are a doorway to the past, and the more one trea-sures the memories, the wider the door will open.* That's what Hope's father used to say, anyway, and like many of the things he'd told her, the passage of time seemed to amplify its wisdom.

But then again, time had a way of changing everything, she thought. As she reflected on her life, it seemed impossible to believe that nearly a quarter century had passed since those days at Sunset Beach. So much had happened since then and she often felt as though she'd become an entirely different person than she once had been.

Now, she was alone. It was early evening, with a hint of winter evident in the brisk air, and she sat on the back porch of her home in Raleigh, North Carolina. Moonlight was casting an eerie glow across the lawn and silvering the leaves that stirred in the breeze. The rustling sound made it seem as though voices of the past were calling to her, as they often did these days. She thought about her children, and as she moved the rocker slowly back and forth, the memories tumbled forth in a kaleidoscope of images. In the darkness, she recalled the awe she'd felt when holding each of them in the hospital; she smiled at the sight of them running naked down the hallway after taking their baths as toddlers. She thought about their gap-toothed smiles after their baby teeth fell out, and relived the mixture of pride and worry she'd experienced as they'd struggled through their teenage years. They were good kids. Great kids. To her surprise, she realized that she could even recall Josh with a fondness that had once seemed impossible. They'd divorced eight years ago, but at sixty, Hope liked to believe that she'd reached the point where forgiveness came easily.

Jacob had dropped by on Friday night, and Rachel had brought over bagels on Sunday morning. Neither of the kids had expressed any curiosity about Hope's announcement that she would be renting a cottage at the coast again, just as she'd done the year before. Their lack of interest wasn't unusual. Like so many young people, they were caught up in their own lives. Rachel had graduated in May, Jacob the year before that, and both had been able to find jobs even before they'd received their diplomas. Jacob sold ads at a local radio station while Rachel worked for an internet marketing firm. They had their own apartments and paid their own bills, which Hope knew was something of a rarity these days. Most of their friends had moved back in with their parents after they'd finished college, and privately, Hope considered her kids' independence even more noteworthy than their graduations.

Even before packing her suitcase earlier that day, Hope had had her hair done. Since her retirement two years ago, she'd been visiting an upscale place near some high-end department stores. It was her one splurge these days. She'd come to know some of the women with the same regular schedule, and she'd sat in the chair, listening as the talk at the salon ran from husbands to kids to the vacations they'd taken over the summer. The easy conversation was a balm to Hope, and while there, she'd found her thoughts drifting to her parents.

They had been gone for a long time now. Her father had passed away from ALS eighteen years earlier; her mom had survived four sad years more. She still missed them, but the pain of their loss had faded over the years into something more manageable, a dull ache that occurred only when she was feeling particularly blue.

When her hair was done, Hope had left the salon, noting the BMWs and Mercedes and the women exiting the department store loaded with bulging bags. She wondered whether their purchases had actually been necessary or whether shopping was an addiction of sorts, the pull from the shelf offering a momentary respite from anxiety or depression. There'd been a time in her life when Hope had occasionally shopped for the same reasons, but those days were long behind her, and she couldn't help but think that the world had changed in recent decades. People seemed more materialistic, more focused on keeping up with the Joneses, but Hope had learned that a meaningful life was seldom about such things. It was about experiences and relationships; it was about health and family and loving someone who loved you in return. She'd done her best to instill these notions in her kids, but who really knew whether she'd succeeded?

These days, answers eluded her. Lately, she'd found herself asking *why* about many things, and while there were people who claimed to have all the answers—daytime television shows were replete with such experts—Hope was rarely persuaded. If there was one question she could have answered by any of them, it was simply this: *Why does love always seem to require sacrifice?*

She didn't know. What she did know was that she'd observed it in her marriage, as a parent, and as the grown child of a father who'd been condemned to slowly waste away. But as much as she'd pondered the question, she still couldn't put her finger on the reason. Was sacrifice a necessary component of love? Were the words actually synonyms? Was the former proof of the latter, and vice versa? She didn't want to think that love had an intrinsic cost—that it required disappointment, or pain, or angst—but there were times when she couldn't help it.

Despite the unforeseen events of her life, Hope wasn't unhappy. She understood that life wasn't easy for anyone, and she felt satisfied that she'd done the best she could. And yet, like everyone, she had regrets, and in the past couple of years, she'd revisited them more frequently. They would crop up unexpectedly, and often at the strangest of times: while she was putting cash into the church basket, for instance, or sweeping up some sugar that had spilled on the floor. When that happened, she would find herself recalling things she wished she could change, arguments that should have been avoided, words of forgiveness that had been left unspoken. Part of her wished she could turn back the clock and make different decisions, but when she was honest with herself, she questioned what she really could have changed. Mistakes were inevitable, and she'd concluded that regrets could impart important lessons in life, if one was willing to learn from them. And in that sense, she realized that her father had been only half-correct about memories. They weren't, after all, only doorways to the past. She wanted to believe that they could also be doorways to a new and different kind of future.

Hope shivered as a chilly gust swept through the back porch, and she knew it was time to head inside.

She'd lived in this house for more than two decades. She and Josh had purchased it shortly after they'd taken their vows, and as she breathed in the familiar surroundings, she thought again how much she'd always adored the place. It was Georgian in style, with large columns out front and wainscoting in most of the rooms on the main floor. Nonetheless, it was probably time to sell it. It was too much, too large for her, and trying to keep all the rooms dusted felt Sisyphean. The stairs, too, were becoming a challenge, but when she'd mentioned the idea of selling, Jacob and Rachel had balked at relinquishing their childhood home.

Whether she sold it or not, it needed work. The hardwood floors were scuffed and scraped; in the dining room, the wallpaper had faded and needed to be replaced. The kitchen and bathrooms were still functional, but definitely outdated and in need of remodeling. There was so much to do; she wondered when, or even if, she'd be up to it.

She moved through the house, turning off lights. Some of the switches on the lamps were notoriously hard to turn, and it took longer than she expected.

Her suitcase stood near the front door, next to the wooden box she'd retrieved from the attic. The sight of them made her think about Tru, but then again, she'd never really stopped thinking about him. He would be sixty-six now. She wondered whether he'd retired from guiding, or still lived in Zimbabwe; perhaps he had moved to Europe or Australia or someplace even more exotic. She speculated about whether he lived near Andrew, and whether he'd become a grandfather in the years they'd been apart. She wondered if he'd married again, whom he had dated, or even if he remembered her at all. Then again, was he even still alive? She liked to think she would have instinctively known if he was gone from this world—that they were somehow linked—but she admitted that might be wishful thinking. Mostly though, she questioned whether the final words in his letter could possibly be true—whether, for them, anything would always be possible.

In the bedroom, she put on the pajamas that Rachel had bought for her last Christmas. They were cozy and warm, exactly what Hope wanted. She slipped into bed and adjusted the covers, hoping for the sleep that so often eluded her these days.

Last year at the beach, she'd lain awake thinking about Tru. She'd willed him to come back to her, reliving the days they'd spent together with vivid intensity. She remembered their encounter on the beach and the coffee they'd shared that very first morning; she replayed for the hundredth time their dinner at Clancy's and their stroll back to the cottage. She felt his gaze on her as they sipped wine on the porch, and the sound of his voice as he read the letter on the bench at Kindred Spirit. More than anything, she recalled the tender and sensual way they'd made love; the intensity of his expression, the words he'd whispered to her.

She wondered at how immediate it all still felt—the tangible weight of his feelings for her; even the implacable guilt. Something had truly broken inside her that morning she left, but she wanted to believe that in the break, a stronger element had eventually taken root. In the aftermath, whenever life seemed unbearably difficult, she would think of Tru and remind herself that if she ever reached the point where she needed him, he would come. He'd told her as much on their last morning together, and that promise was enough for her to carry on.

That night at the beach, as sleep remained out of reach, she'd found herself attempting to rewrite history in a way that gave her peace. She imagined herself turning the car around at the corner and racing back to him; she imagined sitting across the table from Josh and telling him that she'd met someone else. Dreamy images of a later reunion at the airport, where she'd gone to pick up Tru after his flight back from Zimbabwe, played out in her mind; in this fantasy they embraced near the baggage claim and kissed amid throngs of people. He put his arm around her as they walked to her car, and she pictured the casual way he tossed his duffel bag into the trunk as though it had actually happened. She imagined them making love in the apartment she once called home, all those years ago.

But after that, her visions had become clouded. She couldn't visualize the kind of house they would have chosen; when she pictured them in the kitchen, it was either at the cottage her parents had sold long ago or the home she owned with Josh. She couldn't imagine what Tru would do for a living; when she tried, she saw him returning at the end of the day dressed in the same kind of clothing he'd worn the week she'd met him, as though coming in from a game drive. She knew he'd regularly return to Bulawayo to see Andrew, but she had no frame of reference to even conjure up how his home or neighborhood might appear. And always, Andrew remained a ten-year-old, his features forever frozen in time, just as Tru remained forever forty-two.

Strangely, when she fantasized about a life with Tru, Jacob and Rachel were always present. If she and Tru were eating at the table, Jacob was refusing to share his french fries with his sister; if Tru was drawing on the back porch of her parents' cottage, Rachel was finger-painting at the picnic table. In the school auditorium, she sat beside Tru as Jacob and Rachel sang in the choir; on Halloween, she and Tru trailed behind her children, who were dressed as Woody and Jessie from *Toy Story 2*. Always, always, her children were in the life she imagined with Tru, and though she resented the intrusion, Josh was there as well. Jacob in particular bore a strong resemblance to his father, and Rachel had grown up thinking that one day she might become a doctor.

Hope had eventually gotten out of bed. It was chilly at the beach, and, putting on a jacket, she'd retrieved the letter Tru had written to her long ago and seated herself on the back porch. She'd wanted to read it, but couldn't summon the will to do so. Instead, she'd stared at the darkness of the ocean, clutching the well-worn envelope, overwhelmed by a surge of loneliness.

She'd thought to herself that she was alone at the beach, far from anyone she knew. Only Tru was with her; except of course, he was never really there at all.

Hope had returned from her week at the beach the previous year with a mixture of hope and dread. This year, she told herself that things would be different. She had decided that this would be her last trip to the cottage, and in the morning, after placing the box on the back seat, Hope rolled her suitcase to the rear of the car with a determined step. Her neighbor Ben was raking his lawn and came over to put it in the trunk. She was thankful for his help. At her age injuries came more easily and were often slow to heal. Last year, she'd slipped in the kitchen, and though she hadn't fallen, catching herself had left her with a sore shoulder for weeks.

She ran through her mental checklist before getting in the car: the doors were locked, she'd turned out all the lights, the garbage cans stood by the curb, and Ben had agreed to collect her mail and newspapers. The drive would take her a bit less than three hours, but there was no reason to rush. Tomorrow, after all, was the day that mattered. Just thinking about it made her nervous.

Thankfully, traffic was light for most of the trip. She drove past farmland and small towns, keeping a constant speed until she reached the outskirts of Wilmington, where she ate lunch at a bistro she remembered from the year before. Afterward, she swung by a grocery store to stock the refrigerator, stopped at the rental office to pick up the keys, and began the final leg of her journey. She found the cross street she needed, made a few turns, and eventually pulled in the drive.

The cottage resembled the one her parents had once owned, with faded paint, steps leading up to the front door, and a weather-beaten porch out front. Seeing it made her miss the old homestead keenly. As she'd suspected, the new owners had wasted no time in tearing it down and building a newer, larger home similar to the one where Tru had stayed.

Since then, she'd only rarely visited Sunset Beach, as it no longer felt like home. Like many of the small towns dotting the coast, it had changed with the times. The pontoon bridge had been replaced with something more modern, larger homes were now the norm, and Clancy's was gone as well, the old restaurant limping along until a year or two after the century began. Her sister Robin had been the one to tell her about the restaurant's closing; on a trip to Myrtle Beach ten years ago she and her husband had made a detour to the familial island, because she, too, had been curious about the changes time had wrought.

These days, Hope preferred Carolina Beach, an island a little ways to the north, and closer to Wilmington. She'd first visited it upon her counselor's suggestion in December 2005, when the divorce proceedings with Josh were at their worst. Josh had made plans to bring Jacob and Rachel out west for a week during winter break. The kids were young teenagers, moody in general, and the implosion of their parents' marriage had compounded the stress they were feeling. While Hope had recognized that the vacation might be a beneficial distraction for the kids, her counselor pointed out that spending the holidays at home alone wouldn't be good for her own mental state. She had suggested Carolina Beach to Hope; in the winter, she'd said, the island was low-key and relaxing.

Hope had booked a place sight unseen, and the little cottage at the beach had turned out to be exactly what she'd needed. It was there where Hope had begun the process of healing; where she'd gathered the perspective she needed to enter the next phase of her life.

She had known she wouldn't reconcile with Josh. She had cried over him for years, and while his last affair had been the deal breaker, the first one was still the most painful to remember. At the time, the kids weren't yet in school and their needs were constant; meanwhile her father had recently taken a turn for the worse. When Hope learned of the affair, Josh apologized and promised to end it. However, he remained in contact with the woman even as Hope's father got sicker and sicker. She felt as though she was on the verge of panic attacks for months, and it was the first time she'd considered ending the marriage. Instead, overwhelmed at the prospect of upheaval and afraid of the devastating effect divorce could have on her kids, she stuck it out and did her best to forgive. But other affairs followed. There were more tears and too much arguing, and by the time she finally told Josh that she wanted a divorce, they'd been sleeping in separate bedrooms for nearly a year. The day he moved out, he told her she was making the biggest mistake of her life.

Despite her best intentions, bitterness and rancor surfaced in the divorce. She was shocked at the rage and sadness she felt, and Josh was equally angry and defensive. While the custody arrangements had been fairly straightforward, the financial wrangling had been a nightmare. Hope had stayed at home when the kids were young and it wasn't until they were both in school that she went back to work, but no longer as a trauma nurse. Instead, she'd worked part-time with a family practice group so she could be home when the kids finished at school. While the hours were easier, the pay was less, and Josh's attorney argued strenuously that since she had the skills necessary to increase her salary, any alimony should be drastically reduced. Nor, like so many men, did Josh believe in an equal property division. By that point, Josh and Hope were communicating primarily through their lawyers.

She had felt battered by emotion—feelings of failure, loss, anger, resolve, and fear—but as she walked the beach during that Christmas break, she worried mainly about the kids. She wanted to be the best mother she could be, but her counselor had continually reminded her that if she didn't take care of herself first, she wouldn't be able to provide the kids with the solid support they needed.

Deep down, she knew her counselor was right, but the idea felt almost blasphemous. She'd been a mother so long that she wasn't even sure who she really was anymore. While at Carolina Beach, though, she had gradually accepted the notion that her emotional health was as important as the children's. Not more important, but not less important, either.

She also understood how slippery the slope might be if she didn't heed her counselor's advice. She'd seen women lose or gain substantial weight while going through a divorce; she'd heard them talking about Friday and Saturday nights at the bars and admitting to one-night stands with strangers, men they barely remembered. Some remarried quickly, and it was almost always a mistake. Even those who hadn't gone wild often developed self-destructive habits. Hope had seen divorced friends increase the two glasses of wine on the weekend to three or four glasses multiple times during the week. One of those women had come right out and said that drinking was the only way she'd survived her divorce.

Hope didn't want to fall into the same trap, and her time at the beach was clarifying. After returning to Raleigh, she'd joined a gym and started taking spin classes. She'd added yoga to her routine, prepared healthy meals for herself and the kids, and, even on nights she couldn't sleep, forced herself to stay in bed, breathing deeply, trying to discipline her mind. She'd learned to meditate, and put a renewed emphasis on rekindling friendships where contact had lapsed in recent years.

She had also made a vow to never say anything bad about Josh, which hadn't been easy but had probably laid the groundwork for the relationship they had now. These days, most of her friends couldn't understand why she still made time for him in her life, considering all the heartache he'd caused her. The reasons were multifaceted, but also her secret. When asked, she would simply tell them that as terrible a husband as he'd been, he'd always been a good father. Josh had spent a lot of time with the kids when they were young, attending extracurriculars and coaching their youth teams, and he'd spent his weekends with the family instead of with friends. The latter was something she'd insisted upon before agreeing to marry him.

She hadn't, however, accepted Josh's marriage proposal right away. *Let's see how things go for a while*, she'd told him. As he left, he'd paused in the doorway.

"There's something different about you," he'd said to her.

"You're right," she'd said. "I am different."

Eight weeks passed before she finally accepted his proposal, and unlike all her friends, she insisted on a simple wedding a couple of months after that, with only close friends and family in attendance. The reception dinner was potluck, one of her brothers-in-law manned the camera, and the guests finished out the evening dancing at a local nightclub. The short engagement and low-key wedding surprised Josh. He couldn't fathom why she didn't want the kind of wedding that all of her friends had insisted upon. She told him she didn't want to waste the money, but in truth, she suspected she was already pregnant. It turned out she was—with Jacob—and for an instant, she thought perhaps that it might be Tru's, but that was impossible. The timing wasn't right, nor could Tru father a child, but in that moment, she understood that she had no desire to smile through the faux romance of a fairy-tale wedding. By then, after all, she understood the nature of romance, and knew it had little to do with trying to create a fantasy. Real romance was spontaneous, unpredictable, and could be as simple as listening to a man read a love letter found in a lonely mailbox on a stormy September afternoon.

At the cottage, Hope began to settle in. She set the wooden box on the kitchen table, put away the groceries, unpacked her belongings into the drawers so she wouldn't be living out of a suitcase all week, and texted her kids, letting them know she'd arrived. Then, donning a jacket, she stepped onto the back deck and slowly descended the steps to the sand. Her back and legs were stiff from the drive, and though she felt like taking a stroll, she wouldn't go far. She wanted to conserve her energy for the following day.

The sky was the color of cobalt, but the breeze was chilly and she tucked her hands into her jacket pockets. The air smelled of brine, primordial and fresh. Near a truck parked at the water's edge, a man sat in a lawn chair flanked by a row of fishing poles, their lines disappearing into the sea. He was shore fishing, and Hope wondered whether he'd have any luck. Never once had she seen someone at the beach actually reel in a fish from the shallow water, but it seemed to be a popular pastime.

In her pocket, she felt her phone vibrate. Hoping it was one of the kids, she noted instead a missed call from Josh. She put the phone back in her pocket. Unlike Jacob and Rachel, he *had* been interested in her reasons for going to the beach. He thought she hated the beach, since she'd never wanted to vacation there while they'd been married. Whenever Josh had suggested that the family rent a house at the beach, Hope had always offered an alternative: Disney World, Williamsburg, camping trips in the mountains. They went skiing in West Virginia and Colorado, and spent time in New York City, Yellowstone, and the Grand Canyon; eventually they'd purchased a cabin near Asheville, which Josh had kept in the divorce. For years, the thought of being at the beach had just been too painful. In her mind, the beach and Tru were forever linked.

Nonetheless, she sent the kids to summer camps near Myrtle Beach and surfing camps at Nags Head. Both Jacob and Rachel took naturally to surfing, and ironically, it was after one of Rachel's stays at surfing camp that Josh and Hope first began to heal the wounds of the divorce. While at camp, Rachel had complained of difficulty breathing and a racing heart; back at home, they took her to see a pediatric cardiologist, and within a day she was diagnosed with a previously undiscovered congenital defect that would require open-heart surgery.

At the time, Hope and Josh hadn't spoken for nearly four months, but each of them set aside their antagonism for the benefit of their daughter. They alternated spending nights in the hospital and never once raised their voices in anger. The unity of their shared suffering had passed as soon as Rachel was released from the hospital, but it was enough to set in motion a relationship that allowed them to discuss the children in a cordial manner. As time passed, Josh remarried to a woman named Denise, and surprising Hope, something akin to friendship began to slowly renew.

Partly, it had to do with Josh's marriage to Denise. As

that relationship began to disintegrate, Josh began calling Hope. She tried to offer as much support as she could, but in the end, Josh's divorce from Denise ended up being even more acrimonious than his divorce from Hope.

The stress of the divorces had taken a heavy toll on Josh and he no longer resembled the man she'd married. He'd put on weight and his skin was pallid and spotted; he'd lost much of his hair and his once-athletic posture had become stooped. One time, after she hadn't seen him for a few months, it had taken Hope a few seconds to recognize him when he waved at her from across the dining room of their country club. She no longer found him attractive; in more ways than one, she felt sorry for him.

Not long before he'd retired, he'd shown up at her door in a sports jacket and pressed slacks. His freshly showered appearance had signaled that it wasn't a normal visit, and she'd motioned him toward the couch. She made sure to sit at the opposite corner.

It took a while for him to get to the point. He started with small talk, discussing the children, and then a bit about his work. He asked whether she was still doing the *New York Times* crossword puzzles, a habit she'd picked up shortly after the kids started school that had slowly but surely become a minor addiction. She told him that she'd finished one just a few hours ago, and when he brought his hands together, she asked him what was on his mind.

"I was thinking the other day that you're the only real friend I have anymore," he finally said. "I have partners at work, but I can't really talk to any of them the way I do with you."

She said nothing. Waiting.

"We're friends, right?"

"Yes," she said. "I suppose we are."

"We've been through a lot, haven't we?"

She nodded. "Yes."

"I've been thinking about that a lot lately…about you and me. The past. How long we've known each other. Did you realize it's been thirty years? Since we met?"

"I can't say that I've thought about it much."

"Yeah…okay." Though he nodded, she knew he'd wanted a different answer. "I guess what I'm trying to say is that I know I made a lot of mistakes when it came to us. I'm sorry about the things I did. I don't know what was going through my mind at the time."

"You've already apologized," she said. "And besides, that's all in the past. We divorced a long time ago."

"But we were happy, right? When we were married."

"Sometimes," she admitted. "Not always."

He nodded again, a hint of supplication in it. "Do you think we could ever try again? Give it another shot?"

She wasn't sure she'd heard him right. "You mean marriage?"

He raised his hands. "No, not marriage. Like…going on a date. As in, can I take you to dinner on Saturday night? Just to see how it goes. It might not go anywhere, but like I said, you're my closest friend these days—"

"I don't think that's a good idea," she said, cutting him off.

"Why not?"

"I think you're probably in a low spot right now," she said. "And when you're feeling low, sometimes even bad ideas can seem like good ones. It's important for the kids to know that we still get along, and I wouldn't want to jeopardize that."

"I don't want to jeopardize it, either. I'm just wondering

if you'd be willing to give us another chance. Give me a chance."

In that moment, she wondered how well she'd ever known him.

"I can't," she finally said.

"Why not?"

"Because," she told him, "I'm in love with someone else."

As she walked the beach, the damp, cold air began to make her lungs ache, and she decided to turn around. At the sight of the cottage in the distance, a memory of Scottie flashed through her mind. Had he been with her, she knew he would have been disappointed and stared at her with those sweet, sad eyes of his.

The kids had little memory of Scottie. Though he'd been part of the household when they were young, Hope had read once that the part of the brain that processes long-term memory isn't fully developed until a child is seven or so, and Scottie had passed away by then. Instead, they remembered Junior, the Scottish terrier who was part of their lives until both Jacob and Rachel were in college. While Hope had doted upon Junior, she secretly admitted that Scottie would always be her favorite.

For the second time on the walk, she felt her phone vibrate. While Jacob hadn't yet responded, Rachel had texted back, telling Hope to hav fun! Any cute guys? Luv u with a smiley face. Hope knew that kids these days had their own texting protocols, complete with brief responses, acronyms, incorrect spelling and grammar, and a heavy use of emojis. Hope still preferred the old-fashioned way of communicating—either in person, on the phone, or in a letter—but her kids were of a different generation, and she'd learned to do what was easiest for them.

She wondered what they would think if they knew the real reason she'd come to Carolina Beach. She often had the sense that her kids couldn't imagine her wanting more from life than doing crosswords, occasionally visiting the salon, and waiting around for them to visit. But then, Hope recognized that they had never known the real her, the woman she'd been at Sunset Beach so long ago.

Her relationship with Rachel was different than it was with Jacob. Jacob, she thought, had more in common with his father. The two of them could spend an entire Saturday watching football; they went fishing together, enjoyed action movies and target shooting, and could talk about the stock market and investing for hours. With Hope, Jacob mainly spoke about his girlfriend, and often seemed at a loss for words after that.

She was closer with Rachel, particularly since her heart surgery as a teen. Although the cardiologist who oversaw Rachel's case had assured them that repairing her complicated defect was a reasonably safe procedure, Rachel had been terrified. Hope had been equally fearful, but she'd done her best to exude confidence with her daughter. In the days leading up to the operation, Rachel cried often at the thought of dying, and even more bitterly at the idea of having a disfiguring scar on her chest if she did survive. Consumed with anxiety, she babbled as if in a confessional: she told Hope that her boyfriend of three months had begun to pressure Rachel for sex and that she was probably going to say yes, even though she didn't want to; she admitted that she worried constantly about her weight and that she'd been bingeing and purging for several months. She said she worried all the time about almost everything—her looks, popularity, grades, and whether she'd get accepted to the college she wanted to attend, even though the decision was years away. She picked at her cuticles incessantly, ripping at them until they bled. Occasionally, she confided, she even thought about suicide.

While Hope had known that teens were adept at keeping secrets from their parents, what she heard in the days both prior to and after the surgery alarmed her deeply. After Rachel was released from the hospital, Hope found her a good therapist and eventually a psychiatrist who prescribed antidepressants. And slowly but surely, Rachel began to feel more at ease with herself, her acute anxiety and depression finally subsiding.

But those terrible days had also been the start of a new stage in their relationship, one in which Rachel learned she could be honest with her mom without feeling judged, without worrying that Hope would overreact. By the time Rachel went off to college, she seemed to feel as though she could tell her mom almost anything. Though grateful for the honesty, Hope admitted there were some subjects—mainly concerning the quantity of alcohol that college students seemed to drink every weekend—where a little less honesty would have meant less anxiety on Hope's part.

Perhaps their intimacy was the reason for Rachel's text. Like any loyal girlfriend, Rachel reflected her concern for Hope's relationship status by asking about "cute guys."

"Have you ever thought about maybe meeting someone?" Rachel had asked her a little over a year ago.

"Not really."

"Why not? Is it because no one has asked you out?"

"I've been asked out by a few different men. I just told them no."

"Because they were jerks?"

"Not at all. Most of them seemed very kind."

Rachel had frowned at that. "Then what is it? Is it because you were afraid? Because of what happened between Dad and Denise?"

"I had the two of you and my work, and I was content with that."

"But you're retired, we don't live at home anymore, and I don't like the thought of you always being alone. I mean… what if the perfect man is out there just waiting for you?"

Hope's smile bore a trace of melancholy. "Then I suppose I'll have to try to find him, won't I?"

As terrifying as Rachel's heart surgery had been for Hope, the slow-motion death of her father had in some ways been even more difficult to endure.

The first few years after Sunset Beach hadn't been so bad. Her father could still move around, and with every passing month, Hope could remember growing more firm in her conviction that he'd contracted a slower-progressing version of ALS. There were periods when he even seemed to improve, but then, in the course of six or seven weeks, it was as though a switch had suddenly been thrown: Walking became difficult for her father, then unsteady without support, and then altogether impossible.

Along with her sisters, Hope chipped in to help as much as possible. They installed hand railings in the bathtub and hallways and found a used van for disabled people with a wheelchair lift. They hoped it would enable their father to get around town, but his ability to drive lasted less than seven months, and their mother was too nervous to drive the van at all. They sold it at a loss, and in the last year of his life, her father never ventured farther than either the front porch or back deck, unless he was going to see his doctors.

But he wasn't alone. Because he was loved by his family and revered by former students and coworkers, visitors flocked to the house. As was customary in the South, they brought food, and at the end of every week, Hope's mother would plead with her daughters to take some of it home with them because the refrigerator was overstuffed.

Even that relatively uplifting period was short-lived, however, ending for good when her father began losing the ability to speak. In the final few months of his life, he was hooked to an oxygen tank and suffered from violent coughing fits because his muscles were too weak to dislodge the phlegm. Hope could remember the countless times she pounded on his back while her father struggled to breathe. He'd lost so much weight that she sometimes felt as though she would break him in half, but eventually her dad would cough up the phlegm and take long, gasping breaths in the aftermath, his face as pale as rice.

The final weeks seemed like a single extended fever dream—home health nurses were hired, at first for half the day, and then around the clock. Her dad had to be fed liquid through straws. He became so weak that finishing even half a glass took nearly an hour. Incontinence followed as his body rapidly wasted away.

Hope visited him every day during that period. Because speaking had become a challenge for him, she did all the talking. She would tell him about the kids, or confide her struggles with Josh. She confessed that a neighbor had seen Josh at a hotel with a local Realtor; she confirmed that Josh had recently admitted the affair but was still in communication with the woman, and Hope wasn't sure what to do.

Finally, during one of his last lucid periods, six years after her stay at Sunset Beach, Hope told her father about Tru. As she spoke, he maintained eye contact, and when she reached the part of the story where she'd broken down in front of her father on the porch, he moved his hand for the first time in weeks. She reached over, taking it in hers.

He breathed out, long and hard, sounds coming from the back of his throat. They were unintelligible, but she knew him well enough to understand what he was saying.

"Are you sure it's too late?"

Six days later, he passed away.

Hundreds of people attended the funeral, and afterward everyone made their way to the house. When they left later that evening, the house went quiet, as though it had died as well. Hope knew that people reacted to stress and grief in different ways, but she found herself shocked by her mom's downward spiral, which was furious in its intensity and seemingly unstoppable. Her mom fell into bitter fits of unpredictable weeping and started drinking heavily. She stopped tidying up and left dirty clothes strewn about the floors. Dust coated the shelves, and dishes would sit on the counters until Hope came by to clean. Food spoiled in the refrigerator and the television blared nonstop. Then her mom began to complain of various ailments: sensitivity to light, aching joints, waves of pain in her stomach, and difficulty swallowing. Whenever Hope went to visit, she found her fidgety and often unable to complete her thoughts. Other times, she would retreat to her darkened bedroom and lock the door. The silence behind the door was often more unnerving than her fits of weeping.

The passage of time made things worse, not better. Her mom eventually became as housebound as her dad once had been. She left the house only to go to the doctor's office, and four years after her husband's funeral, she was scheduled for a hernia operation. The surgery was considered a minor one, and by all accounts, it went well. The hernia was repaired, and her mother's vitals had remained stable throughout the procedure. In post-op, however, her mother never woke from the anesthesia. She died two days later.

Hope knew the physician, the anesthesiologist, and the nurses. All had taken part in other operations that same day, both before and after Hope's mother's, with no other patients suffering adverse consequences. Hope had spent enough time in the medical world to know that bad things sometimes happened and there wasn't always an easy explanation; part of her wondered whether her mom had simply wanted to die and somehow succeeded.

The following week passed in a blur. Dazed, she remembered little about the wake or the funeral. In the weeks that followed, neither she nor her sisters had the emotional reserves necessary to start going through their mother's belongings. Instead, Hope would sometimes wander the home where she'd grown up, unable to grasp the idea of living without parents. Even though she was an adult, it would take years for her to stop thinking she could pick up the phone and call either one of them.

The loss and melancholy faded slowly, eventually displaced by fonder memories. She would recall the vacations they'd taken as a family and the walks she'd enjoyed with her father. She remembered dinners and birthday parties and cross-country meets and school projects with her mom. Her favorite memories were of her parents as a couple, recalling the way they used to flirt when they thought the kids weren't looking. But the smile would often fade as quickly as it had come, for it would make her think of Tru as well, and the opportunity she'd lost for the two of them to make a life together.

Back at the cottage, Hope took a few minutes to warm her hands over one of the burners on the stove. *Way too cold for October*, she thought. Knowing the temperature would drop further as soon as the sun went down, she considered using the fireplace—gas lines, with gas logs, so a flip of a switch was all it took to light it—but decided instead to raise the thermostat and make herself a cup of hot chocolate. As a child, she'd liked nothing better when she was chilled, but she'd stopped drinking it around the time she became a teenager. Too many calories, she'd worried back then. These days, she no longer cared about such things.

It reminded her of her age, something she'd rather not think about. Fair or not, they lived in a society that placed an emphasis on youth and beauty when it came to women. She liked to think she didn't look her age, but also admitted that she might be fooling herself.

She supposed it really didn't matter. She'd come to the beach for more important reasons. Sipping her hot chocolate, she watched the play of fading sunlight on the water as she reflected on the last twenty-four years. Had Josh ever sensed that she had feelings for another man? As hard as she'd tried to hide it, she wondered whether her secret love for another had in some way undermined her marriage. Had Josh ever intuited that when they were in bed together, Hope sometimes fantasized about Tru? Had he sensed that part of her would always be closed off to him?

She didn't want to think so, but could it have been a factor in his numerous affairs? Not that she was willing to take all the blame, or even most of it, for what he'd done. Josh was an adult and fully in control of his behaviors, but *what if* . . . ?

The questions had plagued her ever since she'd learned of his first affair. She'd known all along she hadn't committed fully to him, just as she now knew that the marriage had been doomed from the instant she'd accepted his proposal. She tried to make up for it with friendship these days, even if she had no desire to rekindle anything between them. In her mind, it was a way to make amends, or atone, even if Josh might never really understand.

She would never confess her guilt to him—she never wanted to hurt anyone again, ever. But no confession meant no chance at forgiveness. She accepted that, just as she accepted the guilt for other wrongs she'd committed in her life. In quiet times, she'd tell herself that most of them would be considered minor when compared to the secret she'd kept from her husband, but there was one that continued to haunt her.

It was the reason she'd come to the beach, and the mirror image of the two great wrongs in her life struck her as both ironic and profound.

To Josh, she'd said nothing about Tru in the hope of sparing his feelings.

To Tru, she'd told the truth about Josh, even while knowing the words would break his heart.

THE BOX

Hope woke to the sight of a sky the color of robins' eggs, peeking through gauzy white curtains. Glancing out the window, she saw that the sun made the beach glow almost white. It was going to be a gorgeous day, except for the temperature. A cold front pushing down from the Ohio Valley was expected to last for a few more days, with gusty winds that would likely steal her breath as she walked the beach. In the past few years, she had begun to understand why Florida and Arizona were such popular retirement destinations.

Stretching her stiff legs, she got up and started some coffee, then showered and dressed. Though she wasn't hungry, she fried an egg for breakfast and forced herself to eat it. Then, putting on her jacket and gloves, she stepped onto the back porch with her second cup of coffee, watching the world slowly come to life.

There were few people on the beach: a man trailing behind a dog in the same way she used to follow Scottie, and a female jogger in the distance who'd left a trail of footprints near the water's edge. The woman had a bouncy stride that kept her ponytail swinging to a lively beat, and as Hope watched, she remembered how much she used to enjoy running. She'd given up the sport when the kids were young, and for whatever reason never resumed. She thought now that it had been a mistake. Nowadays, her physical condition was a source of constant preoccupation—sometimes she longed for the heedless way in which she once took her body for granted. Age revealed so many things about oneself, she mused.

She took a sip of coffee, wondering how the day would unfold. She already felt on edge, even as she cautioned herself against getting her hopes up. Last year when she'd come to the beach, she'd been buoyed by the excitement of her plan, despite its unlikely odds of success. But last year had been the beginning and today it would end...answering once and for all the question of whether miracles really could happen.

When Hope finished her coffee, she went inside and checked the clock. It was time for her to get started.

On the counter was a radio, and she turned it on. Music was always part of the ritual, and she adjusted the dial until she found a station playing soft acoustics. She increased the volume, remembering that she and Tru had been listening to the radio on the night they'd first made love.

In the refrigerator she found the bottle of wine she'd opened the night before and poured herself a small glass, not much more than a swallow. Like the music, wine was part of the ritual she followed whenever opening the box, but because she had to drive, she doubted she would even finish what she'd poured.

She carried the glass to the table and took a seat. The box was where she'd left it the day before. Setting the glass aside, she pulled the box toward her. It was surprisingly heavy. It was constructed of dense wood, both chocolate- and caramel-colored, and had oversize brass hinges. As usual, she took time to admire the intricate carvings on the lid and around the sides—imaginative stylized elephants and lions, zebras and rhinos, giraffes and cheetahs. She'd spotted the box in a booth at a Raleigh street fair, and when she learned that it had been made in Zimbabwe, she knew she had to buy it.

Josh, however, had been less than impressed. "Why on earth would you buy something like that?" he'd said with a snort. At the time, he'd been eating a hot dog while Jacob and Rachel played in a bouncy house. "And where are you going to put it?"

"I haven't decided yet," she'd answered. Once home, she brought the box to the master bedroom, where she stored it under her bed until he went to work on Monday. Then, after adding the contents to it, she'd hidden it at the bottom of a box of baby clothes in the attic, a place she knew Josh would never find it.

Since their time at Sunset Beach, Tru had never tried to contact her. For the first year or two, she'd worried that she might find a letter in the mailbox or hear his voice on the answering machine; when the phone rang in the evenings, she sometimes tensed, steeling herself just in case. Strangely, her relief that it wasn't him was always coupled with a wave of disappointment. However, he'd written that there was no room for three people in the life she would be leading, and as painful as it was, she knew that he'd been right.

Even at the lowest points in her marriage to Josh, she hadn't tried to contact Tru, either. She'd thought about it, come close a few times, but had never succumbed to the temptation. It would have been easy to run to him, but then what? She couldn't face the thought of having to say goodbye a second time, nor was she willing to risk the destruction of her family. Despite Josh's failings, her children remained her priority, and they needed her undivided attention.

So she'd kept him alive in her memories, in the only way she could. She stored her keepsakes in the box, and examined the contents every now and then, when she knew she wouldn't be disturbed. Whenever there was a television show about the majestic game animals in Africa, she would make a point of tuning in; in the late 1990s, she stumbled upon the novels of Alexander McCall Smith and was immediately hooked, since many of the stories were set in Botswana. It wasn't Zimbabwe, but it was close enough, she thought, and it helped further introduce her to a world she knew nothing about. Over the years, there were also occasional articles about Zimbabwe in major news magazines and the Raleigh *News & Observer*. She learned about the land confiscation by the government and wondered what had happened to the farm where Tru had been raised. She also read about the country's hyperinflation, and her first thought was of how it might affect tourism and whether Tru would be able to continue guiding. Occasionally she would receive travel catalogues in the mail, and she would turn to the section that described various safaris. Though most of the safaris were in South Africa, every now and then, she'd read about the lodge at Hwange. When that happened, she would study the photographs, trying to get a better sense of the world he called home. And as she lay in bed afterward, she would admit to herself that her feelings for him were as real and strong as they had been so long ago, when she'd first whispered that she loved him.

In 2006, when her divorce was finalized, Tru would have been fifty-eight years old. She was fifty-two. Jacob and Rachel were teenagers, and Josh was already seeing Denise. Though sixteen years had passed since she'd seen Tru, she'd hoped that there was still time to make things right. By then, practically anything could be found on the internet, but the information about the lodges at Hwange didn't include anything about the guides, other than to note that they were among the most experienced in Zimbabwe. There was, however, an email address, and the woman who answered her query had told Hope that she didn't know Tru, and that he hadn't worked at the lodge in years. The same went for Romy, the friend Tru had mentioned to her. Nonetheless, the woman gave Hope the name of the previous manager, who had transferred to another camp a few years earlier, along with another email address. Hope contacted him there, and while he knew nothing of Tru's whereabouts, he offered the name of yet another camp manager who'd worked at Hwange in the 1990s. There was no current phone number or email address, but he gave Hope a mailing address with the caveat that it might not be up to date, either.

Hope wrote to the manager and waited anxiously for a response. Tru had warned her that time moves more slowly in the bush, and that the mail service wasn't always reliable. Weeks passed without a response, then months, by which point Hope had given up thinking she'd ever hear from him.

It was around that time that a letter had appeared in her mailbox.

The kids had yet to come home from school, and she tore open the letter, devouring the scrawled words. She learned that Tru had left Hwange, but the manager had heard through the grapevine that he may have taken another job in Botswana. He was unsure at which camp, however. The man added that he was also fairly certain that Tru had sold the house in Bulawayo once his son headed off to a university somewhere in Europe. He didn't know the name of the university or even the country where it was located.

With little to go on, Hope began contacting lodges in Botswana. There were dozens of them. She sent email after email, but found no information about Tru.

She didn't bother trying to contact universities in Europe, since that was akin to trying to find a needle in a haystack. Running thin on options, Hope reached out to Air Zimbabwe, hoping to find someone who worked there who had a wife named Kim. Perhaps, through his ex, Hope might learn where Tru was. That, too, led to a dead end. A man named Ken had worked there until 2001 or 2002, but he'd left the company and no one had heard from him since.

After that, Hope tried a more general approach. She contacted various government agencies in Zimbabwe, asking about a massive farm owned by a family named Walls. She'd held this option until last, suspecting that Tru had reduced contact with the family even further after learning what he had from his biological father. The officials there were less than helpful, but by the end of the conversations, she surmised that the farm had been confiscated by the government and redistributed. There was no information at all on the family.

Out of ideas, Hope decided to make it easier for Tru to find her, on the off chance he was looking. In 2009, she had joined Facebook, and she checked it daily for a long time. She heard from old friends and new ones, family members, people she'd known from work. But never once did Tru try to contact her.

The realization that Tru had seemingly vanished—and that they would never see each other again—had put her in a funk for months, and made her reflect on all the other losses in her life. But this was a different kind of grief, one that grew stronger with every passing year. Now, with her children grown, she spent her days and nights alone. Life was passing and all too soon would come to an end; despite herself, Hope began to wonder if she'd be alone when she took her final breaths.

Her house, she sometimes felt, was slowly but surely becoming her tomb.

At the cottage, Hope took a small sip of wine. Though it was light and sweet, it tasted foreign in the morning. Never once in her life had she drunk wine this early, and she doubted she ever would again. But today, she thought she deserved it.

As transporting as the memories were, as much as they'd sustained her, she was tired of feeling trapped by them. She wanted to spend her remaining years waking in the morning without wondering whether Tru would somehow find her again; she wanted to spend as much time with Jacob and Rachel as she could. She longed, more than anything, for peace of mind. She wanted a month to pass without feeling the need to examine the contents of the box that sat on the table in front of her; she wanted to focus instead on crossing a few of the big items off her bucket list. Sit in the audience of *The Ellen DeGeneres Show*. Visit the Biltmore Estate at Christmas. Bet on a horse running at the Kentucky Derby. Watch UNC and Duke play basketball at Cameron Indoor Stadium. That last one would be tough; tickets were nearly impossible to get, but the challenge of that was part of the fun, right?

Not long after her trip to the beach last year, on a day she'd been feeling particularly blue, she'd deleted her Facebook page. Since then, she'd also left the box in the attic, no matter how strongly she'd felt the pull to examine the contents. Now, however, the box was calling to her, and she finally lifted the lid.

On top was Ellen's faded wedding invitation. She stared at the lettering, remembering who she'd been back then and recalling the worries that had plagued her when she first arrived at the beach that week. Sometimes she wished she could speak with the woman she used to be, but she wasn't sure what she would have said. She supposed that she could assure the younger version of herself that she'd have children, but would she add that raising them wasn't anything like the ideal she'd envisioned? That as much as she treasured them, there were countless times when they enraged or disappointed her? That her worries about them were sometimes overwhelming? Or would she tell the younger version of herself that, after having children, there would be times when she wished she could be truly free again?

And what could she possibly say about Josh?

She supposed it didn't matter now, nor was it worth the time it took to even dwell on the questions. But the invitation nonetheless made her reflect that life resembled an infinite number of dominoes set up to topple on the world's largest floor, where one domino leads inevitably to the next. Had the invitation not arrived, Hope may never have argued with Josh, or spent the week without him at Sunset Beach, or even met Tru in the first place. The invitation, she speculated, was the domino that, when toppled, set in motion the rest of her life. The choreography that had led to the most profound experience of love she'd ever had struck her as both scripted and improbable, but she wondered again to what end.

Setting the invitation aside, Hope reached for the first of the drawings. Tru had drawn her the morning after they'd made love, and Hope knew that she no longer resembled the woman in the drawing. In the sketch, her skin was soft and unlined, glowing with the last breath of youth. Her thick hair was shot with sunlit highlights, her breasts were firm and high, her legs toned and unblemished. He'd captured her in a way that no photograph ever had, and as she continued to study it, she mused that she'd never looked prettier. Because he'd drawn her the way he saw her.

Placing it on top of the wedding invitation, she reached for the second drawing. He'd completed it while she'd been at the wedding, and over the years, whenever she went through the contents of the box, she always lingered over this sketch. In it, the two of them stood on the beach, near the water's edge. The pier was in the background and sunlight glinted off the ocean as they stared at each other in profile. Her arms were around his neck and his hands were at her waist. Again, she thought he'd made her more beautiful than she really was, but it was the image of him that captured her. She studied the lines at the corners of his eyes and the dimple in his chin; she traced the shape of his shoulders beneath the loose fabric of his shirt. Most of all, though, she marveled at the expression he'd given himself as he stared at her—that of a man deeply in love with the woman he held in his arms. She pulled the drawing closer, wondering whether he had ever again looked at another woman this way. She would never know, and though there was part of her that wished him happiness, another part wanted to believe that the feelings they'd had for each other were entirely unique.

She set that drawing aside as well. Next came the letter that Tru had written to her, the one she'd found in the glove compartment. The paper had yellowed at the edges and there were small tears in the creases; the letter had become as brittle as she had. The realization brought a lump to her throat as she traced a line between her name at the top and his at the bottom, connecting them once more. She read the words she already knew by heart, never tiring of their power.

Rising from the table, Hope moved to the kitchen window. As her mind wandered, she realized that she could see Tru walking past the cottage with a fishing pole draped over his shoulder, a tackle box in his other hand, and she watched as he turned to face her. He waved, and in response, she reached out, touching the glass.

"I never stopped loving you," she whispered, but the glass was cold and the kitchen was quiet, and when she blinked she realized that the beach was entirely deserted.

Twenty minutes to go, one item left. It was a photocopy of a letter she'd written last year. She'd placed the original in Kindred Spirit on her previous trip to the beach, and as she unfolded the copy, she told herself how silly her gesture had been. A letter means nothing if the intended recipient never receives it, and Tru would never learn of it. Yet in the letter, she'd made a promise to herself, one that she intended to keep. If nothing else, she hoped it would give her the strength she needed to finally say goodbye.

This is a letter to God and the Universe.

I need your help, in what I imagine will be my last attempt to apologize for a decision I made so long ago. My story is both straightforward and complicated. To capture accurately all that happened would require a book, so instead, I will offer only the basics:

In September of 1990, while visiting Sunset Beach, I met a man from Zimbabwe named Tru Walls. At the time, he worked as a safari guide at a camp in the Hwange reserve. He also had a home in Bulawayo, but he'd grown up on a farm near Harare. He was forty-two, divorced, and had a ten-year-old son named Andrew. We met on a Wednesday morning, and I'd fallen in love with him by Thursday evening.

You may think this impossible, that perhaps I'm confusing infatuation with love. All I can say is that I've considered those possibilities a thousand times and rejected them. If you met him, you would understand why he captured my heart; if you had seen the two of us together, you would know that the feelings we had for each other were undeniably real. In the short period we were together, I like to think that we became soul mates, forever intertwined. By Sunday, however, it was over. And I was the one who ended it, for reasons I have agonized over for decades.

It was the right decision at the time; it was also the wrong decision. I would do the same thing again; I would have done it all differently. This confusion remains with me even now, but I have learned to accept that I will never rid myself of the questions.

Needless to say, my decision crushed him. My guilt over this continues to haunt me. I have now reached a point in life where making amends whenever possible feels important. And this is where God and the Universe can help, for my plea is a simple one.

I would like to see Tru again so that I can apologize to him. I want his forgiveness, if something like that is even possible. In my dreams, I'm hopeful that this will give me peace of mind; I need him to understand how much I loved him then, and still love him now. And I want him to know how sorry I am.

Perhaps you are wondering why I did not try to contact him through more conventional means. I did; I tried for years to find him, without luck. Nor do I really believe this letter will reach him, but if it does, then I will ask if he remembers the place that we visited together on Thursday afternoon, right before it began to rain.

This is where I'll be on October 16, 2014. If he remembers the place with the same reverence I do, then he'll also know what time of day I'll be there.

Hope

Eyeing the clock, Hope knew that Kindred Spirit was waiting. She put the items back in the box and closed the lid with finality, already knowing that she wouldn't return the box to the attic, nor would she bring the contents home. The box itself would be left here at the cottage, on the mantel, and the owner could do with it whatever he wanted. Aside from the wedding invitation, the rest of the contents would be left at Kindred Spirit later in the week. She needed a day or two to erase their identities, but she hoped that other visitors would revel in the items, as she and Tru had once treasured Joe's letter to Lena. She wanted people to know that love often lies in wait, ready to bloom when least expected.

The drive was straightforward, a route she knew like the back of her hand. She crossed over the newer bridge at Sunset Beach, drove past the pier to the western edge of the island, and found a place to park.

Bundling up, she trudged slowly through the low-slung dunes, relieved to see that as much as the island had changed, the beach was still the same. Storms and hurricanes as well as currents were continually altering the barrier islands along North Carolina's coast, but Sunset Beach appeared relatively immune, even though she'd heard last year that Bird Island could now be accessed on foot even when it wasn't low tide.

The sand was spongy, leaving her winded, and her legs felt leaden. When she reached the western edge of Sunset Beach, she glanced over her shoulder. She saw no one else walking in the same direction, only a lonely stretch of sand with gentle waves lapping along the shoreline. A brown pelican skimmed the breakers, and she watched until it became nothing but a speck in the distance.

Gathering herself, she started forward again, crossing the hard-packed sand gully that had been submerged only hours before. As soon as she reached Bird Island, the wind, which had been blowing steadily, ceased, as though welcoming her home. The air itself felt thinner and filmy here, and the sun, now ascendant, made her squint as it reflected off the prism of the sea. In the sudden silence, Hope understood that she'd been lying to herself ever since she'd arrived. She wasn't making this trek to say goodbye. She'd come here because she still wanted to believe in the impossible. She'd come because part of her clung irrationally to the belief that Kindred Spirit held the key to their future. She'd come today because she longed with every cell of her body to believe that Tru had somehow learned about her letter and would be here, waiting.

Logically, she understood how crazy it was to wish for such a thing, but she couldn't shake the feeling that Tru would be there. With every step, his presence seemed closer. She heard his voice in the endless roar of the ocean, and despite the chill, she felt herself growing warmer. The sand clawed at her, grabbing every step, but she increased her pace. Her breath came out in little puffs; her heart began to race, but still she pressed onward. Terns and gulls clustered in groups while sandpipers darted in and out of the gently lapping waves. She felt a sudden kinship with them, for she knew they would be the only witnesses to a reunion that had been twenty-four years in the making. They would watch as she fell into his arms; they would hear him proclaim that he'd never stopped loving her. He would spin her around and kiss her, and they would rush back to the cottage, eager to make up for lost time...

A sudden gust of wind broke her from her reverie. A hard

gust, enough to make her feel unsteady on her feet, and she thought:

Who am I kidding?

She was a fool, a believer in fairy tales, in thrall to memories that now kept her prisoner. There was no one standing near the water's edge or approaching in the distance. She was alone out here, and the certainty she'd felt regarding Tru's presence slipped away as quickly as it had come. *He won't be here*, she chided herself. He couldn't be here, because he knew nothing about the letter.

Breathing hard, Hope slowed, focusing her energy blindly on placing one foot in front of the other. Minutes passed. Ten, then fifteen. By this point, she felt she was progressing by mere inches with every step. Finally, she was able to spot the American flag in the distance, furling and unfurling in the breeze, and knew it was time to start angling away from the water's edge.

Just beyond the curve of the dune, she spotted the mailbox and bench, as lonely and abandoned as ever. She headed for the bench, nearly collapsing onto it as soon as she arrived.

Tru was nowhere to be seen.

The day had continued to brighten, and she shielded her eyes against the glare. Last year when she'd come, it had been cloudy, similar to the day she'd visited with Tru. She'd felt a sense of déjà vu, but now the high and steady sun seemed to taunt her for her foolishness.

The angle of the dune blocked her view of the sandy stretch of beach she'd just traversed, so she trained her gaze in the opposite direction. The flag. The waves. Shore birds, and the gently swaying saw grass capping the dunes. She marveled at how little the landscape had changed since her father had first brought her here, in contrast to how much had changed within her. She'd lived almost an entire life, but had accomplished nothing extraordinary. She'd made no permanent mark on the world, nor would she ever, but if love was all that really mattered, she understood that she'd been singularly blessed.

She decided to rest before heading back. But first she would check the mailbox. Her fingers tingled as she pulled it open and reached for the stack of letters. Carrying them back to the bench, she used her scarf to weight down the stack.

For the next half hour, she immersed herself in reading the missives that others had left. Nearly all dealt with loss, as if in keeping with some sort of theme. Two letters were from a father and daughter, who had written to a wife and mother who had died four months prior of ovarian cancer. Another was written by a woman named Valentina who was grieving the husband she'd lost; still another described the loss of a grandchild who'd passed away from a drug over-dose. A particularly well-written letter described the fears associated with the loss of a job and the eventual loss of the person's home through foreclosure. Three of them were from recent widows. And though she wished it were oth-erwise, all of them served as a reminder that Tru was gone forever, too.

She set aside the pile she'd read; there were only two let-ters left. Thinking she might as well finish, she reached for yet another envelope. It had been opened and she pulled the letter free, unfolding it in the sun. It was written on yellow legal paper and she glanced at the name at the top, unable to believe what she was seeing.

Hope

She blinked, continuing to stare at her name.

Hope

It couldn't be, but...*it was*, and she felt a wave of dizziness. She recognized the handwriting; she'd seen it earlier that morning in the letter Tru had written long ago. She would have recognized it anywhere, but if that was the case, where was he?

Why wasn't he here?

Her mind continued to race, nothing making sense at all, except for the letter she held in her hand. There was a date at the top—October 2, which was twelve days ago...

Twelve days?

Had he been twelve days early?

She didn't understand, and her confusion led to even more questions. Had he gotten the date wrong? Had he learned of her letter, or was the whole thing a coincidence? Was the letter even for her? Had she really recognized the handwriting? And if so...

Where was he?

Where was he?

Where was he?

Her hands began to shake and she closed her eyes, trying to slow her thoughts and the cascade of questions. She drew several long, deep breaths, telling herself that she'd been imagining all of it. When she opened her eyes, there would be a different name at the top; when she really examined the letter, she would see that the handwriting didn't match at all.

When she had regained a semblance of self-control, she lowered her gaze to the page.

Hope

Nor, she realized, had she been mistaken about the

handwriting. It was his, no one's but his, and she felt a catch
in her throat as she finally began to read.

Hope,

*The destiny that matters most in life is the one concerning
love.*

   *I write those words as I sit in a room where I've been
staying for more than a month. It's a bed and breakfast
called the Stanley House, and it's located in the historic district of Wilmington. The owners are very kind, it's quiet
most of the time, and the food is good.*

   *I know these details may feel irrelevant, but I'm ner-
vous, so let me start with the obvious: I learned about your
letter on August 23, and I flew to North Carolina two days
later. I knew where you wanted to meet me and guessed
that you would visit at low tide, but for reasons I can best
explain later, I didn't know the exact date you would be
there. I had only vague references to work from, which is
why I chose to stay at a bed and breakfast. If I was going to
be in North Carolina for a while, I wanted someplace more
comfortable than a hotel, but I didn't want the trouble of
renting a place. I wasn't even sure how to go about something like that in a foreign country, to tell you the truth. All
I knew was that I had to come, since I'd promised you that
I would.*

   *Despite the lack of particulars, I assumed that you'd
picked a date in September. That's when we met, after
all. I've visited Kindred Spirit every day this past month. I
watched and waited for you without success, all the while
wondering whether I'd missed you, or whether you had
changed your mind. I wondered if fate had conspired to*

keep us apart once more. When September gave way to October, I made the decision to leave you a letter, with the hope that you may one day learn of it in the same inexplicable way I had learned of yours.

You see, I also learned that you wanted to apologize for what had happened between us, for making the decision that you did so long ago. I told you then, and I still believe now, that no apology is necessary. Meeting you and falling in love with you was an experience I would relive a thousand times in a thousand different lives, if I was ever given that chance.

You are, and always have been, forgiven.
Tru

After finishing the letter, Hope continued to stare at the page, her heart pounding in her chest. The world seemed to be closing in, collapsing from all sides. The letter offered no clues as to whether he'd stayed, no means of contacting him if he'd returned to Africa...

"Did you leave?" she cried aloud. "Please don't tell me you've already left..."

As she spoke the words, she lifted her eyes from the page and caught sight of a man standing no more than ten feet away. The sun cast him in shadow, making it hard to see his features, but she had visualized his image so many thousands of times over the years that she recognized him anyway. Her mouth opened, and as he took a hesitant step toward her, she saw that he'd begun to smile.

"I didn't leave," Tru said to her. "I'm still here."

REUNION

———✉———

Staring at him, Hope felt frozen to the bench. It couldn't be happening—there was no way that Tru could really be here—and yet she couldn't hold back the avalanche of emotions that crashed over her. Wonder and joy were coupled with absolute shock, making it impossible for her to speak, and a tiny part of her feared that if she did, the illusion would be shattered.

He was here. She could see him. She'd heard him speak, and with the sound of his voice, the memories of their time together materialized with vivid force. Her first thought was that he'd changed little in the years since she'd seen him last. He was still lean, his broad shoulders unbent by age, and while his hair had thinned and turned silver-gray, it had the same careless, tousled look she'd always adored. He was dressed the same as he'd dressed back then, in a neatly tucked-in button-up shirt, jeans, and boots; she remembered him being impervious to the cold, but today he was wearing a jacket that reached his hips, though he hadn't bothered to zip it up.

He hadn't moved any closer, seemingly as stunned as she. Eventually he broke the spell.

"Hello, Hope."

Hearing him say her name made her heart slam in her chest. "Tru?" she breathed.

He started toward her. "I see you found the letter I left you."

Only then did she realize she was still holding it.

"I did." She nodded. She folded it and absently slipped it into the pocket of her jacket, her mind a jumble of colliding images, past and present. "Were you behind me on the beach? I didn't see you."

He hooked a thumb over his shoulder. "I walked over from Sunset Beach, but I didn't see you, either. Not until the mailbox came into view, anyway. I'm sorry if I startled you."

She shook her head as she rose from the bench. "I still can't believe you're here...I feel like I'm dreaming."

"You're not dreaming."

"How do you know?"

"Because," he responded gently, his accent exactly as she remembered, "both of us can't be dreaming.

"It's been a long time," he added.

"Yes, it has."

"You're still beautiful," he said, a note of wonder in his voice.

She felt the blood rise in her cheeks, a sensation she'd almost forgotten. "Hardly..." She pushed a windblown lock of hair out of her face. "But thank you."

He closed the gap between them and gently took her hand in his. The warmth of his grip spread throughout her, and while he was close enough to kiss her, he didn't.

Instead, he traced his thumb slowly across her skin, the feeling electric.

"How are you?" he asked.

Every cell in her body seemed to be vibrating. "I'm..." She brought her lips together before going on. "Actually, I don't know how I'm doing. Other than feeling...shell-shocked."

His eyes captured hers, collapsing the years they'd lost. "There's so much I want to ask you," he said.

"Me too," she whispered.

"It's so good to see you again."

As he spoke, her vision began to telescope, the wider world shrinking to the dimensions of that singular moment: Tru suddenly standing before her after so many years apart, and without another word, they went together. He put his arms around her, drawing her close, and all at once, she felt as if she were thirty-six again, dissolving in the shelter of his body as the autumn sunlight streamed down around them.

They stayed like that for a long time, until she finally pulled back to look at him. Really look. Though the lines had grown deeper in his face, the dimple on his chin and the color of his eyes were the same as she remembered. She found herself foolishly relieved that she'd had her hair done recently, and that she'd taken time with her appearance this morning. The clash of memory and immediate sensation was roiling her thoughts, and she felt her eyes inexplicably well with tears. She swiped at them, embarrassed.

"Are you all right?" he asked.

"I'm fine." She sniffed. "I'm sorry for crying, but I...I just...I never really believed that you would be here."

He offered a wry smile. "I'll admit that it was a fairly extraordinary sequence of events that led me back to you."

Despite her tears, she laughed under her breath at the phrasing. He sounded like he always had, making it a bit easier to regain her bearings.

"How did you find my letter?" she wondered. "Were you here in the last year?"

"No," he said. "And I didn't actually find it, or even read it. I was told about it. But... more importantly, how are you? What happened to you during all these years?"

"I'm fine," she answered automatically. "I..." She trailed off, suddenly blank. What does one say to a former lover after twenty-four years? When she'd been fantasizing about this moment ever since they'd said goodbye? "A lot happened" was all she could think to say.

"Really?" He raised an eyebrow in jest, and she couldn't help but smile. They had always felt a natural ease with each other, and that, at least, remained unchanged.

"I wouldn't even know where to start," she admitted.

"How about where we left off?"

"I'm not sure what that means."

"All right. Let's start with this: I assume you went through with the wedding?"

He must have guessed, because she'd never contacted him. But there was no sadness or bitterness in his tone, only curiosity.

"I did," she admitted. "Josh and I got married, but..." She wasn't ready to delve into details. "We didn't make it. We divorced eight years ago."

He glanced down at the sand, then back up again. "That must have been difficult for you. I'm sorry."

"Don't be," she said. "The marriage had run its course and it was time to end it. How about you? Did you ever get married again?"

"No," he answered. "Things never quite worked out that way. It's just me these days."

Though it was selfish of her, she felt a wave of relief. "You still have Andrew, right? He must be in his thirties by now."

"He's thirty-four," Tru answered. "I see him a few times a year. He lives in Antwerp these days."

"Is he married?"

"Yes," Tru said. "Three years."

Amazing, she thought. It was difficult to imagine. "Does he have children yet?"

"His wife, Annette, is pregnant with their first."

"So you'll be a grandfather soon."

"I suppose I will be," he admitted. "How about you? Did you ever have the children you wanted?"

"Two." She nodded. "A boy and a girl. Well, actually, I suppose they're a man and woman now. They're in their twenties. Jacob and Rachel."

He squeezed her hand gently. "I'm happy for you."

"Thank you. It's been the thing I'm most proud of," she said. "Do you still guide?"

"No," he answered. "I retired three years ago."

"Do you miss it?"

"Not at all," he said. "I've grown to enjoy sleeping past dawn without wondering whether lions will be at my doorstep."

She knew it was small talk, skimming the surface of things, but it felt unforced and easy, like the conversations she had with her closest friends. They could go months, sometimes a year without speaking, then pick up exactly where they'd left off the last time they'd spoken. She hadn't imagined it would be the same with Tru, but the pleasant realization was interrupted by an arctic blast of wind. It cut through her jacket and kicked up the sand on the dunes. Over his shoulder, she saw her scarf shift on the bench while the letters beneath fluttered at the edges. "Hold on. I'd better put the letters back before they blow away."

She hurried to the mailbox. While her legs had felt like jelly when she'd arrived, they now felt rejuvenated, as if time were moving backward. Which, in a way, it was.

Closing the mouth of the mailbox, she noticed that Tru had followed her.

"I'm going to keep the letter you wrote to me," she told him. "Unless you don't want me to."

"Why wouldn't I? I wrote it for you."

She wrapped the scarf around her neck. "Why didn't you mention in the letter that you were still here? You could have simply written, *wait for me*."

"I wasn't exactly sure how long I was going to stay in the area. When I wrote to you, I didn't know the date that you would be here, and the original letter you wrote was no longer in the mailbox when I arrived."

She tilted her head. "How long were you thinking you'd stay?"

"Through the end of the year."

At first, not sure she'd heard him right, she couldn't respond. Then: "You were planning to come here every day until January? And then go back to Africa?"

"You're half-correct. I was planning to stay through January. But no, even then, I wasn't going to return to Africa. Not immediately, anyway."

"Where were you planning to go?"

"I intended to stay here in the States."

"Why?"

He seemed puzzled by the question. "So I could look for you," he finally answered.

She opened her mouth, trying to respond, but again, no words would come. It made no sense at all, she thought. She didn't deserve this devotion. She'd left him. She'd seen him break down and continued to drive away; she'd chosen to destroy his hopes and make a life with Josh instead.

And yet, as he gazed at her, she realized that his love remained undimmed, even if he hadn't yet grasped how much she'd missed him. Or how much she still cared for him now. In her mind, she heard a voice warning her to be careful, to be completely honest about everything so he wouldn't be hurt again. But in the throes of their reunion, the voice seemed distant, an echo that faded away to a whisper.

"What are you doing this afternoon?" she asked.

"Nothing. What did you have in mind?"

Instead of answering, she smiled, knowing exactly where to go.

They started back the way they'd come, eventually reaching the sandy gully that separated Bird Island from Sunset Beach. In the distance they could see the outline of the pier, its details lost in the glare off the water. The waves were long and gentle, rolling toward the shore in steady rhythm. Up ahead, Hope noted that there were more people on the beach now, tiny figures moving along the water's edge. The air was sharp, carrying with it the scent of pine and wind, and in the chill she felt her fingers beginning to tingle.

They moved at a leisurely pace, though Tru didn't seem to mind. She caught the hint of a limp in his stride, no-ticeable enough to make her wonder what had happened to him. It might be nothing—perhaps a touch of arthritis, or simply the by-product of an active life—but it reminded her that despite their shared history, they were in many ways strangers. She'd cherished a memory, but that wasn't necessarily the man he was today.

Or was it?

Walking beside him, she wasn't sure. All she knew was that being with him felt as easy and comforting as it had back then, and glancing over at Tru, she suspected he felt the same way. Like her, he'd tucked his hands into his pockets, his cheeks turning pink in the chill, and there was a contented air about him, like a man just returned home after a long journey. Because the tide was slowly coming in, they walked at the very edge of the hard-packed sand, both of them watching for waves that might soak their shoes.

They drifted into conversation, the words flowing unchecked, like an old habit rediscovered. She did most of the talking. She told him about the deaths of her parents, touched briefly on work, along with her marriage and subsequent divorce from Josh, but mainly found herself telling him about Jacob and Rachel. She told countless stories about their childhoods and their teen years, and admitted how terrified she'd been when Rachel had her open-heart surgery. Often she read reactions of warmth or concern on Tru's face, his empathy plain. She couldn't recall everything, of course; some of the details of her life were lost to her, but she felt that Tru instinctively grasped the patterns and threads of her past. By the time they'd passed beneath the pier, she suspected there was little about her life as a mother that he didn't already know.

As they moved through the softer sand and began to angle toward the path that led through the dunes, she walked ahead of him, realizing that unlike the arduous hike out to Kindred Spirit, she'd barely noticed the trek back. Her fingers felt warm and supple in her pockets, and despite doing almost all of the talking, she wasn't winded.

After skirting the path, they reached the street and she noticed a car parked in the spot next to hers.

"Yours?" she asked, pointing.

"A rental," he said.

It made sense that he'd rented a car, she supposed, but she couldn't help but realize that their cars were close to each other, as if drawn together by the same magical forces that had allowed Hope and Tru to reunite. She found that oddly touching.

"How about you follow me?" she offered. "It's a bit of a drive."

"Lead the way."

She hit the button to unlock the doors and slipped behind the wheel. The car was cold, and after starting the engine, she cranked the heater to maximum. Beyond the glass, Tru got into his rental. She backed out, then stopped in the street to wait for him. When he was ready, she removed her foot from the brake and the car began to roll forward, toward an afternoon she couldn't have foreseen and a future she couldn't imagine.

Alone in the car, her thoughts began to wander and she continued to peek in the rearview mirror, making sure Tru didn't disappear. Making sure she hadn't been hallucinating, because part of her still couldn't believe that he'd learned of her letter.

But he had learned of it, she thought.

He was here. He'd come back because she'd wanted him to. And he still cared for her.

She took a breath, steadying herself as the car finally began to warm. His car trailed behind hers through the turns and over the bridge. Onto the highway, where, thankfully, most of the lights were green, then finally toward the turnoff that led to Carolina Beach. Another small bridge and a few turns later, she pulled into the driveway of the cottage she'd rented.

She left room for Tru to pull in alongside her, watching as he finally came to a stop. She stepped out, listening to the ticking of her engine as it cooled. In his car, Tru was turned around, reaching for something in the back seat, his hair silver through the glass.

As she waited, thin strands of clouds drifted overhead, softening the glare. The breeze was steady, and after the warmth of the car, she felt herself suddenly shiver. As she crossed her arms, she heard a cardinal call from the trees, and when she spotted it, she flashed to the memory of Joe's letter to Lena that Tru had read to her when they'd visited Kindred Spirit long ago. *Cardinals*, she thought, *mate for life.* The idea made her smile.

Tru stepped out of the car, moving as gracefully as he had in the past. Holding a canvas bag in his hand, he squinted toward the cottage.

"Is this where you're staying?"

"I rented it for a week."

He scrutinized the cottage again, then turned back to her. "It reminds me of your parents' cottage."

She smiled, feeling a sense of déjà vu. "That's exactly what I thought when I first saw it, too."

The autumn sun slanted down on them as Tru followed her to the front door. Once inside, Hope set her hat, gloves, and scarf on the end table and hung her jacket in the closet. Tru hung his jacket beside hers. The canvas bag went onto the end table, next to her things. There was something reassuringly domestic about the ease with which they entered the house, she thought, as if they'd been doing it together all their lives.

She could feel a draft coming through the windows. Though she'd adjusted the thermostat earlier, the house was struggling against the elements, and she rubbed her arms to keep the blood flowing. She watched as Tru took in the surroundings, and she had the sense that his eyes still missed nothing.

"I can't believe you're really here," she said. "I never thought in a million years you'd come."

"And yet, you were waiting for me at the mailbox."

She acknowledged his observation with a sheepish smile, combing her fingers through her windblown hair. "I've done most of the talking, so now I want to hear about you."

"My life hasn't been all that interesting."

"So you say," she said, her expression skeptical. She touched his arm. "Are you hungry? Can I make you some lunch?"

"Only if you'll join me. I had a late breakfast, so I'm not famished."

"Then how about a glass of wine? I think this calls for a little celebration."

"I agree," he said. "Do you need help?"

"No, but if you wouldn't mind getting the fire going, that

would be great. Just flip the switch near the mantel. It's automatic. And then make yourself at home. I'll be back in a minute."

Hope went to the kitchen and peered into the refrigerator. Pulling out the bottle of wine, she poured two glasses and returned to the living room. By then, the fire was going and Tru was on the couch. After handing him a glass, she set hers on the coffee table.

"Do you need a blanket? Even with the fire going, I'm still kind of chilled."

"I'm all right," he said.

She gathered up a throw from the bed in her room, then took a seat on the couch, adjusting the blanket over herself before reaching for her glass. The heat from the fireplace was already seeping into the room.

"This is nice," she commented, thinking he was as handsome as when they'd first met. "Wildly unbelievable, but nice."

He laughed, a familiar rumble. "It's more than nice. It's miraculous." Lifting his glass, he said, "To...Kindred Spirit."

After clinking glasses, they both took a sip. When Tru lowered his glass, he gave a faint smile.

"I'm surprised that you're not staying at Sunset Beach."

"It's not the same," she said. *Nor has it been since I met you*, she added silently.

"Have you been here before?"

She nodded. "I came here the first time after I separated from Josh." She told him a bit about what she'd been going through back then and how much the visit had helped her clear her mind, before going on. "At the time, it was all I could do to keep a lid on all the emotions I was experiencing. But the time alone also reminded me how much the kids were struggling with the divorce, too, even if they weren't showing it. They really needed me, and it helped me refocus on that."

"You sound like you were a great mother."

"I tried." She shrugged. "But I made mistakes, too."

"I think that's part of the description. At least when it comes to being a parent. I still wonder whether I should have spent more time with Andrew."

"Has he said anything?"

"No, but he wouldn't. And yet, the years went by too quickly. One day, he was a little boy, and the next thing I knew, he was heading off to Oxford."

"Did you stay at Hwange until then?"

"I did."

"But then you left."

"How did you know that?"

"I looked for you," she said. "Before putting the letter in the mailbox, I mean."

"When?"

"In 2006. After I divorced from Josh, probably a year after my first visit to Carolina Beach. I remembered where you worked and I contacted the lodge. Other places, too. But I couldn't find you."

He seemed to contemplate that, his eyes unfocused for a few seconds. She had the sense there was something he wanted to say but couldn't. Instead, after a few beats, he offered a gentle smile. "I wish I'd known," he said finally. "And I wish you would have."

Me too, she thought. "What happened? I thought you liked working at Hwange."

"I did," he said. "But I was there for a long time and it was time to move on."

"Why?"

"There was new management at the camp, and a lot of the other guides had left, including my friend Romy. He'd retired a couple of years earlier. The lodge was going through a transition period, and with Andrew off to college, there was really nothing to keep me in the area. I thought that if I wanted to start over someplace else, it was better sooner rather than later. So I sold my place in Bulawayo and moved to Botswana. I'd found a job at a camp that sounded interesting."

So he went to Botswana after all, she thought.

"They all sound interesting to me."

"A good number of them actually are," he agreed. "Did you ever get to go on safari? You had said that you wanted to one day."

"Not yet. I'm still hoping to, though." Then, circling back to what he'd said earlier and remembering how many camps she'd contacted, she asked: "What was so interesting about the camp in Botswana? Was it well known?"

"Not at all. It's more of a middle-tier camp. The accommodations are a bit rustic. Bagged lunches instead of prepared meals, things like that. And the game can be fairly sporadic. But I'd heard about the lions in the area. Or rather, a specific pride of them."

"I thought you saw lions all the time."

"I did," he said. "But not like this. I'd heard a rumor that the lions had learned to hunt and bring down elephants."

"How could lions bring down an elephant?"

"I had no idea, and I didn't believe it at the time, but eventually I met a guide who used to work there. He told me that while he hadn't actually seen an attack, he'd come across an elephant carcass the following day. And it was clear to him that lions had been feasting most of the night."

She squinted at him doubtfully. "Maybe the elephant was sick and the lions came across it?"

"That's what I thought initially. People always talk about the lion as being the king of the jungle—even that Disney movie *The Lion King* played up the mythology—but I knew from experience that it wasn't true. Elephants are, and always have been, the king of the bush. They're massive and scary, truly dominant. In the hundreds of times I watched an elephant approach lions, the lions always backed off. But if the guide was right, I knew it was something I had to see for myself. The thought of it became something of an obsession. And again, with Andrew gone, I thought, why not?"

He took a swallow of wine before going on. "When I started working there, I learned that none of the guides had ever seen it, but they all believed it, too. Because every now and then, a carcass would turn up. If it was happening, it was incredibly rare, which made sense. Even if a pride of lions could take down an elephant, they would undoubtedly prefer easier prey. And during my first few years there, that's all I ever saw. The main source of food for the pride was what I'd always seen in the past—impalas, warthogs, zebras, and giraffes. I never encountered a single elephant carcass. Halfway through my third year there, though, a drought set in. A bad one. It lasted months, and a lot of the regular game either died off or began migrating toward the Okavango Delta. Meanwhile, the lions were still around, and gradually grew more desperate. Then late one afternoon, while on a game drive, I saw it happen."

"You did?"

He nodded, retreating into the past. She watched as he

swirled his wineglass before going on. "It was a smaller elephant, not one of the big bulls, but the lions separated it from the herd and went to work. One at a time, almost like a military operation. One of them attacking the leg, another jumping on the elephant's back, while the others surrounded it. Just sort of wearing the elephant down over time. It wasn't violent, either. It was very calm, very methodical. The pride was cautious and the entire attack probably took thirty minutes. And then, when the elephant was weakening, they ganged up, several attacking at once. The elephant went down, and it didn't take long after that."

He shrugged, his voice growing softer. "I know you might feel bad for the elephant. But by the end, I was awed by the lions. It was certainly one of the most memorable experiences of my guiding career."

"Unbelievable," she said. "Were you alone when it happened?"

"No," he said. "There were six guests in the jeep. I think one of them ended up selling the video footage he took to CNN. I never saw it, but over the next few years, I heard from a lot of people who did. The lodge where I was working became very popular for a while after that. But eventually the rains resumed and the drought ended. The game returned, and the lions went back to easier prey. I never saw it happen again, nor did I see another carcass. I heard that there was another occurrence some years later, but by then I was no longer there."

She smiled. "I'll say the same thing to you that I did when we first met: You definitely have the most interesting job of anyone I've ever known."

"It had its moments." He shrugged.

She cocked her head. "And you mentioned that Andrew went to Oxford?"

Tru nodded. "He certainly ended up being a better student than I ever was. Incredibly bright. He excelled in science."

"You must be proud."

"I am. But truly, it had more to do with him—and Kim, of course—than me."

"How's she doing? Is she still married?"

"She is. Her other children are grown now, too. Ironically, she actually lives near me again. After I settled in Bantry Bay, she and her husband moved to Cape Town."

"I've heard it's beautiful there."

"It is. The coastline is gorgeous. Beautiful sunsets."

She stared into her glass. "I can't tell you how many times I found myself wondering about you over the years. How you spent your days, what you saw, how Andrew was doing."

"For a long time, my life wasn't all that different from the life I had led before. It was mostly centered on work and Andrew. I went on two, sometimes three game drives a day, played my guitar or made sketches in the evening when I was in the bush; and in Bulawayo, I watched my son grow up. Saw him become interested in model trains for a year, then skateboards, then the electric guitar, then chemistry, and then girls. In that order."

She nodded, remembering the phases Jacob and Rachel had gone through.

"How were his teenage years?"

"Like most teens, he had his own social life by then. Friends, a girlfriend for a year. There was a period there when I felt a bit like a hotelier whenever he was around, but I recognized his desire for independence and accepted it more than Kim did. It was harder for her to let go of the little boy he once had been, I think."

"It was the same with me," Hope admitted. "I think it's a mother thing."

"I suppose the most difficult time for me was when he went off to university. He was a long way from home, and I couldn't visit often. Nor did he want me to. So I'd see him over the holidays or between terms. But it wasn't the same, especially whenever I returned from the bush. I felt restless in Bulawayo. I wasn't sure what to do with myself, so when I heard the rumor about the lions, I just picked up and left for Botswana."

"Did Andrew visit you there?"

"He did, but not as frequently. I sometimes think I shouldn't have sold the house in Bulawayo. He didn't know anyone in Gaborone—I had an apartment there—and when he was on break, he wanted to see his friends. Of course, Kim wanted time with him, too. Sometimes I would return to Bulawayo and stay in a hotel, but that wasn't the same, either. He was an adult by then. A young one, but I could see he was beginning his own life."

"What did he study?"

"He ended up taking a first in chemistry, and talked about becoming an engineer. But after he graduated, he became interested in precious gems, especially colored diamonds. He's a diamond broker now, which means he travels to New York City and Beijing regularly. He was a good lad who turned into a fine young man."

"I'd like to meet him one day."

"I'd like that, too," he said.

"Does he ever go back to Zimbabwe?"

"Not often. Nor do Kim or I. Zimbabwe is experiencing some difficult times."

"I read about the land confiscation. Did that affect your family farm?"

Tru nodded. "It did. You should understand that there's been a long history of wrongs committed in that country by people like my grandfather. Even so, the transition was brutal. My stepfather knew a lot of people in the government, and because of that, he thought that he would be protected. But one morning, a group of soldiers and government officials showed up and surrounded the property. The officials had legal documents stating that the farm had been seized, along with all of its assets. Everything. My stepfather and half brothers were given twenty minutes to gather their personal things, and were escorted off the property at gunpoint. A few of our workers protested and they were shot on the spot. And just like that, the farm and all the land was no longer theirs. There was nothing they could do. That was in 2002. I was in Botswana by then, and I was told that my stepfather went downhill pretty quickly. He started drinking heavily, and he committed suicide about a year later."

She thought back to Tru's family history. It felt epic and dark, almost Shakespearean. "That's terrible."

"It was. And still is, even for the people who received the land. They didn't know what to do with it, didn't know how to maintain the equipment or the irrigation methods, and they didn't rotate the crops correctly. Now nothing is being grown at all. Our farm turned into a squatters' camp, and the same thing has happened all over the country. Add in the currency collapse, and..."

When he trailed off, Hope tried to imagine it. "It sounds like you got out just in time."

"It makes me sad, though. Zimbabwe will always be my home."

"What about your half brothers?"

Tru drained his glass and set it on the table. "Both are in Tanzania. Both are farming again, but it's nothing like it was before. They don't have much land, and what they do have isn't nearly as fertile as the old farm. But the only reason I know that is because they had to borrow money from me, and they're not always able to make the payments."

"That was kind of you. To help them, I mean."

"They had no more ability to choose the family they were born into than I did. Beyond that, though, I think it's what my mum would have wanted me to do."

"What about your biological father? Did you ever see him again?"

"No," Tru said. "We spoke on the phone a couple of weeks after I returned to Zimbabwe, but he passed away not long after that."

"How about his other children? Did you ever change your mind about meeting them?"

"No," Tru answered. "And I'm fairly sure they didn't want to get to know me, either. The letter from the attorney informing me of my father's death made that clear. I don't know their reasons—maybe it was because I was a reminder that their mother wasn't the only woman our father loved, or maybe they were worried about an inheritance, but I saw no reason to ignore their wishes. Like my father, they were strangers."

"I'm still glad you had a chance to meet him."

He turned his gaze toward the fire. "I am, too. I still have the photographs and drawings he gave me. It seems like so long ago," he said.

"It has been a long time," she said quietly.

"Too long," he said, taking her hand, and she knew that

he was talking about her. She felt her cheeks flush, even as his thumb began to caress her skin, his touch achingly familiar. How was it possible that they'd found each other again? And what was happening to them now? He seemed unchanged from the man she'd once fallen for, but it made her think again how different her own life had become. Where he was as handsome as ever, she felt her age; where he seemed at ease in her presence, his touch triggered another wave of emotion. It was overwhelming, almost too much, and she squeezed his hand before releasing it. She wasn't ready for that much intimacy yet, but she gave an encouraging smile before sitting up straight.

"So, let me see if I have this straight. You were in Hwange until... 1999 or 2000? And then you moved to Botswana?"

He nodded. "1999. I was in Botswana for five years."

"And then?"

"I think, for that, I'll probably need another glass of wine."

"Let me get it." Taking his glass, she retreated to the kitchen before returning a minute later. She got comfortable beneath the blanket again, thinking the room was warming up nicely. Cozy. In many ways, it had already been a perfect afternoon.

"All right," she said, "what year was this?"

"2004."

"What happened?"

"I was in an accident," he said. "A rather bad one."

"How bad?"

He took a sip of wine, his eyes on hers. "I died."

DYING

As he lay in the ditch by the side of the highway, Tru could feel his life slipping away. He was only dimly aware of his overturned truck with the demolished front end, and of the way one of the tires was finally rotating to a stop; he barely noticed the people rushing toward him. He wasn't sure where he was or what had happened, or why the world seemed blurry. He didn't understand why he couldn't seem to move his legs, or what was causing the relentless waves of pain throughout his entire body.

Nor, when he finally woke in a hospital he didn't recognize in an entirely different country, would he remember the accident at all. He remembered that he had been returning to the lodge after spending a few days in Gaborone, but only learned later from the nurse that an oncoming supply truck in the opposite lane had suddenly crossed into the path of his pickup. Tru hadn't been wearing his seat belt, and in the collision, he'd rocketed through the windshield, cracking his skull and landing forty feet away, which caused eighteen more bones to break, including both femurs, all the bones in his right arm, three vertebrae, and five ribs. He was loaded into a vegetable cart by strangers and rushed to a temporary NGO clinic that was offering vaccinations at a nearby village. It had neither the equipment, medicine, or supplies that Tru needed, nor was a doctor even present. The floor was dirt, and the room was filled with children who had learned to ignore the flies that swarmed over their faces and limbs. The nurse was from Sweden, young and overwhelmed, and had no idea what to do when Tru was rolled into the waiting room. But people expected her to do something—anything—so she moved toward the cart and checked for a pulse. There was nothing. She checked the carotid artery. Still nothing. She put her ear to Tru's mouth and checked for breathing. She heard and felt nothing, then raced toward her bag for a stethoscope. She placed it on his chest and listened carefully for the faintest murmur without hearing anything before finally giving up. Tru was dead.

The owner of the vegetable cart asked that the body be placed elsewhere, so he could go back and retrieve his vegetables before they were all stolen. There was an argument about whether he should wait for the police, but the owner shouted the loudest and his opinion carried the day. He and the father of one of the children lifted Tru's body from the cart. The bones clicked and made grinding noises as Tru was placed on the floor in the corner, and the nurse draped a blanket over his body. People made room for the corpse, but otherwise ignored it. The owner of the vegetable cart vanished back onto the street and the nurse continued to administer injections.

Sometime later, Tru coughed.

He was brought to the hospital in Gaborone in the bed of someone's truck. From the village, it took more than an hour to get there. When he was admitted, there was little the emergency doctor thought he could do. It was a wonder Tru remained alive. His stretcher was left in a crowded hallway while the hospital staff waited for him to die. Maybe minutes, they thought, no more than half an hour. By then, the sun was going down.

Tru didn't die. He survived overnight, but soon an infection set in. The hospital was short on antibiotics and didn't want to waste them. Tru's fever rose and his brain began to swell. Two days passed, then three, and still he lingered somewhere between life and death. By then, Andrew had been contacted through his listing as next of kin on his ID, and had flown from England to be with his father. Alerted by Andrew, Kim also flew in from Johannesburg, where she was living at the time. An emergency medical flight was arranged, and Tru was flown to a trauma hospital in South Africa. He somehow survived that flight, too, and was given massive infusions of antibiotics while the doctors drained the fluid from his brain. He remained unconscious for eight days. On day nine, his fever broke, and he woke to see Andrew by his bedside.

He stayed in the hospital for seven more weeks while one by one his bones were reset, casted, and healed. Afterward, unable to walk, fighting double vision, and constantly plagued by vertigo, he was moved to a rehabilitation facility.

He was there for nearly three years.

At the cottage, the firelight flickered in Hope's eyes like candles, and Tru thought again that she was as beautiful as she'd been so long ago. Maybe more so. In the soft lines near her eyes, he saw wisdom and a hard-won serenity. Her face was full of grace.

He knew the years hadn't been easy for her. Though she hadn't spoken much about her marriage to Josh, he guessed she was avoiding the subject to spare not only Tru's feelings but her own.

Meanwhile, she stared at him as though she was seeing him for the first time.

"Oh my God," she said. "That's...one of the most terrible things I've ever heard. How did you survive?"

"I don't know."

"Were you really dead?"

"That's what I was told. I called the nurse at the vaccination clinic about a year after the accident, and she swore that I had no vitals at all. She said that when I coughed, half of the patients in the room screamed. It made me laugh at the time."

"You're trying to be funny, but there's nothing funny about any of that."

"No," he agreed. "There wasn't." He touched his temple, where his hair had turned white. "I had a traumatic brain injury. Some pieces of my skull were driven into my brain, and for a long time, the wiring was all messed up. After I finally woke, I would talk to Andrew or the doctors, thinking that I was saying one thing, but actually I was saying something entirely different. I'd think I was saying, 'Good morning,' and what the doctors would hear was 'Plums cry on boats.' It was incredibly frustrating, and because my right arm was so smashed up, I couldn't write, either. Eventually, some of the wiring started to get straightened out. It was slow going, but even when I could speak and made sense, there were ridiculous gaps in my memory. I'd forget words, usually the simple things. I'd have to say 'that thing you use to eat, the pokey silver thing you hold in your hand,' instead of 'fork.' While that was occurring, the doctors also weren't sure whether my paralysis was temporary or permanent. There was a lot of lingering swelling in my spine because of the broken vertebrae, and even after they put in rods, it took a long time for the swelling to go down."

"Oh, Tru...I wish I would have known," she said, her voice beginning to crack.

"There was nothing you could have done," he pointed out.

"Still," she said, drawing her knees up under the blanket. "That's when I was trying to find you. I never thought to check the hospitals."

He nodded. "I know."

"I wish I could have been there for you."

"I wasn't alone," he said. "Andrew would come to visit whenever he had the chance. Kim visited from time to time as well. And Romy somehow learned what had happened. It took him five days on a bus to reach the rehabilitation center, but he stayed for a week. All their visits were hard for me, though. Especially during the first year. I was in a lot of pain, I couldn't really communicate, and I knew they were as frightened as I was. I knew they had the same questions I did: Would I ever walk again? Would I be able to speak normally? Would I ever be able to live on my own? It was hard enough already, without feeling their worries, too."

"How long was it until you started getting better?"

"The double vision improved within a month, but everything was still miserably out of focus for maybe six months after that. I was able to sit up in bed after three or four months. Movement in my toes came next, but some of the bones in my legs hadn't been set properly, so they had to re-break and reset them. Then there were the brain surgeries, and the spinal surgery, and... it was an experience I'd rather not repeat."

"When did you realize that you'd be able to walk again?"

"Moving my toes was a good start, but it seemed to take forever to be able to move my feet. And walking was out of the question, at least in the beginning. I had to learn how to stand again, but the muscles in my legs had atrophied and my nerves still weren't firing correctly. I'd experience intense, shooting pains all the way down the sciatic nerve. Sometimes I'd take a supported step—with bars on either side of me—but then I suddenly wouldn't be able to move my rear leg at all. Like the connection between my brain and my legs had suddenly been severed. Sometime around the year mark, I was finally able to cross the room with sup-port. It was only ten feet or so and my left foot dragged a bit... but I actually wept. It was the first time I began to see a light at the end of the tunnel. I knew that if I kept work-ing at it, I might one day be able to leave the clinic."

"That must have been nightmarish for you."

"Actually, I have trouble remembering all of it. It feels so distant now... those days and weeks and months and years sort of run together."

She studied him. "I would never have known any of this unless you told me. You seem... the same as you were back then. I noticed the limp, but it's so slight..."

"I have to stay active, which means I keep to a rather stringent exercise routine. I walk a lot. That helps with the pain."

"Is there a lot of pain anymore?"

"Some, but the exercise makes a big difference."

"It must have been really hard for Andrew to see you like that."

"It's still hard for him to talk about how I looked when he saw me in the hospital in Botswana. Or how worried he'd been on the flight, and while waiting for me to wake at the hospital in South Africa. He remained by my side for the duration of my stay at the hospital. I will say that he and Kim kept their wits about them. Had they not made arrangements for a medical flight, I doubt I would have survived. But once I was in the rehabilitation facility, Andrew was always more optimistic than I was whenever he saw me. Because he only saw me once every two or three months, my improvement, to him, was proceeding in leaps and bounds. To me, obviously, it felt altogether different."

"And you said you were there for three years?"

"In the last year, I no longer lived on-site. I still had hours of therapy every day, but it felt as if I'd been released from jail. I'd gone outside only rarely in the first two years. If I never see another fluorescent tube again in my life, it'll still be too soon."

"I feel so bad for you."

"Don't," he said. "I'm doing well now. And believe it or not, I met some wonderful people. The physical therapist, the speech therapist, my doctors and nurses. They were outstanding. But it's a strange period to remember, because it sometimes feels as if I took a three-year pause on actually living my life. Which in a way I did, I suppose."

She inhaled slowly, as though absorbing the warmth of the fire. Then: "You're a lot stronger than I probably would have been about the whole thing."

"Not really. Don't think for a second that I was unfazed. I was on antidepressants for almost a year."

"I think that's understandable," she said. "You were traumatized in every way."

For a while they both stared into the fire, Hope's feet snuggled close to his legs under the blanket. He had the feeling that she was still trying to make sense of the things he'd told her and how close they'd come to losing each other forever. Here and now, the idea felt incomprehensible to him, a near miss too harrowing to grasp, but then again, everything about today was unfathomable. That they were sitting beside each other on the couch right now felt both surreal and wildly romantic until Tru's stomach gave an audible growl.

Hope laughed. "You must be starving." She threw off the blanket. "I'm getting hungry, too. Are you up for some chicken salad? Over some greens? If you'd rather, I also have salmon or shrimp."

"A salad sounds perfect," he said.

She stood. "I'll get it started."

"Can I help?" Tru asked, stretching.

"I really don't need much help, but I wouldn't mind the company."

Hope draped the blanket on the couch and they carried their wineglasses into the kitchen. As Hope opened the refrigerator, he leaned against the counter, watching her. She pulled out romaine lettuce, cherry tomatoes, and sliced peppers of various colors, and he reflected on what she'd told him that afternoon. The disappointments she'd experienced hadn't hardened into either anger or bitterness, but rather acceptance that life seldom turns out the way that one imagines it will.

She seemed to sense what he was thinking because she smiled. Reaching into the drawer, she pulled out a small knife, then a cutting board.

"Are you sure I can't help?" he asked.

"This won't take long at all, but how about you grab the plates and forks? They're in the cabinet by the sink."

At her instruction, he placed the plates next to the cutting board and watched as she sliced the vegetables. Next, she tossed and dressed the salad in a bowl with a little lemon juice and olive oil before arranging two servings on the plates. Finally, she added a scoop of chicken salad to each. He'd imagined being in a kitchen with her a thousand times in the last twenty-four years, just like this.

"Voilà."

"It looks delicious," he said, following her to the table.

After putting her plate down, she motioned toward the refrigerator. "Do you want some more wine?" she asked.

"No, thank you. Two glasses is my limit these days."

"I'm closer to one," she said. She reached for her fork. "Do you remember when we had dinner at Clancy's? And then went back and had a glass of wine at my parents' cottage?"

"How could I forget?" he said. "That was the night we first got to know each other. You took my breath away."

She nodded, a hint of color staining her cheeks. She bent over her salad and he did the same.

Tru nodded at the carved box sitting on the table. "What's in there?"

"Memories," she said, a mysterious lilt in her voice. "I'll show you later, but for now, let's keep talking about you. I think we're up to around 2007? What happened after you finished your rehabilitation?"

He hesitated, as though trying to figure out what to say. "I found a job in Namibia. Guiding. Well-kept lodge and huge reserve, with one of the largest concentrations of cheetahs on the continent. And Namibia is a beautiful country. The Skeleton Coast and Sossusvlei desert are ... among the most otherworldly places on the planet. When I wasn't working or flying to Europe to see Andrew, I played the tourist, exploring whenever I could. I stayed at the camp until I retired and moved to Cape Town. Or rather, Bantry Bay. It's on the outskirts, right on the coast. I have a small place there with a spectacular view. And it's walking distance to cafés, bookstores, and the market. It suits me."

"Did you ever think about moving to Europe to be closer to Andrew?"

He shook his head. "I get up there from time to time, and work brings him to Cape Town regularly. If he could, he'd move to Cape Town, but Annette won't let him. Most of her family lives in Belgium. But Africa has a hold on him, the same way it does on me. Unless you were raised there, it's hard to understand."

Her gaze was full of wonder. "Your life sounds incredibly romantic to me. Aside from that awful three-year period, I mean."

"I've lived the life I wanted. Mostly, anyway." He ran a hand through his hair. "Did you ever think about getting married again? After your divorce?"

"No," she answered. "I didn't even feel like dating. I told myself that it was because of the kids, but ... "

"But what?"

Instead of answering, she shook her head. "It's not important. Let's finish with you. Now that you're retired, how do you spend your days?"

"I don't do much. But I do enjoy being able to walk without carrying a rifle."

She smiled. "Do you have hobbies?" She rested her chin

in her hand, striking a girlish pose as she fixed her attention on him. "Aside from drawing and guitar?"

"I visit a gym most mornings for an hour, and usually follow that with a long walk or a hike. I do a lot of reading, too. I've probably read more books in the last three years than I'd read in the previous sixty-three combined. I haven't broken down and bought a computer yet, but Andrew keeps insisting that I need to catch up with the times."

"You don't have a computer?"

"What would I do with it?" He seemed genuinely bemused.

"I don't know…read online newspapers, order something you need, email. Stay connected to the world?"

"Maybe one day. I still prefer reading a regular newspaper, I have everything I need, and there's no one I want to email."

"Do you know what Facebook is?"

"I've heard of it," Tru conceded. "As I mentioned, I do read the paper."

"I had a Facebook account for a few years. In case you wanted to contact me."

He didn't respond right away. Instead, he watched her, wondering how much to say, knowing he wasn't ready to tell her everything just yet.

"I thought about trying to reach out," he finally offered. "More times than you can imagine. But I didn't know if you were still married, or remarried, or whether you were interested in hearing from me. I didn't want to disrupt your life. And really, I don't know how well I would do with a computer anyway. Or with Facebook. What do Americans say? 'Can't teach an old dog new tricks'?" He grinned. "It was a big step for me to get a cell phone. But I only did that so Andrew could reach me when he needed to."

"You didn't have a cell phone?"

"I never felt like I needed one until recently. There's no service in the bush, and besides, the only one who would ever call was Andrew."

"How about Kim? Don't you still speak with her?"

"Not very often, these days. Andrew is grown now, so there's not as much reason for us to speak. And you? Do you still speak with Josh?"

"Sometimes," she said. "Maybe too much."

Tru's expression was quizzical.

"A few months ago, he suggested we try to make a go of it again. Him and me, I mean."

"That didn't interest you?"

"Not in the slightest," she responded. "And I was a bit shocked that he had the nerve to bring it up."

"Why?"

While they finished their salads, Hope shared more detail about Josh. His affairs and the divorce battles, his subsequent marriage and divorce, and the toll that life had taken on him. Tru listened, hearing only a trace of the anguish that all of Josh's actions must have caused her, and thinking to himself that Josh was a fool. That she was somehow able to forgive him struck Tru as remarkable, but then it was just another thing he admired about her.

They lingered at the kitchen table, filling in blanks and answering questions about each other's past. When they eventually brought their dishes to the sink, Hope turned on the radio, letting the music drift out of the kitchen as they wandered back to the couch. The fire was still burning, casting a yellow glow through the room. Tru watched as she took a seat and tucked the blanket around herself, thinking that he never wanted this day to end.

Until he'd learned that Hope had placed a letter in Kindred Spirit, Tru had sometimes thought that he'd died twice, not just once, in his lifetime.

Upon his return to Zimbabwe in 1990, he'd spent time with Andrew, but he could remember feeling numb to the world, even as he'd played soccer or cooked or watched TV with his son. When he went back to the bush, working with the guests was a distraction, but he could never escape thoughts of her. When he would stop the jeep on game drives so the guests could photograph whatever animal they were seeing, he would sometimes imagine that she was in the front seat beside him, marveling at his world in the same way he continued to marvel at the world they'd briefly inhabited together.

The evenings were hardest. He couldn't concentrate long enough to either draw or play the guitar. Nor did he socialize with the other guides; instead, he would lie in bed and stare at the ceiling. Eventually his friend Romy grew concerned enough to mention it, but it was a long time before Tru could even bring himself to say Hope's name.

It took months for Tru to return to his normal habits, but even then, he knew he was no longer fully himself. Prior to meeting Hope, he'd dated occasionally; afterward, he lost all desire to do so. Nor did that feeling ever change. It was as though that part of him, the desire for female companionship or the spark of human attraction, had been left behind on the sandy shores of Sunset Beach, North Carolina.

It was Andrew who finally got him drawing again. During one of Tru's visits to Bulawayo, his son asked whether Tru was angry with him. When Tru squatted lower and asked why he would ever think such a thing, Andrew mumbled that he hadn't received a drawing in months. Tru promised to start sketching again, but on most evenings, when he put pencil to paper, it was Hope he sketched. Usually he recreated from memory something from their time together: the sight of her staring at him as he held Scottie that first day on the beach, or how ravishing she'd looked on the night of the rehearsal dinner. Only after he'd made good progress on a drawing of Hope would he turn his attention to something he suspected Andrew would like.

The drawings of Hope took weeks to complete, not days. There was a newfound desire within him to match them perfectly with his memories, to capture those images with precision and care. When he was finally satisfied, he would save the drawing and start on the next. Over the years, the project became something of a compulsion, feeding an unconscious belief, perhaps, that re-creating Hope's likeness perfectly would somehow bring her back to him. He made more than fifty detailed sketches, each of them documenting a different memory. When he was finished, he put them in order, a chronicle of their time together. At that point, he started to draw the corresponding sketches of himself, or how he imagined he'd looked to her in those same moments. In the end, he had them bound in a book—drawings of himself on the left-hand pages, and Hope on the right— but he had never shown it to anyone. He'd finished it the year after Andrew went to college. It had taken nearly nine years to complete.

That was another reason he lost much of his sense of purpose as the century wound down. He paced the house with nothing to do, leafed through the book every night, and dwelt on the fact that everyone who mattered in his life was gone. His mother. His grandfather. Kim, and now Andrew. Hope. He was alone, he thought, and would always be alone. It was a hard time, maybe as hard as his recovery from the accident would later be, but in a different way.

Botswana and the lion quest, as he referred to it then, had been good for him; but always, he kept the book of sketches at hand, among his most vital possessions. After the accident, the book was the only thing he really wanted, but he didn't want to ask Andrew to bring it. He had never told Andrew about it, and he didn't want to lie to him or Kim. Instead, he had his ex-wife make arrangements to box up all of his things in Botswana and place them in storage. She did, but he spent much of the next two years worrying that the book had somehow been lost or damaged. The first thing he did after moving out of the rehab facility was make a short trip to Botswana. He hired some youths to help him open box after box until the book was found. Aside from being dusty, it was in perfect condition.

But the compulsion to relive in images the days that they'd shared together began to dim not long after that. For his own good, he knew he couldn't keep dreaming that they would someday be together again. He had no idea that around that time, Hope had been trying to find him.

Had he known, and despite his lingering injuries, he told himself he would have moved heaven and earth to go to her. And there'd been a moment when he'd come close to doing exactly that.

Twilight came softly to Carolina Beach.

Hope and Tru, their limbs brushing occasionally, sat on

the couch, continuing to talk, heedless of the waning light as they delved deeper and deeper into each other's lives. The glasses of wine, long since empty, gave way to cups of tea, and generalities gave way to intimate details. Staring at her profile in the lengthening shadows, Tru could hardly grasp that Hope was actually with him. She was, and always had been, his dream.

"I have a confession to make," he finally began. "There's something I haven't told you. About something that happened before I took the job in Namibia. I wanted to tell you earlier, but when you told me that you tried to find me..."

"What is it?"

He stared into his glass. "I almost came back to North Carolina. To look for you. It was right after I finished my rehabilitation, and I bought a ticket and packed my bags and actually made it to the airport. But when it came time to head through security...I couldn't do it." He swallowed, as if recalling his paralysis. "I'm ashamed to say that in the end, I just...walked back to my car."

It took a moment for understanding to dawn on her. "You mean that when I was looking for you, you were trying to find me, too?"

He nodded, conscious of the dryness in his throat, knowing she was thinking about the years they'd lost—not once, but twice.

"I don't know what to say," she said slowly.

"I don't think there's anything to say, other than that it breaks my heart."

"Oh, Tru," she said, her eyes growing moist. "Why didn't you get on that plane?"

"I didn't know if I could find you." He shook his head. "But the truth is, I was afraid of what would happen if I did. I kept imagining that I'd finally catch sight of you in a restaurant, or on the street, or maybe in your yard. You'd be holding hands with another man, or laughing with your kids, and after all I'd just been through, there was part of me that knew I wouldn't be able to endure that. It wasn't that I didn't want you to be happy, because I did. I wanted that for you every single day in the last twenty-four years, if only because I knew that I wasn't happy. It felt like part of me was missing, and always would be. But I was too afraid to do anything about it, and now—after hearing about your life—all I can think is that I should have had more courage when it mattered the most. Because it means I wouldn't have wasted the last eight years."

When he finished, Hope glanced away before pushing the blanket aside. Rising from the couch, she went to the front window. Her face was in shadow, but he saw the wet shine of her cheeks glowing in the moonlight.

"Why did fate always seem to conspire against us?" she asked, turning to look at him over her shoulder. "Do you think there's a greater plan at work, one we can't even fathom?"

"I don't know," he said hoarsely.

Her shoulders slumped ever so slightly and she turned away again. She stared out the window without speaking until finally drawing a long breath. Returning to the couch, she took a seat beside him.

Up close, he thought, her face looked the same as it had in all the drawings he'd ever done of her. "I'm sorry, Hope. More sorry than you know."

She swiped at her cheeks. "I am, too."

"What now? Do you need some time alone?"

"No," she said. "That's the last thing I want right now."

"Is there anything I can do for you?"

Instead of answering his question, she scooted closer and readjusted the blanket over her legs. She reached for his hand, and he cradled it, relishing the softness of her skin. He traced the tender, birdlike bones on top, marveling that the last time he'd held a woman's hand, it had been hers.

"I want you to tell me how you learned about my letter," she said. "The one I put in Kindred Spirit. The thing that finally allowed us to find each other again."

Tru closed his eyes for a moment. "It's hard to explain in a way that makes sense, even to me."

"How so?"

"Because," he said, "it started with a dream."

"You dreamed about the letter?"

"No," he said. "I dreamed about a place—a café…a real place, just down the hill from where I live." He gave a wistful smile. "I go there when I'm in the mood to be among people, and it's got a fantastic view of the coast. Usually I'll bring a book with me and while away a couple of hours in the afternoon. The owner knows me and doesn't mind how long I stay." He leaned forward, resting his elbows on his knees. "Anyway, I woke one morning, knowing I'd just dreamed about the place, but unlike a lot of dreams, the images didn't fizzle away. I kept seeing myself sitting at a table, like I was seeing myself on camera. I had a book with me, and there was a glass of iced tea on the table, both of which are ordinary parts of my life. It was afternoon and the sun was shining, and that's typical as well. But in the dream, I remember noticing a couple walk in and take a seat at a nearby table. They were strangely out of focus, and I couldn't make out their conversation, and yet I felt this urgent need to speak with them. I just knew they had something important to tell me, so I got up from the table and started to approach, but with every step I took, their table seemed to get farther and farther away. I can remember feeling a rising panic about that—I had to speak with them—and it was in that moment that I suddenly woke. It wasn't a nightmare, exactly, but it left me a bit unsettled the rest of the day. A week later, I went to the café."

"Because of the dream?"

"No," he said. "By then, I'd largely forgotten about it. As I mentioned, I eat there frequently. I'd had a late lunch, and was sipping a glass of iced tea and reading a book on the Boer wars. At that point, a couple came into the restaurant. Almost every other table in the place was free, but they sat down right near me."

"Kind of like the dream," she said.

"No," he said with a shake of his head, "everything to that point was *exactly* like the dream."

Hope leaned forward, her features softened by the firelight. Outside, night gathered at the window, collecting darkness, as Tru went on with his story.

Like everyone, Tru had experienced feelings of déjà vu in the past, but in the moment he glanced up from the book, he felt the previous week's dream come rushing back with utter clarity. For a moment, the world seemed to swim at the edges, almost as if he were back in the dream again.

However, unlike in his dream, he could see the couple clearly. The woman was blond and thin, attractive, and somewhere in her forties; the man sitting across from her was a few years older and tall, with dark hair and a gold watch that glinted in the sunlight. He realized he could also hear them, and decided he must have subliminally picked up bits and pieces of their conversation, which was the reason he'd glanced up from his book in the first place. They were talking about their upcoming safaris, and he heard them mention their plans to visit not only Kruger—a massive reserve in South Africa—but Mombo Camp and Jack's Camp, both of which were in Botswana. They were speculating about the accommodations and the animals they might see, topics he'd heard discussed thousands of times over the past forty years.

Tru didn't recognize the couple. He'd always had a good memory for faces, but these people were strangers. There was no further reason to be interested in them at all, and yet he couldn't look away. Not because of the dream. It was something else, and it wasn't until he zeroed in on the soft twang of the woman's accent that he felt a jolt of recognition, one that made the feeling of déjà vu come rushing back again, even as it mingled with his memories of another time and place.

Hope, he'd immediately thought. The woman sounded exactly like Hope.

In the years since his visit to Sunset Beach, he'd met thousands of guests. A few had been from North Carolina, and there was something unique about the accent when compared to other southern states, a softer roll to the vowels, perhaps.

They had something important to tell him.

Before he even realized that he'd risen from his seat, he was at their table. Normally, he would never think of interrupting strangers at lunch, but like a puppet on a string, he felt as though he had no choice.

"Pardon me," Tru began. "I hate to interrupt, but you wouldn't happen to be from North Carolina?" he asked them.

If either the man or woman was bothered by his sudden appearance at their table, they didn't show it.

"Why, as a matter of fact, we are," said the woman. She smiled expectantly. "Have we met?"

"I don't believe we have."

"Then how on earth would you know where we're from?"

"I recognized the accent," Tru responded.

"But clearly you're not a Tar Heel."

"No," he said. "I'm originally from Zimbabwe. But I spent some time in Sunset Beach once."

"Small world!" the woman exclaimed. "We have a house there. When did you visit?"

"1990," Tru answered.

"That's long before our time," she said. "We just bought the beach house two years ago. I'm Sharon Wheddon, and this is my husband, Bill."

Bill reached his hand out, and Tru shook it.

"Tru Walls," he said. "I heard you talking about Mombo Camp and Jack's Camp. Before I retired, I used to be a safari guide, and I can assure you that both are outstanding. You'll see plenty of game at Mombo. But the camps are different. Jack's is in the Kalahari, and it's one of the best places in the world to see meerkats."

As he spoke, the woman stared at him, her head cocked slightly to the side, a slight frown of concentration on her face. Her mouth opened, then closed before she leaned across the table.

"Did you say your name was Tru Walls, and that you're from Zimbabwe? And that you used to guide?"

"Yes."

Sharon turned from Tru to Bill. "Do you remember what we found last spring? When we were staying at the beach house and went on that long walk? And I made a joke, because we were going to Africa?"

As she spoke, Bill began to nod. "Now I do."

Sharon faced Tru with a delighted expression.

"Have you ever heard of Kindred Spirit?"

At her comment, Tru felt suddenly dizzy. How long had it been since he'd heard anyone mention the name of the mailbox? Though it was a place Tru had remembered a thousand times over the years, it had been until now a knowledge that felt in some way only his and Hope's to share. "You mean the mailbox?" he croaked out.

"Yes!" Sharon cried, "I can't believe this! Honey, can you believe this?"

Bill shook his head, seemingly as amazed as she was, while she clapped her hands in excitement.

"When you were at Sunset Beach, you met a woman there named...Helen? Hannah?" She frowned. "No, Hope—that was it, wasn't it?"

The world beyond their table went blurry and the floor suddenly felt unsteady. "I did," he finally stammered, "but you seem to have me at a disadvantage."

"Maybe you should sit," Sharon said. "There was a letter at Kindred Spirit that I need to tell you about."

By the time he concluded, darkness had pressed close around the house, the fire the only source of light. He could just make out the faint sounds of music drifting from the radio in the kitchen. Hope's eyes gleamed in the firelight.

"Two days later, I was here, in North Carolina. Obviously,

they didn't remember everything about the letter—critically, the date or even the month you would be here—but my name and background were enough for them to remember the basics."

"Why didn't you start looking for me as soon as you got to North Carolina?"

He was quiet for a moment. "Do you realize that during the week we spent together, you never told me Josh's last name?"

"Of course I did," she said. "I must have."

"No," he said, with an almost sad smile. "You didn't. And I never asked. Nor did I know your sisters' last names. I didn't even realize it until after I got back to Africa, not that it mattered back then, of course. And after twenty-four years, without last names, I didn't have much to go on. I knew your maiden name, but Anderson is a fairly common name, I quickly learned, even in North Carolina. And besides, I had no idea where you were living, or even if you'd stayed in North Carolina at all. I did remember that Josh was an orthopedic surgeon, and I must have called every orthopedic office and hospital all the way to Greensboro, asking about doctors named Josh, but that didn't get me anywhere."

She brought her lips together. "Then how on earth would you have found me years ago? When you almost got on the plane?"

"At the time, I hadn't really thought that far ahead. But I suppose I would have probably hired a private investigator. And if you hadn't shown up by the end of the year, that's what I was planning to do. But..." He grinned. "I knew you'd come. I knew I'd find you at Kindred Spirit, because that's where you said you'd be. Every day in September, I woke up thinking that today would be the day."

"And every day was a disappointment."

"Yes," he said. "But it also made it more likely that the next day would be the one."

"What if I'd decided to come in July or August? Weren't you worried that you'd missed me?"

"Not really," he said. "I didn't think you'd want to meet me in the summer, because of all the vacationers. I suspected you'd pick a day more like the one on which we visited the mailbox, when it was likely we could have some privacy. Autumn or winter seemed most likely."

Hope gave a rueful smile. "You've always known me, haven't you?"

In response, Tru lifted her hand and kissed it. "I believed in us."

She felt herself flush again. "Would you like to read the letter?"

"You still have it?"

"I have a copy," she said. "It's in the box on the table."

When she started to get up, Tru raised his hands to stop her. Rising from the couch, he fetched the carved box from the kitchen and was about to set it on the coffee table when Hope shook her head.

"No," she said. "Put it here on the couch. Between us."

"It's heavy," he observed, taking a seat again.

"It's from Zimbabwe," she said. "Open it. The letter is at the bottom."

Tru lifted the lid. On top, he saw the wedding invitation, and he touched it with a questioning look; beneath it were the drawings, as well as the letter he'd written to her. At the bottom was an envelope, plain and unmarked. He was strangely affected by the sight of the drawings and letter.

"You kept them," he murmured, almost in disbelief.

"Of course," she answered.

"Why?"

"Don't you know?" She touched his arm gently. "Even when I married Josh, I was still in love with you. I knew that as I took my vows. My feelings for you were passionate, but...peaceful. Because that's how you made me feel during the week we spent together. At peace. Being with you felt like coming home."

Tru swallowed through the lump in his throat. "It was the same for me." He stared down at the letter. "Losing you was like feeling the earth fall away beneath my feet."

"Read," she said, nodding at the envelope. "It's short."

Tru returned the other items to the box before sliding the letter from the envelope. He read it slowly, rolling the words around in his mind, hearing her voice in every line. His chest filled, brimming now with unspoken emotion. He wanted to kiss her then, but didn't. "I have something to give you."

He got up and went to the end table near the door. Reaching into the canvas knapsack, he pulled out the book of bound sketches he'd made. Returning to the couch, he handed her the book. *Kindred Spirit*, the gold-stamped lettering on the cover read.

Hope looked from him to the book and back again, curiosity getting the better of her. Tru settled next to her as she ran her finger over the wording.

"I'm almost afraid to see what it is," she said.

"Don't be," he urged as Hope finally opened the book. On the first page, there was a portrait of Hope at the edge of the pier, a place he'd never seen her. It was a sketch that seemed to capture everything about her, but since it had no role in their story, he viewed it as a title page of sorts.

He was silent as Hope turned the page, studying on the left an image of him walking the beach, and on the right,

Hope trailing behind, some distance back. Scottie could be seen racing for the dune.

The next pages showed the two of them on the first morning they'd ever spoken; in the sketches, he was holding Scottie and her concern was evident in her worried expression. The next two pages showed them walking back toward the cottage; those were followed by drawings of the two of them drinking coffee on the back deck. The images blended together like a series of screen shots in a movie. Hope took a long time to work her way through to the end. When she finally did, he noted a tear track on her cheek.

"You captured all of it," she said.

"Yes," he said. "I tried to, anyway. It's for you."

"No," she said. "This is a work of art."

"It's us," he said.

"When did you…"

"It took years," he said.

She ran her hand over the cover again. "I don't know what to say. But there's no way you can give this to me. It's…a treasure."

"I can always make another one. And ever since I finished, I've been dreaming of the day I would see you again, so I could show you how you've lived on in my soul."

She continued to hold the book in her lap, clutching it as though she never wanted to let it go. "You even added that moment on the beach, after I told you Josh had proposed, when you held me…"

He waited as she searched for the words.

"I can't tell you how many times I've thought about that," she said in a low voice. "As we walked, I was trying to figure out a way to tell you, and I was so confused and scared. I could feel this void already beginning to form because I knew we were going to say goodbye. But I wanted it to be on our terms, whatever that meant, and it felt like Josh took that away from me..."

He could hear the plea in her tone. "I thought I understood how much I hurt you that day, but seeing the drawing of you in that moment is devastating. The expression on your face—the way you drew yourself..."

Her voice trembled, and she trailed off. Tru swallowed, acknowledging the truth of her words. It had been one of the most painful renderings in the entire book, one he'd had to walk away from more than once.

"And then, do you know what you did? You didn't argue, or get angry, or make demands. Instead, your first instinct was just to hold me. To comfort me, even when it should have been the other way around. I didn't deserve it, but you knew it was something that I needed." She fought to keep her composure. "That's what I feel like I missed out on when I married Josh—having someone who would comfort me when things were at their worst. And then, today, at the mailbox, when I was in shock and had no idea what to say or do, you took me in your arms again. Because you knew I felt like I had fallen off a cliff and needed you to catch me." She shook her head sadly. "I don't know if Josh ever held me like that—with perfect empathy. It made me think again how much I gave up when I drove away that day."

He watched her without moving, then finally reached for the box and placed it on the table. He put his hand on the book of sketches he'd created, loosening it from her grip, and set it beside the box before putting his arm around her. Hope leaned into him. He kissed her hair softly, just as he'd done so long ago.

"I'm here now," he whispered. "We were in love, but the

timing wasn't right. And all the love in the world can't alter timing."

"I know," she said, "but I think we would have been good together. I think we could have made each other happy..." He watched as she closed her eyes before slowly opening them again. "And now it's too late," she said, her voice desolate.

Tru used a finger to gently lift her chin. She faced him, as beautiful as any woman he'd ever seen. He leaned closer, their lips coming together. Her mouth was warm and eager.

"It's never too late to hold you," he murmured.

Rising from the couch, he reached for her hand. The moon had risen, casting a silvery beam through the window to compete with the molten glow of the fire. She rose, slowly, and he kissed the hand he'd been holding. Languorously, he pulled her toward him. He wrapped his arms around her, feeling as her arms twined around his neck. She rested her head against his shoulder, her breath fluttering against his collarbone, and he thought to himself that this was all he'd ever wanted. *She* was all he'd ever wanted. He'd known she was the one since the moment he'd met her; he'd known since then that there would never be another.

From the porch, he heard the distant tinkle of wind chimes. Hope's body swayed against his, beckoning and warm, and he gave in to everything he was feeling.

Her mouth opened beneath his, her tongue flicking against his. It was hot and moist, the sensation unchanged after all this time, ageless and elemental. He tightened his arms around her, melding her body to his. His hand roved over her back and into her hair, then caressed her back again. He'd waited so long for this, reliving it on so many lonely nights. When the kiss ended, Hope rested her head on his chest, her body beginning to shake.

He heard her sniff, and with alarm, he realized she was crying. When he pulled back, she refused to meet his gaze. Instead, she kept her face buried in his chest.

"What's wrong?" he asked.

"I'm sorry," she said. "I'm so, so sorry. I wish I had never left you. I wish I had found you earlier, I wish you had gotten on that plane..."

There was something in her voice, a fear he hadn't expected. "I'm here now," he said, "and I'm not going anywhere."

"It's too late," she said, her voice cracking. "I'm sorry, but it's too late now. I can't do this to you."

"It's all right," he whispered, feeling the first inkling of panic. He didn't know what was wrong; he didn't know what he'd done to upset her. "I understand why you had to leave. And you have two wonderful children...Hope, it's all right. I understand the choice you made."

"It's not that." She shook her head, a deep weariness weighting her words. "But it's still too late."

"What are you talking about?" he cried, gripping her arms and pulling back. "I don't understand what you're trying to tell me. Please talk to me, Hope." Desperate, he tried to peer into her face.

"I'm afraid...and I have no idea what to say to my kids..."

"There's nothing to be afraid of. I'm sure they'll understand."

"But they won't," she said. "I remember how hard it was for me."

Tru felt a shiver go through him. He forced himself to take a deep breath. "I don't understand."

Hope began to cry harder, great gasping sobs that left her clinging to him for support. "I'm dying," she finally said. "I have ALS like my father did, and now I'm dying."

With her words, Tru's mind emptied, and all he could think about were the shadows cast by the fire and the way they seemed almost alive. Her words seemed to ricochet inside him...*I have ALS like my father did, and now I'm dying.*

He closed his eyes, trying to offer strength, but his body seemed to be weakening. She squeezed him hard, whispering, "Oh, Tru...I'm so sorry...It's all my fault..."

He felt a pressure behind his eyes as he heard her voice again.

I'm dying...She'd told him how heartbreaking her father's decline had been; that he had lost so much weight in the last few months that Hope could carry him to the bed. It was a ruthless and unstoppable illness, finally stealing even his very breath. Tru didn't know what to say as Hope rocked and sobbed against him, and it was all he could do to simply remain upright.

Beyond the windows, the world was black. A cold night, but Tru felt even colder. He had waited a lifetime for Hope and had found her, but all too soon, she would be stolen from him again. His thoughts were racing and he ached inside, and he remembered again the last line in the note he'd written to her after she'd invited him to Kindred Spirit the very first time.

I'm anticipating surprise with you as my guide.

He didn't know why those words leaped to mind, or what they were supposed to mean right now, nor did they seem to make any sense at all. Hope was his dream, all he'd ever wanted, and she'd told him that she was dying. Tru felt on the verge of shattering as they clung to each other and wept, the sounds muffled in the cocoon of the silent house.

DAY BY DAY

———— ✉ ————

I knew I had it, even before my first diagnostic test," Hope said.

It had taken her a while to stop crying, and when her tears had finally abated, Tru had wiped his own face as well. He'd gone to the kitchen to make more tea and brought a fresh cup to her as she sat on the couch. Her knees were drawn up, swaddled in the blanket.

Gripping the mug with both hands, she said, "I remembered what my father had told me it was like in the very beginning. Just this overall run-down feeling, like a cold, except that it never got any better. I was the one who suggested the diagnosis to my doctor, but she was skeptical. Because ALS generally doesn't run in families. Only one in ten cases has any kind of family history. But when I went in for the tests and the results were slow to come back, I knew."

"When did you find out?"

"The July before last. So a little less than a year and a half ago. I'd only been retired six months and was looking forward to a new life." Then, knowing what his next question would be, she added, "My dad lasted a little less than seven years. And I think I'm doing better than he was, for now, anyway. By that, I mean I think it's progressing more slowly than his did, but I can tell that it's worse now than when I first found out. I struggled to make it to Kindred Spirit this morning."

"I can't imagine what it's like to face this, Hope."

"It's awful," she admitted. "And I haven't figured out a way to tell the kids yet. They were so young when my dad passed away that they don't really remember him. Nor do they remember the toll it took on the family. I know that when I finally do tell them, they're going to react in the same way I did. They're going to be terrified and spend a lot of time hovering over me, but I don't want them to put their lives on hold for me. I was thirty-six when I found out, but they're just starting out. I don't want that—I want them to live their own lives. But once they know, that will become impossible. The only reason I didn't fall apart when my dad was sick was because the kids were young and needed all my attention. I didn't have a choice. But I told you what it was like with my dad...how hard it was to watch him die."

"You did." Tru nodded.

"That was one of the reasons I put the letter in the mail-box last year. Because I realized that..."

When she trailed off, Tru reached for her hand. "You realized...?"

"Because I realized that while it was too late for us, maybe it wasn't too late to apologize to you, and I needed to do that. Because I saw you standing in the road and I just kept going. I've had to live with that, which might be punishment enough, but...part of me wanted your forgiveness, too."

"You've always had it," he said, wrapping his other hand around hers, cradling it like a broken bird. "I wrote it in my letter—meeting you was something I would have done a thousand times over, if given the chance, even if I knew it had to end. I've never been angry at you because of the choice you made."

"But I hurt you."

He leaned closer and raised a hand to touch her cheek.

"Grief is always the price we pay for love," he said. "I learned that with my mum and when Andrew moved away. It's the nature of things."

Hope was silent as she contemplated this. She stared up at him. "You know what the worst part is?" she said in a subdued voice. "About knowing that you're dying?"

"I have no idea."

"Your dreams start dying, too. When I received the diagnosis, one of the first things that went through my mind was that it meant I'd probably never be a grandmother. Rocking a baby to sleep, or doing paint-by-numbers at the picnic table, or giving them baths. Little things, things that haven't even happened and might not ever happen, seemed to be what I missed the most. Which I'll admit makes no sense, but I can't help it."

Tru was quiet as he reflected on what she'd said. "When I was in the hospital," he finally responded, "I felt the same way. I dreamed about going hiking in Europe or taking up painting, and then I'd get massively depressed when I realized that I might not be able to do those things. But the batty thing is that once I got better, hiking and painting no longer interested me. I think it's human nature to want what we might not be able to have."

"I know you're right, but still... I was really looking

forward to being a grandmother." She managed a small laugh. "Assuming that Jacob and Rachel get married, of course. Which I doubt will happen anytime soon. They seem to enjoy their independence."

He smiled. "I know you said the walk this morning was tough, but you seemed all right on the way back."

"I felt good," she agreed. "Sometimes it's like that. And physically, I feel all right most of the time, as long as I don't overdo it. I don't think there's been much change lately. I want to believe that I've come to terms with it. It's enlightening, because it makes it easier to decide what's important to me and what isn't. I know how I want to spend my time, and what I'd rather avoid. But there are still days when I get frightened or sad. Especially for my kids."

"I would, too. When I was in the hospital, Andrew's terrified expression when he sat with me almost broke my heart."

"Which is why I've kept it a secret so far," she said. "Even my sisters don't know. Or my friends."

He leaned in and touched his forehead to hers. "I'm honored you shared it with me," he whispered.

"I thought about telling you earlier," she confessed. "After you told me about your accident. But I was having such a wonderful time, I didn't want it to end."

"It still hasn't ended," he said. "I'd rather be here with you than anywhere else. And despite what you just told me, it's been one of the best days of my life."

"You're a sweet man, Tru." She smiled sadly. "You always were."

She angled her face slightly to give him a gentle kiss, the brush of his whiskers triggering a sense of déjà vu. "I know you said that two glasses of wine is your limit, but I think I'd like another glass. Would you care to join me? There's another bottle in the refrigerator."

"I'll get it," he said.

While he was in the kitchen, Hope rubbed her face wearily, hardly able to believe that her secret was finally out. She'd hated telling Tru, but having spoken the words once, she knew she would be able to say them again. To Jacob and Rachel and her sisters. Her friends. Even Josh. But none of them would react like Tru, who had somehow eased her fears, if only for a moment.

Tru returned from the kitchen with a pair of glasses and handed one to her. As soon as he took his seat, he lifted his arm and she snuggled within his embrace. For a while they sat in silence, staring into the fire. Hope's mind reeled with all the events of the day: Tru's return, the book of sketches, telling him her secret. It was almost too much to process.

"I should have gotten on the plane," Tru said into the silence. "I should have tried harder to find you."

"I feel like I should have tried harder, too," she said. "But knowing that you thought about me all these years means everything to me."

"Me too. Just like today . . . it's been all I ever dreamed of."

"But I'm dying."

"I think you're living," he said with surprising firmness. "And day by day, that's all any of us can ever do. I can't guarantee that I'll be alive a year from now, or a month from now. Or even tomorrow."

She let her head drop back against his arm. "That's what people say, and I know there's truth to it. But it's different when you know for certain that you only have so much time left. If my dad is any guide, I have five, maybe five and a half years. And the last year isn't so good."

"In four and a half years, I'll be seventy."

"So what?"

"I don't know. Anything can happen, and that's the point. What I do know is that I've spent the last twenty-four years dreaming of you. Wanting to hold your hand and talk and listen and cook dinners and lie beside you at night. I haven't had the life that you did. I've been alone, and when I learned about your letter, I realized that I was alone because I was waiting for you. I love you, Hope."

"I love you, too."

"Then let's not waste any more time. It's finally time for us. For you and me. No matter what the future has in store for either of us."

"What are you saying?"

He kissed her neck softly, and she felt the blood rush to her stomach, like it had so long ago. Tucking some strands of hair behind her ear, he murmured, "Marry me. Or don't, and just be with me. I'll move to North Carolina and we can live wherever you want. We can travel, but we don't have to. We can cook together, or eat out every meal. It doesn't matter to me. I just want to hold you, and love you with every breath that you or I ever take. I don't care how long it lasts, and I don't care how sick you get. I just want you. Will you do that for me?"

Hope stared at him, stunned, before finally breaking into a smile.

"Do you mean that?"

"I'll do anything you want," he said. "As long as it's with you."

Without a word, she reached for his hand. Rising from the couch, she led him to the bedroom, and that night they rediscovered each other, their bodies moving to the memory of another time, familiar and yet tenderly, impossibly new. When they were finished, she lay next to Tru, staring at him with the same deep contentment she saw in his eyes. It was a look she'd missed all her life.

"I'd like that," she finally whispered.

"Like what?" he asked.

She moved closer, kissing him on the nose, then on the lips. "I'd like," she whispered, "to marry you."

EPILOGUE

I struggled with the ending of Tru and Hope's story. I didn't want to catalogue Hope's drawn-out battle with ALS, or the countless ways in which Tru tried to ease her decline. I did, however, write an additional chapter about the week that Hope and Tru spent at Carolina Beach, as well as Hope's conversation with her children, their wedding the following February, and the safari that they enjoyed on their honeymoon. I concluded the chapter with a description of their annual treks to Kindred Spirit, where they left the manila envelope in the mailbox so that others might share in their story. In the end, though, I discarded the pages I'd written—in my talks with them, it was clear that the story they wanted to share was a simple one: They fell in love, were separated for years, but found a way to reunite, partly because of the magic associated with Kindred Spirit. I didn't want to distract from the almost fable-like quality of their tale.

Still, their story didn't quite feel complete to me. The writer in me couldn't help feeling that there was a gap concerning Tru's life in the years prior to his reunion with Hope. For that reason, in the months immediately prior to publication, I called Tru to secure his approval for another trip to Zimbabwe. I wanted to meet Romy, a man who had played a minor, almost inconsequential role in the love story of Tru and Hope.

Romy had retired to a small village in Chegutu District in northern Zimbabwe, and the journey was a story in and of itself. Guns were plentiful in that part of the country, and I was worried about being kidnapped, but the driver I hired happened to be well connected to the tribes who controlled the area and ensured my safe passage. I note this only because it was a reminder of the lawlessness now present in a country that I nonetheless regard as one of the most remarkable places on earth.

Romy was thin and gray-haired, his skin darker than most of the other villagers'. He was missing a front tooth, but like Tru, he still moved with surprising agility. We spoke while sitting on a bench that had been assembled from cinder blocks and what had once been the bed of a pickup truck. After I introduced myself, I told him about the book that I'd written and explained that I was hoping for more background on his friend Tru Walls.

A slow smile spread across his face. "So he found her, yeah?"

"I think they found each other."

Romy bent forward and picked up a stick from the ground.

"How many times you been to Zimbabwe?"

"This is my second trip here."

"You know what happens to the trees after the elephants knock them over? Why you don't see trees lying on the ground everywhere?"

I shook my head, intrigued.

"Termites," he said. "They eat everything, until there's nothing left. Good for the bush, but bad for anything made of wood. That's why this bench has cinder blocks and metal. Because termites just eat and eat, and they never stop."

"I'm not sure what you're trying to tell me."

Romy rested his elbows on his bony knees and leaned toward me, still holding the stick. "Tru was like that after he came back from America... like he was being eaten up from the inside. He'd always liked to be by himself, but now it was more... he was always alone. He would stay in his room, drawing pictures, but he didn't show me his pictures anymore. For a long time, I didn't know what was wrong, just that every September, he would start acting sad again."

Romy cracked the stick in half and let the pieces fall to the ground.

"Then, one night in September—five or six years after the trip to America?—I saw him sitting outside. He was drinking. I was having a smoke and went to join him. He turned to me, and his face... I'd never seen him look that way before. I asked him, 'How are you doing?' But he didn't say anything. He didn't tell me to go away, so I sat down next to him. After a while, he gave me a drink. He always had good whiskey. His family was rich, you know."

I nodded.

"After some time, he finally asked me what was the hardest thing I ever did. I said I didn't know, life is full of hard things. Why did he want to know? He said that he knew the hardest thing he had to do, and that nothing would ever be greater than that."

Romy let out a wheezy breath before going on. "It wasn't the words... it was how he said it. There was so much sadness, so much pain, like those termites had eaten his soul. And then he told me about that trip to America... and the woman. Hope."

Romy turned to face me.

"I've loved some women in my life," he said with a grin. But then the grin faded. "When he talked, I knew I never loved anyone that way. And when he told me how he said goodbye..."

Romy stared at the ground. "He cried, like a person broken. And I felt his heart aching inside me, too." He shook his head. "After that, whenever I saw him I would think, he's still feeling pain, just hiding it."

Romy grew quiet, and for a while we just sat together and watched twilight descend over the village. "He never talked about it no more. I retired then, and I didn't see Tru for a long time, not until he had the big accident. I went to see him at the hospital. Did you know about that?"

"Yes," I said.

"He looked terrible, so terrible. But the doctors said he was a lot better than before! He was mixing up his words a lot of the time, so I did a lot of talking. And I was trying to be cheerful, to make jokes, and I asked him, did he see Jesus or God when he died? He made a sad smile, one that nearly broke my heart. 'No,' he said to me, 'I saw Hope.'"

When I returned from Zimbabwe, I drove to the beach where Tru and Hope now live. I had taken nearly a year to research and write the book, and was reluctant to intrude on them anymore. Nonetheless, I found myself walking near the water's edge, past their cottage. I didn't see them.

It was midafternoon. I continued to walk up the beach, eventually reaching the pier, and strolled to the end of it. There were a handful of people fishing, but I found a clear spot in the corner. I stared at the ocean, feeling the breeze in my hair, knowing that writing their story had changed me.

I hadn't seen either of them in months, and I missed them. I drew comfort from the knowledge that they were together, the way they were supposed to be. Later, as I passed by their cottage *a second time on the way back, my eyes were drawn automatically to their home. Still no sight of them.*

It was getting late by then, the sky a mixture of violets, blues, and grays, but on the horizon, the moon had begun its rise from the sea, as if it had spent the day hiding at the ocean floor.

Twilight began to deepen and I found myself scanning the beach again. I could see their house in the distance, and though the beach had largely emptied, I saw that Tru and Hope had emerged to enjoy the evening. My heart leaped at the sight of them, and I thought again about the years they'd spent apart. I thought about their future, the walks they would miss and the adventures they would never have. I thought about sacrifice and miracles. And I thought also about the love they'd always felt for each other—like stars in the daytime sky, unseen, but always present.

They were at the bottom of the ramp, the one that Tru had been building the first time I met him. Hope was in her wheelchair, a blanket over her legs. Tru was standing beside her, his hand resting gently on her shoulder. There was a lifetime of love in that simple gesture, and I felt my throat close up. As I continued to stare, he must have sensed my presence in the distance, for he turned in my direction.

He waved a greeting. Though I waved back, I knew it was a farewell of sorts. While I considered them friends, I doubted we would speak again.

It was their time, at last.

AUTHOR'S NOTE

Dear Reader,

While my novels generally hew to certain expected norms (they're usually set in North Carolina, feature a love story, etc.), I do try to vary the themes, characters, or devices in interesting ways with every book. I've always loved the literary device of "self-insertion," in which the author himself makes an appearance in a fictional work—sometimes as a thinly veiled autobiographical narrator, like Vonnegut in *Slaughterhouse Five*, or merely incidentally, like the character of Stephen King in *The Dark Tower: Volume VI*, whose entirely fictional diary plays a role in the story (and whose death is mentioned in the novel as occurring in 1997). One of my favorite novelists, Herman Wouk, wrote a novel at age ninety-seven, *The Lawgiver*, in which he fictitiously gets involved in a disastrous attempt to make a movie in Hollywood, over the misgivings of his real-life wife, Betty. This layered, "story-within-a-story" device involving the author always felt intriguing to me—the novelistic equivalent of Renaissance painters mischievously inserting themselves into their tableaux. I hope you agree that the bookends I wrote in my own voice added an interesting dimension to what is in other ways a classic story of lovers long denied.

While my "discovery" of Tru and Hope's story is entirely fictional, the inspiration and setting of the novel are drawn directly from my own experiences. I first traveled to Africa in 2010, and on that trip fell head over heels in love with the countries I was lucky enough to visit—the utterly spectacular landscapes, the fascinating and varied cultures, the turbulent political histories, and curious sense of timelessness I experienced there. I've since returned to Africa several more times, each time exploring different regions and visiting a rapidly disappearing natural environment. These trips were nothing short of life-changing, expanding my awareness of the places far removed from my staid existence in small-town North Carolina. On each of these trips, I met dozens of safari guides whose rich knowledge and fascinating life stories provided grist for my creative mill, and eventually inspired me to create a character whose fate was entwined with and governed by his life growing up in Africa.

Carolina Beach also holds a special place in my heart, as I have retreated to its simple, restorative pleasures on many occasions when I was in need of introspection or healing. In the off-season in particular, its windswept beaches and easygoing year-round residents provide the perfect antidote to life's stresses: long walks on deserted, sandy stretches, simple meals at unpretentious locales, and the unceasing roar of ocean waves. I recommend it to anyone looking for a quieter alternative to the typical resort vacation.

And finally, Kindred Spirit: It actually does exist on the nature reserve of Bird Island, near Sunset Beach, North Carolina. As a veteran letter-writer, I found a natural appeal in the lonely mailbox that served as a central location in my story. Perhaps one day, you too will find a way to visit this picturesque destination and share your own thoughts and stories...

Nicholas Sparks

THE LOST ART OF LETTER WRITING

by Nicholas Sparks

THE NOTEBOOK

Even if the only book you've ever read of mine is *The Notebook*, you probably already know that I am a passionate believer in the lost art of letter writing. Noah's youthful letters to Allie after she moves away from New Bern are an outpouring of his undying love for her, and they continue for two years, unanswered. In Noah's desperate, poetic, and gradually hopeless efforts to reach Allie, I wanted to capture the near-obsessive nature of young love. We never forget our first loves, and after memorializing his feelings in countless letters, Noah clearly never does.

But the letter that forms the emotional linchpin of this very short novel is actually Allie's last letter to Noah, which she pens early in the progression of her Alzheimer's, during a lucid moment in the middle of the night. In it, she promises to find a way to come back to Noah despite the ravages and losses of her disease. She already knows that there will soon come a time when she no longer recognizes him, but in an effort to keep her feelings for Noah alive forever, she writes, "And if you save this letter to read again, then believe what I am writing for you now. Noah, wherever you are and whenever this is, I love you. I love you now as I write this, and I love you now as you read this. And I am so sorry if I am not able to tell you. I love you deeply, my husband. You are, and always have been, my dream."

Our memories may fade and be altered with time, but committing words to paper keeps them pristine forever. For Allie, it is the only means she has of ensuring that Noah will truly remember her voice.

THE WEDDING

We can't all be as romantic and eloquent as Noah, and in *The Wedding*, I wanted to portray the struggles of an ordinary man—a good man, a faithful man, but as far removed from Noah Calhoun as you could imagine—to save his marriage. Wilson, a middle-aged trusts and estates lawyer, realizes at the beginning of the novel that he has forgotten his and his wife Jane's twenty-ninth wedding anniversary. Jane's obvious disappointment caps off what Wilson soon realizes has been a gradual erosion of their decades-long bond. In fact, Wilson fears that Jane is no longer in love with him.

For his part, Wilson knows that his love for Jane is just as deep and alive as it ever was—deeper, perhaps. So, what to do? Well, when your father-in-law is Noah Calhoun, who better to ask for advice about keeping a lifelong love alive? Noah's advice, while oblique, resonates deeply for Wilson: court his wife the way he once did when they were young, and make her fall in love with him all over again.

The novel culminates with a surprise on their thirtieth wedding anniversary, and a letter from Wilson to Jane that accompanies a priceless gift: "I once made a vow to you on the steps outside the courthouse, and as your husband of thirty years, it's time I finally made another: From this point on, I will become the man I always should have been. I'll become a more romantic husband, and make the most of the years we have left together. And in each precious moment, my hope is that I'll do or say something that lets you know that I could never have cherished another as much as I've always cherished you..."

By telling the story of an older couple that has lost the spark of their early connection, I wanted to show that romance isn't always the equivalent of being struck by lightning. It often takes conscious work and appreciation, and letters are a powerful way to show your appreciation. You don't have to be a poet to make someone feel loved (Wilson certainly wasn't!)...you only need to be sincere.

THE LAST SONG

People often refer to me as a "romance writer," but I think it would be more accurate to describe me as a writer who is preoccupied with all kinds of love—between amorous couples, of course, but also between friends, between siblings, and between parents and children. In *The Last Song*, the seventeen-year-old protagonist, Ronnie, falls in love with a young man while reluctantly spending a summer with her divorced father in North Carolina. But in many ways, the most heart-wrenching and deeply emotional thread of this novel has to do with Ronnie's relationship with her father, Steve. An angry young woman who blames her father for the demise of her parents' marriage, she arrives in Wrightsville Beach hostile and, in many ways, a stranger to her own parent. It proves to be a revelatory summer, however, as it turns out that the reason she and her younger brother, Jonah, have been "banished" to live with their father for the summer is because Steve is terminally ill. A man with countless regrets of his own, he grasps desperately for ways to connect with his young son and estranged daughter.

In the end, it is Ronnie who remains with him at the very end, when her father is too weak to speak or move. In those final days, she summons the strength to read the letter her father has left behind for her: "...Thank you for staying. I know it's hard for you, surely harder than you imagined it would be, and I'm sorry for the hours that you're going to inevitably spend alone. But I'm especially sorry because I haven't always been the father you've needed me to be. I know I've made mistakes. I wish I could change so many things in my life. I suppose that's normal, considering what's happening to me, but there's something else I want you to know... You and Jonah have always been the greatest blessings in my life. I love you, Ronnie, and I've always loved you. And never, ever forget that I am, and always have been, proud of you."

Letters have often been used to express the regrets and feelings that are so difficult to articulate in person. And what parent is not familiar with the jumble of regrets, questions, and profound love that wells up at the sight of your child on the brink of adulthood— much less an adulthood you might not be around to see?

DEAR JOHN

What is more classic than the fabled "Dear John" letter of countless wars? How many young men have gone off to war with a beloved in their hearts, only to have the prolonged separation and horrors of battle take their toll on their most precious relationships?

Although most soldiers rely on email and Skype these days to stay in touch with loved ones, in 2000, John Tyree and Savannah Curtis write letters constantly to keep the flame of their passion alive. Savannah, a college student in North Carolina, is waiting endlessly for John to return from his army posting in Germany...In truth, they've both been counting down the days until he can return. Deeply in love, Savannah sees John off at the airport after a blissful leave spent together, pressing a letter on him that he reads on the plane: "I love you, John Tyree, and I'm going to hold you to the promise you once made to me. If you come back, I'll marry you. If you break your promise, you'll break my heart."

Despite their best intentions, the events of 9/11 change everything for John and Savannah. John's reenlistment and deployment to Iraq force the lovers to make impossible choices, putting them on different paths. But the bittersweet memories of their love live on in their letters...bringing them back to each other in heartbreaking ways.

SAFE HAVEN

Millions of readers around the world were captivated last year by a terminally ill woman's *New York Times* Modern Love essay, "You May Want to Marry My Husband," written like a personal ad seeking a new spouse for her husband once she passed. My novel *Safe Haven* (published back in 2010) featured something in the same vein, in the form of a letter left behind by a deceased woman. "To the woman my husband loves," the letter begins. In it, the deceased wife of widower Alex implores his new love Katie: "If you love Alex now, then love him forever. Make him laugh again, and cherish the time you spend together....Kiss him and make love to him, and consider yourself lucky for having met him, for he's the kind of man who'll prove you right....I also want you to love my children the same way I do...Adore them, laugh with them, help them grow into kind, independent adults. What you give them in love, they'll return tenfold in time, if only because Alex is their father."

Who hasn't imagined what message we would want to leave behind for our loved ones, if we knew that the end of our lives was imminently approaching? In *Safe Haven*, I got to explore not only the stages of grief that people go through after losing a spouse, but also the challenges of being a single parent (something I revisited in *Two by Two*, in a totally different context). It also gave me a chance to wonder about the intense desire that many terminally ill people experience to exert some kind of protective force over their loved ones, even after death. If only there were a way to shelter our children, nurture our spouses, and be present for dear friends, in spirit if not in body...

Having lost my parents and my sister early in life, I have always wished that before passing, everyone had the chance to write a heartfelt letter to each of the people most important to them. Words—especially written ones, meant only for us—have a power to comfort, tell truths, and communicate profound emotions in a way that few things can.

And that's why I still believe in the lost art of letter writing.